SAGRAMANDA

SAGRAMANDA

A NOVEL OF NEAR-FUTURE INDIA

ALAN DEAN FOSTER

an imprint of **Prometheus Books**
Amherst, NY

Published 2008 by Pyr®, an imprint of Prometheus Books

Inquiries should be addressed to
Pyr
59 John Glenn Drive
Amherst, New York 14228–2119
VOICE: 716–691–0133, ext. 210
FAX: 716–691–0137
WWW.PYRSF.COM

12 11 10 09 08   5 4 3 2 1

Library of Congress Cataloging-in-Publication Data

Foster, Alan Dean, 1946–
    Sagramanda : a novel of near-future India / by Alan Dean Foster.
        p. cm.
    ISBN 978–1–59102–645–7 (paperback : alk. paper)
    ISBN 978–1–59102–488–0 (hardcover : alk. paper)
    1. India—Fiction. I. Title.

PS3556.O756S24 2006
813'.54—dc22

2006020966

Printed in the United States of America on acid-free paper

To the young people of India, who are waking up.

To Kali at Kolkata, apologies for *Gunga Din*.

To the tigers and barasingha of Kanha, thanks for the memories.

To Dimple at Kanha, who taught me how to make pakhoras.

To Kiran Moktan at Darjeeling, for letting me spend time with the snow leopards.

To the carvers of Khajuraho, eternal life.

To the silent stories of Orchha.

To the friendly rats of Deshnok, more milk and cookies.

To the people of Jaisalmer, more water and less heat.

Most especially, to Nagy, for his patience and skill.

Four weeks, 3000 kilometers, drive on the right, and remember:

Camels and elephants have the right of way.

chapter i

There are the poor, and there are the terribly poor. Below them are the wretchedly poor. And then there are those who literally have nothing, not even hope. To them, the term is not even any longer applicable. That so many of these utterly forgotten manage to reach adulthood is itself amazing. To belong to this class of humanity is to view the alley as mansion, the street as home, and to live most if not all of one's miserable life in the gutter.

Taneer had once seen such a man, not much older than himself, walk quietly up to others, hand outstretched, one finger upraised. Not as an insult, but as a silent request. The man was asking for a single rupee. One rupee. About two American cents. Taneer had watched as the man stopped outside an eating place. Not a restaurant, really. A few rough wooden tables and chairs, not even a roof over the stall where the food was cooked in sizzling open skillets and pans. The man had stood there with his suppliant, petitioning, upraised finger until the exasperated proprietor had heaved a very large pot brimming with dirty dishwater square in the man's face. The patrons, most of whom were not a great deal better off than the beggar, had laughed heartily.

The man had blinked away the dirty water coursing down his face and seeping into his eyes. He'd said nothing, had not wiped at the two-legged column of walking filth that was himself. He had not cursed, or started to cry. Instead, he had remained as he had prior to the polluted dousing, finger upthrust, waiting. After another ten minutes of being ignored he had moved on, the white and brown rags that cloaked his slender form held together with sweat and grime, wearing little more than his dignity.

That was India.

That was Sagramanda.

It like to broke Taneer's heart.

Remembering the dignified beggar, Taneer gave rupees when he could safely do so, without fear of being mobbed. He could not do so at present because he dare not do anything that might attract attention to himself. If they caught him, those who were after him would break him much more than emotionally. They would break his bones.

What he had discovered after all those days and nights spent slaving in the lab, what he had subsequently stolen from it and from his outraged employers, could not destroy the world—but it could remake it. Because of his discovery, and his decision to abscond with it, he was going to end up either very rich or very dead. For Depahli's sake as much as his own, it had to be the former.

Right now, more than anything else, he needed time. Time to consolidate his thoughts as well as his gains. Time to determine whether he would be more successful as a scientist or as a thief. He had to find a place to hide, where he could think, and plan, and decide on his next move. Fortunately, his home was Sagramanda.

In a city of more than one hundred million people, even a formerly honest man like Taneer Buthlahee stood a fair chance of losing himself.

Sanjay Ghosh had determined to leave the village for good when the leopard ate his dog. The household canine was not the first local children's favorite the leopard had eaten. The uninvited occasional visitor had acquired a taste for defenseless family pets, and the Ghoshes' dog was either the tenth or eleventh it had snatched from the village, depending on whether or not the Toshwahlas' cat had been taken by it or killed by a snake.

The leopard lived high up in the hills that were still covered by jungle and had not yet been cut and burned for cooking charcoal. Years ago, the state government had added the hills to an existing wildlife preserve and had forbidden the cutting of trees within the new boundaries. While it was true that the stream that ran by the village subsequently ran clearer and purer than ever, and did not flood nearly so often, the animals that lived in the forest had grown bolder with time and had lost their fear of being hunted. One could tolerate monkeys, Sanjay believed. They were always fun to watch, even when they were making trouble or trying to raid the fields, and were sacred to Hanuman besides. But a leopard . . .

The big cat was protected, local officials had insisted when the village headman had gone to town to complain. It was in hope of seeing such animals that money-spending tourists came to visit the preserve. But Sanjay and his family and friends never saw any of the foreign money that they suspected ended up, like so much similar money, in politicians' pockets in Delhi and Mumbai and Sagramanda.

Would the village sacrifice its cleaner, fresher water to get rid of the leopard? A wandering priest had taken a poll on his PDA. The verdict was that Sanjay's fellow villagers would tolerate the big cat until and unless it switched from eating kittens and dogs and chickens to the villagers themselves. Perhaps then they could interest a local news-paper, if not a local government official, in their ongoing predicament.

Sanjay, however, was determined not to wait around to find out if he was to be the one signifying a step up in the leopard's diet. Small, dark, and tough, with a mustache as fine as any in the village, he had spent hour after hour late into the nights at the village computer ter-minal. He had learned English, and even some German. English and computers were the keys to everything, he knew.

Now he felt that he was at last ready to take the big step, to move away from subsistence farming and to join the modern economy. He was going to earn real money. The incident of the leopard and the family dog had only been the final push he needed.

"We have to find a way to make a better life for our children than can be found in this village," he had told his wife on more than one occasion. "To do that, a man needs money. There is no money here. In Sagramanda, there is money."

"There is also death." Chakra had spoken to him from her side of the bed. She had the face of a Bollywood star and the body of a whore, which not even long days of hard work in the fields had been able to diminish. Yet. One of Sanjay's goals was to preserve both—for her self-image as well as for his own pleasure. The only reason he had not left the village for the city earlier was his fear of leaving her behind. In his absence, other men would be tempted by her apparent availability. The world would not be a natural place if it were otherwise.

Even with worry in her voice and fear in her eyes for his prospects, she had repeatedly reassured him on that score.

"I love only you, Sanjay," she had cooed as she had stroked him to hardness. "I love that you love only me, and I know you will be true to our family even should you find yourself among the many temptations of Sagramanda. Also," she had added with a smile while giving him a painful twist, "if I find out that you have cheated on me, or spent the money you are so desperate to make for us on another woman, I will find you and feed your balls to the leopard, may it make an interesting change of diet for him."

With a woman like that waiting for him, he had mused, how could he become anything other than a success?

It had been almost two years since he had left the village. The first months in Sagramanda had been horrible. As it did to all who struggled to embrace it, the city had overwhelmed him; with its size, the fury of the competition just to survive, the traditional threats and new dangers. But the two weapons he had brought with him—his studied command of English and his slight but steadily growing knowledge of computers—had soon raised him up above the millions of lost and abandoned souls who populated the streets.

It was as true as the government announcements that repeatedly played on the village computer back home had claimed: education was the key to everything.

Within six months, he had a dry place to live. Within a year, he was sending money home. The email he received from Chakra via the village terminal, the glowing photos of his son and daughter, and the pride inherent in their words at his success, were more than enough to inspire him to keep going, though the regular communications did less to assuage the loneliness he felt.

Next month, he promised Chakra. By next month he would have saved enough, and secured enough, to allow him to come home for a visit. What a celebration there would be then! Everyone was anxious to see him again, to hear the stories of his adventures and experiences in the city. Through sheer determination and force of will he had become, if not a Bollywood movie star, certainly a village success story.

"*Chakra*," he whispered to himself. Chakra *sundar*; beautiful Chakra. Her name was poetry. The village celebration would have to wait. Sanjay was a modest man, even shy. But back in Chakra's arms again, after nearly two years, he intended not to stir from his house, newly renovated by her with some of the money he had succeeded in sending, for at least two days. It would be two days they would not spend sleeping. He smiled, and his fellow passengers could only stare at him and wonder at the source of his contentment.

The maglev was not only the fastest way into the heart of the city, it was the safest. More expensive than the old subway to be sure, but Sanjay felt he could afford it now. Peering out from the confines of the economy carriage at the endless expanse of conurbation, he could for the duration of the journey feel that he had risen figuratively as well as literally above the uncountable masses that swelled the city to unmanageable size. Yet unmanageable or no, somehow it all held together. Somehow, it worked.

That was India, too. Knowing it gave him a feeling of pride.

From Mahout Station he took a bus. Fuel-cell powered, electric-engine driven, it contributed no emissions to befoul the already dangerously polluted urban air. Sanjay was able to breathe freely as he stepped off, however. It was nearing the end of the monsoon season, and recent rains had washed the atmosphere above the city blissfully free of contaminants. If the climate was kind, he would not have to wear his face mask for another month or two.

As if to bless the new day a light rain began to fall. Not the kind of thunderous torrent of a downpour that characterized the full monsoon. This was more of a last parting kiss. It would be a good day. Around him, towering new skyscrapers blocked the morning light from the city's half-restored historical district. His destination, his shop, lay nearby, chosen as much for its proximity to public transport as for its commercial viability.

Being located near the historical district, with its venerable old buildings and museums, meant tourists. Tourists meant money. Since most of them had not the slightest idea how to bargain properly, good money.

His tiny souvenir shop stood untouched, one of several dozen similar shops located in the old, single-story block. Ghosh's Keepsakes had a middling location, squashed tightly between Ardath's Souvenir Shop and Shankrashma's T-shirt Emporium (and souvenirs). Taxis and buses, scooters and powered three-wheeled covered rickshaws, trucks and motorcycles and bicycles and tricycles choked the streets. Private vehicles were, of course, banned from this part of the city between the hours of six in the morning and nine at night in favor of public transport, government vehicles, and delivery trucks. Otherwise everything would come to a complete standstill and nothing would move at all.

As he removed the electronic key that would unlock his front door and disarm the alarm he had to scurry sideways to avoid the familiar warning beep of a municipal cattle remover. The hulking vehicle slowed as it neared the pair of cows who had settled themselves atop and alongside the grassy median that divided the several lanes of traffic. He did not bother to stop and watch as the driver went about the business of gently slipping the teflon-coated metal scoop beneath the first animal. As its sides came up to gently enfold and secure the mildly irritated bovine, the scoop rose upward, over the cab of the mover, to deposit the unharmed animal in the holding pen in back. By the time the process had been repeated with the remaining animal, Sanjay was already opening the door to his establishment. The achievement of which he was perhaps most proud and for which he was certainly the most thankful greeted him with a soft whine as the air-conditioning sprang to life.

"Namaste—assalam aleikum—good morning." The shop's voice greeted him in Hindi, Urdu, and English, as it would any of his customers should he find himself busy with stock in the back room.

It was a long way from having to rise before dawn to eat dirt and dust in the village fields, he reminded himself gratefully. He tried to make a moment most every morning to render such thanks.

The register's box tunnel sprang to life at the touch of his fingers. There was nothing much more to do except set the tea to boiling, which he did with a verbal command to the shelf-mounted unit.

Ready, alert, and open for business, he called forth the morning's *Times* in the tunnel. Indulging in an addiction that was common to hundreds of millions of his fellow citizens, he went straight to the Entertainment pages. Outside, traffic flowed a little more smoothly now that the morning's wandering cattle had been relocated. Afternoon might see a family of curious monkeys ambling down the boulevard, though with the rain the local troops of langurs might choose to remain among the trees in the nearby park.

Confirmation that it was going to be a good day came when his first buying customers turned out to be a quartet of visiting Japanese. They were young, energetic, and chatty. As expected, the first thing they did was have their picture taken inside the shop. Sanjay had grown sufficiently sophisticated in the ways of foreigners to know that the Japanese never took pictures of places they visited. They only took pictures of *themselves* standing in front of places they visited.

Obsequious shopkeeper and eager tourists communicated in broken English, of which Sanjay's command was by far the greater. He was careful to defer to his visitors, of course: admiring their attire, complimenting them on their English, expressing astonishment at their bargaining abilities, remarking favorably on their taste, and being sure to add a ten percent surcharge onto their purchases for ship-ping costs as well as another seven percent for the use of credit cards. Not to mention the thirty percent overall profit he made on the entire sale once they had worn him down to half his initial asking price on every item.

While they went away happy, he treated himself to a cup of second-pick green Darjeeling, with extra sugar and cream. Sealed tightly nearby was the hand-wrapped packet of Ruby Clonal first pick, but such exclusive tea was reserved for customers who purchased only the best his poor shop had to offer. That meant trinkets of gold and gemstones, not mass-produced sandalwood carvings or inlaid marble boxes from Agra.

He made several additional sales before lunch, which put him in a more contented mood than usual when Bindar arrived. The two men smiled at one another. Or at least, Sanjay smiled. Bindar's expression was more of a furtive grimace. It suited the man. In stature he was as short as Sanjay but far thinner. Cousin to the rats that still infested parts of the city, some would say. Brother to the mongoose would have been Bindar's preferred comparison.

"You had a pleasant journey from the north?" Sanjay inquired conversationally as he flicked a switch on the shop controller. In response, the window and door darkened while a glowing "Closed" sign written in a multiplicity of languages materialized, ghostlike, within the light-altering depths of the polycrylic panels.

"I'm not missing any body parts, am I?" As the visitor flopped himself down in the single chair that stood opposite Sanjay's front counter, he swung a small backpack off his bony shoulders and onto the glass countertop, blocking the view of rings and necklaces and bangles within. It was a view not missed. Bindar was a supplier of goods, not a customer.

Sanjay maintained his smile. "Nothing that is readily visible, anyway. Tea?"

The wiry visitor seated before him nodded briskly. Both men drank. There followed brief but intense conversation involving the cricket of the previous day, during which the Sri Lankan national team had nearly managed to beat the Australians. In India, few things could displace business. Cricket was one of them. Talk of batsmen and bowlers concluded, Bindar sneaked a last glance at the darkened storefront before opening his pack.

This involved considerably more than simply unsnapping a strap or untying a couple of knots. First, Sanjay's lean visitor entered a code into the hand unit he extracted from the pocket of his ragged shorts. An LED on the pack, which was woven of impenetrable carbon fiber composite camouflaged to look like cheap burlap, flashed green. Entry and broadcast of a second code brought forth another green light plus a soft click from somewhere within. Had anyone else tried to force their way into the pack without successfully entering both codes, the amount of C-4 explosive integrated into its inner lining was sufficient in quantity and purity to scatter the would-be intruder's body parts plus those of anyone in his immediate vicinity over a distance more expansive than the standard cricket field. As the pack's owner unsealed the top flap Sanjay leaned forward, the better to see what the man with the mongoose countenance had brought for him.

There were a dozen small packets, every one as neatly wrapped and bound as a Chinese New Year present. Each was hand-identified in English, that being as much the language of general commerce throughout the subcontinent as it was in the rest of the wider world. One package said "Acetaminophen syntase—Pandeswami Industries, Guwahati." The two next to the first declared their contents to be "Multivitamin with proprietary Ayurvedic herbs and supplements." All three packages contained nothing of the kind, unless one counted as a similarity the fact that they were packed tight with synthesized pharmaceuticals.

Illegal recreational pharmaceuticals.

Sanjay had always been a very fast learner. He had been the first in his village age group to master English verbs, the first to inquire about how to use a computer keyboard, the first to try voice recognition commands. Once he obtained the small business loan that had enabled him to open his little shop, it had not taken him long to learn that even when dealing with ignorant tourists, the profit margin on T-shirts and silver anklets and carved wooden elephants was small. Much smaller than on other things that could be sold to travelers out of a shop such as his.

He prided himself on never selling such items to Indians. Well, not to Hindus, anyway. He was a strong BJP man, firmly believing them to be corrupt but less corrupt than the members of the Congress and other parties. When resigned to a life in hell always vote for the lesser devil, his father had once told him. Though considering himself to be completely unprejudiced, he was happy enough to sell drugs to Buddhists, and Muslims, and the occasional Sikh, as well as to eager tourists.

You are throwing away your lives as well as your money, he wanted to tell them when they came looking for his shop (he had already gained a modest reputation for availability of certain chemical combinants). You were born with all these advantages, and you are casting them to the winds for a few moments of false pleasure, he felt the urge to say.

But he did not. Because he had a wife, and two children, and had not the brutal ancestors of his fresh-faced customers raped and stolen from his own progenitors whatever had taken their fancy? Ghosh's Keepsakes was not exactly a front for a reprise of the Sepoy Rebellion, but neither did his misgivings over what he was doing cause him to lose much sleep. Especially not when some smart-mouthed French or Italian kid wearing fake Indian clothing and sporting long dreads ambled in off the street, acting as if he owned the place, and flashed a wallet stuffed with more rupees than Sanjay's long-suffering father was used to seeing in a year.

So he beamed at Bindar, who was forever looking over his shoulder as if Durga herself was on his tail with a knife in each of her eight arms, and selected one of the packets at random. His visitor simply nodded, knowing in advance what Sanjay intended to do with the package. Unless, of course, the shopkeeper had taken leave of his rural but carefully honed senses.

Using his remote, Sanjay unlocked the bottom drawer of his counter. It did not look like a drawer, but like a section of the counter base itself. Recognizing his thumbprint, the drawer slid out. It contained not trinkets and bangles, not even the good 22k gold jewelry he kept for knowledgeable customers, but several pieces of gleaming white electronics.

Carefully puncturing the packet he had selected he used a small spoon to tip a tiny bit of the beige powder it contained into an open receptacle atop one such device. Practiced fingers manipulated a set of buttons. Sanjay did not know how the instruments worked. It was not necessary that he did. While lights flickered and danced, Bindar struggled as he always did not to lean forward and peer over the counter.

As a matter of professional regard, Sanjay was not smiling now. He liked Bindar, who had come to Sagramanda from a village even poorer than Sanjay's and who had chosen a profession far more dangerous than that of shopkeeper. But it was hard to keep a straight face when his restless visitor was twisting and squirming in the chair like a man whose previous night's meal of curried goat was threatening to come back on him.

It took only a couple of minutes for the precision instrument to render its verdict and end the courier's agony.

"Quite satisfactory," Sanjay declared. The drawer shut down and locked automatically when he pushed it closed. A second touch on the remote would have opened a panel in a dirty section of floor behind him. Storing the merchandise could wait until Bindar's departure. After all, if the courier, good man though he was, saw the location of Sanjay's hiding place, then it would be a hiding place no longer.

Though even Sanjay's small shop accepted a wide range of credcards there were some transactions to be made in this world where cash was still preferred. Bindar's tension eased when Sanjay returned from a back room with a small box. Opening the box, the whippet-thin courier thumbed rapidly through the wad of bills it contained; a comforting masala of rupees, euros, yen, and dollars. He didn't count it all, just as Sanjay had not tested every packet. If the total was short, someone would accost the shopkeeper one day and have a word with him about the discrepancy. Perhaps break a bone or two. Or put out an eye. The same thing could happen to Bindar if one of the packets Sanjay had accepted turned out to be full of, say, turbinado sugar instead of fashionable hallucinogenics.

The transaction completed, the two men exchanged gossip, further sports talk, political conversation, and more tea. Bindar did not linger.

He had other deliveries to make, other collections to pursue. Both men found themselves discussing the disappearance of a mutual acquaintance who had shorted a certain midlevel distributor in the district of High Hooghly. The acquaintance had been found just last week. In three different parts of the city. Simultaneously. It was an object lesson no one needed to dwell upon.

Bindar finished the last of his tea, rose, and moved toward the door. Fingering his remote, Sanjay unlocked it, at the same time reopening his shop for business and brightening the windows so passing customers could once more see inside as soon as he had safely locked away the delivery.

"Take care of yourself, my friend," he told the departing courier. "Watch out for evil spirits and loose women."

"Every chance I get." Bindar smirked. They were bound together by business and a common heritage. Neither of which would keep Bindar from having Sanjay's throat cut if he ever felt the shopkeeper had cheated him: a purely businesslike sentiment Sanjay silently reciprocated.

But—business was good, and there was no reason this day for such dark thoughts to trouble either man. Bidding Bindar good-bye, Sanjay returned to his chair behind the counter; the one that circulated a permanent cooling fluid throughout its seat and frame. There was no need to advertise that he had just restocked a certain singular portion of his inventory. His regular customers would know, and travelers would find out. Switching on the store box, he settled back and relaxed as a schedule of available entertainment materialized in the tunnel that opened in front of him.

He chose an old movie. He liked the old movies, even if they were in black and white. Three-dimensionalized, the figures appeared in front of him, one-quarter actual size, whirling and dancing and singing something about love and fate and the caprices of the Gods. Business was good, life was good, he told himself as he directed the brewer to make another cup of chai—iced, this time.

Next year, he told himself. Next year he would bring Chakra and the children to Sagramanda to live with him. Would get them out of the hot, stinking, poverty-stricken countryside forever.

One man's picturesque village is another man's slum.

chapter ii

Even dressed for protection from the appalling afternoon heat, Depahli De turned heads in the mall. For most of her life it was a place she would never even have thought of entering, much less have felt comfortable in. Then she had met Taneer, and her life had changed forever.

Now she walked proudly, breasts thrust forward against her fancy sari, perfect hips switching just so, a little of the 22k gold that Taneer had lavished on her the equal of all but the richest women perusing the expensive goods on the tenth floor. Her eyes sparkled beneath radiant color-shifting makeup she had only recently learned how to apply. Her blemishless pale skin, just tinged with hues of coffee, glistened as if peeled from an apsara. Lightly applied floral perfume mixed with her own natural pheromones left a trail of lavender and musk in her wake, an invisible plume of eroticism, like a locomotive puffing out sex instead of steam. Men gaped in spite of themselves while their women silently gritted their teeth and tried not to make their envious glares too obvious.

Depahli didn't care. Let the Brahmin bitches growl and curse under their breath! She had taken enough shit from their kind from the time she had been old enough to understand what it meant to be born the lowest of the low. Now she could ignore them. Soon, with luck, it would be *her* turn to look down on *them*.

Depahli De had been born a Dalit. An outcaste, or Untouchable.

Of course, that supposedly meant nothing in today's India. Caste had long ago officially been abolished as a method of discrimination. Officially. Real life, just as in the matrimonial ads that filled the pages of the country's newspapers and magazines and websites, was another matter entirely.

Like so many Untouchables, as a young girl Depahli had considered herself condemned to a life of degradation and poverty. A male member of a higher caste, one of the four varnas, might opt to drop down in caste and marry her, but this happened only very rarely. Despite the beauty that was apparent from a very early age she could not even find work as a prostitute except among her own kind. For a member of a higher caste to touch her would be to pollute himself. For one to sleep with her would be to pollute himself irredeemably. She smiled to herself as she stopped to finger the material of a fine carbon-silk business suit imported from Italy.

Dear, sweet Taneer was irredeemably polluted indeed.

They had only met because she'd had the guts to flee the squalid surroundings of her home in a run-down industrial section of Nagpur after her uncle Chamudi had raped her. That was ten years ago. She had been fourteen. With virtually no money but a great deal of determination she had walked, hitched, and begged her way to Sagramanda. Glorious, steaming, pulsing, fetid Sagramanda, where it was said that anything was possible, even for one born an outcaste. Where, surrounded by a hundred million fellow seeking souls, it was even possible to shrug off a question about caste as irrelevant and deftly turn a discussion to other matters.

And wonder of wonders, she had managed to do all of it without having to sell herself. Not wholly, anyway.

She had modeled. Both nude and clothed. She was not ashamed of having a body men admired. So extraordinary was her appearance that by the time she was seventeen she had steady work in the trivit studios. On only one thing had she insisted: no intercourse, no penetration. Dry fucking she would consent to, but she wouldn't do hardcore. It cost her a great deal of money, but she had remained firm in her private principles. Or as one disappointed but grudgingly admiring vitographer had told her, firm in her principal privates.

Still, she had managed. One man's appetite might be limited, but that of the box and the Net, she had learned, was insatiable. Even among stiff competition she had stood out as exceptional.

She knew she had stumbled across an exceptional man when, collapsing in his arms one day while sobbing uncontrollably, she had revealed the nature of her career to Taneer. How much more damage could it do, she had argued with herself, when he already knew she was an outcaste? Her instincts had been proven right and her trust rewarded. Astonishingly, he had only smiled reassuringly at her and said, "One day you must show me some of your better virtuals." Ecstatic at his plain-spoken acceptance of her unsavory past, she had spent all that night showing him the reality.

That was the day when she realized she would do more than love Taneer Buthlahee forever. If necessary, she would die for him. In acknowledging her ancestry and her work, he had in a sense already died for her. Could she do no less for him?

The attendant who wandered over to see if he could help was young and trim, neatly dressed in natty gray and blue. It was amusing to watch him try to control his eyes. Struggling to remain locked on her own, they found themselves wandering all over her like a security scanner at the airport. Not to tease but to please the poor fellow, who despite the attention paid to his appearance was anything but handsome, she took a deeper breath and leaned close.

"I would like this suit, but in forest green. Do you have anything like that?" She had discovered that whenever she chose to deliberately lower it, her voice could make even confident conversationalists stammer.

The young salesman was no orator. "I—I'll check the imben—the inventory." He stepped back. Or rather, retreated helplessly as he gestured to the nearest female clerk. "If you'd like to step into our scanner, please?"

Please. She had spent an entire childhood never hearing the word. Though it was commonly directed her way now, she never tired of it. "Of course," she murmured obligingly.

The department's scanner raced red lights up and down her form, penetrating her sari to take her measurements. Yes, they did have the suit she had selected available in a dark green. Would she care to view the color? Checking the sample, she condescended to approve. The appropriate suit was pulled from inventory and sent to the store's tailor. Half an hour later, after the material had been melted, reformed, rewoven, and cooled, she returned to pick up her package.

She paid with cash. Ever since Taneer had gone into hiding they had paid for everything with cash. Her beloved had told her that in some parts of the world cash was no longer accepted for large purchases. To the best of his knowledge, however, that was not yet true anywhere in Asia. The bag containing her purchase slung deftly over one arm, she left the store and sauntered out into the mall's towering atrium. It was a wonderland that as a child she had not even imagined could exist, except in dreams.

Like translucent balloons, automated ads drifted through the multiple converging halls of the mall, rising and falling from floor to floor as easily as they negotiated side passages and entryways. Electronics kept them banned from certain areas such as the children's playground and the food court. The latter was a favorite stop of hers. Growing up, she had never imagined there could be so many different kinds of food. Growing up, she had never imagined there could be so much food.

Though she could now pay for whatever kind of dish she wanted, as often as she wanted, she never left as much as a crumb on her plate. Not even when sampling such exotic cuisine as game from Africa or chili from America. Even when venturing into Starbeans, she made herself finish every last sip of coffee concoctions that were sometimes too rich for a digestive system that had evolved to cope with far simpler fare.

Employing built-in aerogel cameras, adverts designed to appeal specifically to the young, female, and middle-to-upper-class zeroed in on her repeatedly. The constant battle between manufacturers of pocket-sized ad-blockers and the designers of mobile advertisements had spurred technological leaps among both. Depahli rarely used the blocker that Taneer had bought for her. Truth be told, she enjoyed enough of the ads to allow them access. Even the ones for the omnipresent matrimonial services that allowed her to compare, fancifully of course, other prospective suitors to Taneer. Invariably, all were found wanting.

Not all the ads she walked through were gender-specific. The expensive three-dimensional one for the new Maruti Hathi 4×4 skirted the edge of acceptability. Until appropriate regulations had been put in place, mobile adverts had diverted some people to their deaths by blocking their vision or unsettling their sense of balance.

More noise than usual in front of her drew her attention. It was coming from the vicinity of the food court, her intended destination. Suddenly the milling, well-dressed crowd that had been promenading noisily in both directions surged toward her. The shouts of angry men formed a low counterpoint to the screams of women and the anxious cries of confused children.

A handful of men and women formed a tight knot that forced its way through the crowd. Most but not all of them were young. As she ducked to one side and sought shelter against the transparent polycarbonate wall that kept patrons from tumbling into the open, multistory atrium, several loud pops were distinctly audible above the noise of the crowd.

Ignoring the scattering, panicky mallers, the retreating men and women kept up a continuous running fire on their pursuers—half a dozen khaki-clad mall security personnel. Dark as an African but wearing a multihued cap over his shaved skull, one squat, mustachioed runner took a stun pellet in the right leg. Grimacing, he went down in the center of the walkway, right in front of the crouching Depahli. A moment later two of the security guards were all over him. The look on their faces was known to her. It was one she recognized all too well from her childhood. They very much wanted to beat and kick the man with the now paralyzed leg. But there were too many witnesses, and they had to settle for roughly taking him into custody.

The moving fight flowed in a steady curve around the fourth-floor level, finally petering out near the carpark exit. Security made one more arrest, but the other intruders managed to get away. All around Depahli shaken couples and families with crying children were rising to their feet. Talk of what had happened was terse and quickly put aside. After all, it was not as if such things didn't happen in Sagramanda every day.

The nature of the intruders and their offense became clear as soon as she entered the food court. McDonald's and Pizza Hut had been targets, but so had Cum-In Chicken, Flash Satay, and other non-American fast food outlets. A quick survey of those that had been vandalized and those that had been spared gave more than a subtle clue to the agenda of the attackers. All of those outlets that had been despoiled served meat. Those whose offerings were strictly vegetarian had been spared.

The attackers had been members of one of several underground but well-known radical vegan groups. Perhaps the Pushkar Commandos, she mused. Their members had been much in the news lately, ever since their fire-bomb attack on the offices of a certain national concern that had its headquarters on the east coast and specialized in the cloning and genetic engineering of avian foodstock. Having no sympathy for their aims, she deliberately and defiantly sought out an undamaged outlet that served not only meat, but beef. Bright, stinging memories of preadolescent starvation tend to trump whatever philosophies purport to discredit particular kinds of nourishment.

She ordered a double burger and fries, and to wash it all down, a Nathmull's teacola.

Sitting there, watching the crowd recover from the shock of the intrusion and temporarily free from the persistent drifting ads that were kept outside the dining area, she had time to ponder how drastically her life had changed. From a future promising nothing better than an arranged marriage to another Untouchable like herself, or worse, indentured servitude in a child sweatshop or outright sale as a lifetime servant to an abusive family, she had come to this. Sitting in the Chowringhee Mall eating American-style food, gold dangling from her ears and neck and encircling her fingers, a bag of designer clothing resting at her feet. Her perfectly made-up mouth contorted into a grimace of self-reflection, but not even that could distort her beauty. Not too many years ago she would have been abysmally grateful had someone just given her the shopping bag.

Gold, jewelry, clothing. An apartment, albeit a secret one, with a real induction stove, and a vit, and a molly player. A car, surely, was in her future, though until things were resolved her beloved insisted it was safer for the both of them to continue to rely on public transportation, where their movements would be far more difficult to track. And Taneer Buthlahee. She had him, too. Nothing would or could make her let go of any of that.

The two men did not ask permission to sit down opposite her. Like her, they were in their mid-twenties. They were fashionably dressed. Both wore gleaming wrist communicator/chronographs that reeked of money. So did their attitudes.

"I don't think I've seen in you in here before," said the first. He made it sound like a challenge.

His companion grinned, showing perfectly capped (or regenerated) white teeth. He had a very thin, movie-star mustache and was to all appearances as confident in his looks as in his money. "I know I haven't. There is no way I would forget you, if I had seen you."

She bit down into the last of the hamburger, wishing the curried ketchup were hot enough to match the heat rising inside her. But she kept her voice level. "That's all right. You can pretend."

Sudden confusion did not diminish the man's smile. "Pretend what?"

"That you've never seen me."

Now the smile did fade, though the man's companion laughed appreciatively. "Looks *and* wit! Where are you from, beautiful?" Resting his chin in one hand, he leaned over the table and did his best to establish unbreakable eye contact with her.

"From the place to which I am now going." Flashing a quick, tight smile of her own, she swallowed the last of the teacola and reached down with one hand to pick up her shopping bag. Before she could rise, the disappointed smiler had grabbed her other wrist. Not painfully. Just hard enough to restrain her. As her uncle Chamudi had often restrained her. Gently but irresistibly, his grin returning to its full enhanced orthodontic brilliance, the man started to pull her across the table toward him.

Somewhat less gently and just as irresistibly, she raised her left leg, locked it out straight, and pushed the heel of her foot against his crotch underneath the table. "Keep pulling," she suggested encouragingly

The smile drained away from the man's face. So did some of the color. Letting go of her wrist, he sat back in his chair and affected the air of the unaffected as he looked around to see if anyone else noticed what was happening. In this he had only partial success.

She withdrew her foot. What she wanted to do was ram it into him hard enough so that it came out his asshole, with his balls balanced on her heel. But it would do no good to antagonize this spoiled pair any further. Mall security might take an interest in any more expansive confrontation, and if there was one thing Taneer had impressed on her more than anything else it was a need right now to avoid attracting any kind of official attention.

So she fought off the urge to make a point, drew back her leg, and rose. At least she could enjoy the look on the face of Mr. Smiley's now bewildered companion. As for Mr. Smiley himself, he was looking increasingly unwell.

"So interesting to make your acquaintance. Not seeing you again soon, I think." She sashayed off, lengthening her stride as she reached the boundaries of the food court, deliberately refusing to look back. When she finally did so, her smarmy, self-confident accosters were nowhere to be seen. She started to shake: with anger, not with fear. Getting herself back under control, she began working her way toward the exit that linked the mall to its proprietary subway terminal.

Never again would a man, any man, treat her the way Uncle Chamudi had done. Touch her the way he had. The pop-out ceramic blade that was built into and took the shape of the heel of her shoe remained sheathed. Smiley-face would never know how lucky he had been that she had decided only to make an impression on him.

She did not go straight home. Taneer's instructions as to how she needed to travel had been very explicit. He had only to tell her something once and she would remember it. Halfway across the city she got out of the subway, took the escalator up to the street, and began to walk. Baroghly was a border area. As she covered ground, her surroundings changed very quickly from lower middle-class to poor. Not to abject poor. She did not go as far as the antiquated hovels of Outer Sealadhan. She did not have to. There was enough of a mix in the human crush of Baroghly to suit her needs.

The reek from the public restroom was almost overpowering. No tourists could have stood it for more than a few seconds, and few respectable citizens of the city would have tried. Waiting until the entrance to the women's section was deserted, Depahli did not hesitate, but walked straight toward it and entered. She did not like the stench, but she had no trouble tolerating it. It was more than familiar to her from her childhood as well as from her early years in Sagramanda.

On the third try she found an empty plastic stall that was not over-whelmed with the stain of urine, the slickness of vomit, and the smear of human feces. Removing the collapsible, lightweight garment holder from her bag, she undressed as quickly as possible. Every gleam of gold went into a small box. The contents of a can of deodorized antiseptic played over her naked body. From the bottom of the bag she extracted a second, airtight container. The pre-stained, simple cotton sari it held fit her loosely, badly, thoroughly obscuring her figure. Today's veil was beige, with strategic yet unrevealing rips and tears.

She stood thus inside the stall, listening to the comings and goings of poor women and their chattering, bawling, screaming children, before finally emerging. The stink of the restroom clung to her clothing but, thanks to the spray, not to her skin. No one looked in her direction when she stepped outside the overwhelmed public facility. No covetous female or lustful male eyes followed her progress as she limped up the street.

A short stroll through the sultry, steaming early evening would bring her to a bus stop. The creaking fuel-cell bus would carry her to the terminal for an older subway line, one that did not cross the gleaming tracks of the line that ran past Chowringhee Mall. One more change to another line, suffering the disapproving stares of irritated middle-class commuters, would deposit her a few blocks from the innocuous apartment building that was home. That would be followed by another foray into a much cleaner public restroom where she would change again, finally able to walk free and clean back to the temporary home she and Taneer shared.

It was a lot of effort simply to get home from a day of shopping, but she did not mind. She knew what real work was, and having to endure repeated changes of clothing and public transportation was not

work. Operating a hand loom until your fingertips bled and your fin-
gernails fell out in a poorly ventilated, un-air-conditioned sweatshop
surrounded by dozens of other vacant-eyed children, that was work.
Begging in the streets for the occasional pitiful rupee or two while
fighting off the come-ons of fat, leering, sweaty old men, that was
work. Complying with Taneer's directives to repeatedly change her
clothing and return home by multiple devious routes, that was not
work. It was a game. An important game, to be sure. He had impressed
that on her. But not work, nonetheless.

There were people who very badly wanted to take what he had, he
had explained to her as he had held both her hands in his and stared
solemnly into her eyes. People who would do terrible things to both of
them to learn the secret he knew. Better to avoid such people until he
could make arrangements to sell the valuable knowledge the details of
which only he knew. He was in the process of organizing that sale. It
would make them rich. Once the sale was an accomplished fact, there
would be no point in anyone hunting them any longer. They would be
able to go anywhere they wanted, in confidence and safety. To Delhi, perhaps, or Mumbai, or Hyderabad, or even overseas. In America, Taneer
had a distant cousin on his mother's side. Perhaps they could go there.
The cousin had told Taneer's father Anil that there were many people of
Indian extraction in America, and that life there was very good indeed.

Of course, they were in hiding from Anil Buthlahee too. Taneer's
father had not been shy in expressing his disapproval of their relationship. But he could not reach them, could not harm them, in America.

Live in America. Depahli had seen America. In movies, on television, on the Net. It was a place of wonders. Violent, yes. Confusing,
yes. But she had not seen anything that suggested she would not be
able to adapt to it or that was likely to give her problems.

She lived in Sagramanda.

The tiger had come out of the Sundarbans. That was certain. Under cover of night, it had worked its way into the southeastern suburbs of the city. This was not as difficult to do as a visitor from elsewhere might imagine. Sagramanda was full of parks and residential greenbelts; a necessary if permanently insufficient counterweight to the burgeoning pressure of its swollen and always growing population. Eternally in need of land, the expanding megalopolis had long ago pushed and shoved its way up against the immense delta complex where the Ganges and the Brahmaputra merged to form the world's largest remaining mangrove swamp. The ever-shifting waterways on the western side of the border with Bangladesh constituted the Indian portion of the Sundarbans Preserve. Traveling only at night, it was possible for large animals to migrate, to work their way into the outskirts of the metropolis itself. Monkeys did so with ease. The chital and sambar deer that populated many of the city's green areas moved freely between parks and the delta of the Sundarbans.

But not usually a tiger.

Three meters long and twelve years old, the big male weighed more than a quarter of a ton. Among the trees and paved pathways and benches and fountains he drifted silently, a striped wraith invisible beneath the wan illumination of a splinter of moon. He was strong and experienced—but he had also lived a long time. He was old enough to hope for easier prey than the skittish sambar and the swift chital. Also, he had not fed in some time, and was very hungry.

The wildlife division of the municipal authority was as aware of animal movements as were the monkeys and mongooses. Steps had been taken long ago. Though in a city of a hundred million other demands took budgetary precedence over wildlife considerations, some few millions of rupees still trickled down for observation and reaction.

The tiger's approach to the outermost city limits did not go unnoticed. Its heat signature was detected by one of the dozens of automated monitoring stations located on the border between inhabited suburb and unpopulated Sundarbans. Identified as a *Panthera tigris tigris* large enough to present a potential danger should it continue on its present path, the station automatically activated the two interceptors nearest the big cat.

Quarter ton or not, the tiger moved in utter silence, advancing with less noise than the wind. On a nearly moonless night it was all but invisible. Movement directly ahead made it pause.

Two figures stood staring into the woodland, trying to penetrate a night that was dark as smoke. Both held rifles. Their eyes scanned the tree line intently, unblinkingly. Another person might have found the lack of any eye-blinks unnerving, but they were characteristic of the interceptors. The big cat's nostrils flared; the tips of his whiskers rose. The night air was suffused with the distinctive scent of human. He hesitated.

Ordinarily, a tiger confronted with a pair of armed human shapes would have turned and retreated. Ordinarily, the scent alone would have been enough to send it loping swiftly back the way it had come. But the tigers of the Sundarbans were and always had been particularly bold. The emptiness in the male's belly was profound.

It charged.

Both figures turned immediately to confront it. Rifle muzzles rose, and the sound of gunfire split the night. Flying through the air, two hundred and forty kilos of wide-eyed, gaping-mouthed cat struck the nearer of the two interceptors.

And passed completely through it.

Surprised, the tiger hit the ground, dug in powerful claws, and whirled. Both interceptors had turned to face it. The echo of large-caliber weapons had grown repetitive. Puzzled but not frightened, the tiger attacked again. This time a massive paw swiped directly through the middle of the other interceptor. Its gun muzzle dropped until it passed right through the tiger's head and neck.

The interceptors were virtuals. Like their images, the strong stink of human was projected from a small, tracked vehicle the size of a lawnmower. The autonomous vehicles could go where no human watchman could go, stay on duty twenty-four hours a day, never grew tired, did not need bathroom or meal breaks, and did not go on strike over the lack of a comprehensive health plan.

Reaching down with a paw, the inquisitive tiger batted hard at the nearest of the motorized devices. The projection of an armed human hunter was skewed sideways, then flickered out entirely as the vehicle was knocked completely over on its side. Half the lights within the device went dark. Meanwhile, the second vehicle had turned toward the tiger, aiming its virtual in the cat's direction. Nose in the air, the tiger turned away and, ignoring the repeated recorded sounds of a heavy weapon being fired, resumed pacing along its original path.

The children should not have been out that late. There were six of them, evenly divided between boys and girls, all friends, all giggling and laughing at their special adventure. They had the playground area on the edge of the housing development all to themselves. It was an upscale complex, benefiting from its proximity to the wildlife preserve, offering its fortunate residents views toward Bangladesh of trees and water and birds instead of the seething urban stew that was the city interior.

One of the girls tripped one of the boys as he was heading for the gel-coated spiral slide. Uttering a mildly shocking grown-up word, he rose, brushed sand off his pants, and began to chase her. The other boys urged him on while the remaining girls encouraged their darting, weaving companion in her flight. She was a good soccer player and at first avoided his pursuit easily, leaving him frustrated and half angry, half exhilarated. But he was a little faster. Closing on her, he reached for the long, flying, fashionably blue-and-green streaked black hair that trailed behind his teaser.

An enormous dark mass erupted out of a clump of bushes just to their left. It struck silently: no growls, no intimidating roars designed to stop prey in its tracks with blood-chilling sonics. That kind of hunting the tiger left to its cousin the lion. It did not even have to bite. The force of the charge and the weight behind it snapped the girl's neck on impact.

The boy who had nearly caught her stumbled and went down onto his knees, then his face, wrapping both hands protectively over his head as he pushed his face into the sandy soil. Behind him his friends were screaming, girls and boys alike. He did not, could not, look up, so he did not see the tiger carrying the girl off, her neck in its mouth. Bobbing loosely, her head hung straight down, the tips of her carefully streaked hair just brushing the ground. She had died instantly, on impact, so fast it was mercifully doubtful she had even known what had happened.

One of the other boys finally summoned up enough courage to run forward and check on his friend. He was able to comfort him somewhat, but he could do nothing to still the shaking that was convulsing the other boy's body. Behind them, the surviving girls could not stop screaming.

Farther back, across from the playground, a few lights were starting to wink to life within the nearest apartment building. Anxious adults who were not virtuals were hurrying toward the children. They were not armed, and there was nothing they could do.

Living close to Nature sometimes brought with it things that were not benefits.

The killing would be reported, but it was unlikely anything would be done. Hunting tigers took time and money the city did not have. Furthermore, the status accorded to large predators was inviolate. Cold as it seemed on paper, there were far more children in India than tigers. The incident in the night was an isolated one. It would soon, however, prove itself to be that rare exception to the rule.

Because the tiger had now acquired a taste.

chapter iii

It made the news, of course. The next day, free readers
drifted among the morning commuters, teasing them to purchase
and download the body of the report as well as the rest of the paper.
Getting off at the museum, Jena Chalmette took note of the flashing,
hovering words as they flicked past her in search of paying downloaders.
She did not buy the report, or the paper that contained it. Not because
it was potentially too distressing, or too gory. Actually, she was very
much interested in death and its many manifestations. She envied the
unknown tiger capabilities that were so much greater than her own.

Not that she hadn't done all right with what small talent she had.

Tall and decidedly non-Indian, Jena had been born in France. In
the south of France, to be precise, near the Pyrenees and the border
with Andorra. She had become interested in India and its rich history
and multifarious cultures as a teenager. Unhappily, as a teenager she

had also become deeply interested in assorted threads of mysticism. This had been the despair of her quiet mother and the outrage of her loud father. Her mother had reacted to the situation by becoming more and more withdrawn and by making ever more frequent trips to an online pharmacy, from which she drew enervation if not real peace. Her father, considering himself a practical man, had tried to beat the impractical obsession out of his daughter.

Predictably, Jena had reacted by running away, to Outer Marseilles. There she had met Jean-Paul, who had introduced her to many things seventeen-year-old girls think they know all about but soon come to realize are entirely new to them. Among the delights the languorous, swarthy, serpentine Jean-Paul had introduced her to were group sex, wherein she was expected to share herself freely with his acquaintances; pharmaceuticals even her mother had never thought to try; and petty theft to support their respective habits—his that was well developed, and hers that was new and growing.

Eventually she had settled on rapture-4. It sharply enhanced her emotions and heightened her perceptions. She believed it also altered the reality around her, allowing her to see things the sight of which was otherwise denied to mere mortals.

It was while semicomatose in the throes of a particularly deep and spiritual rapture-4-induced mental trip that she found herself face-to-face with Kali.

She knew Kali quite well, from her years of reading. But she had certainly never expected to encounter the goddess in person. Confronting the wide-eyed, gaping Jena, the goddess held a sword in one hand and the head of a recently slain demon in another while her other two hands beckoned encouragingly to the young woman kneeling at her feet. A necklace of fifty skulls garlanded her neck, one for each of the fifty letters of the Sanskrit alphabet, and each of her earrings was a dead body. She wore only a girdle comprised of the hands of dead men. Her eyes were red and her breasts and body smeared with blood. She was *nigurna*, the ultimate reality, beyond name and form. The bright fire of truth that burns away everything, including clothing.

Her ivory-white teeth symbolized purity, while her red, extended tongue signified her delight in the enjoyment of everything that society considers forbidden. Smiling, she extended a welcoming hand downward. Taking it, Jena rose, utterly entranced.

"Dance with me," the goddess invited her. "The world is created and destroyed in my dancing. Your redemption lies in awareness that you are invited to take part in my dance, to yield yourself to the beat of my dance of life and death."

So Jena danced with the goddess. Entering the squalid fourth-floor walk-up they shared, a startled Jean-Paul nearly swallowed his Galois before trying his best to bring her out of her daze. He'd seen people on bad trips before, had partaken of a few himself. All he had to do was take one look at Jena's enraptured, glowing, thoroughly stoned expression to know that his girlfriend of the moment was way, way gone. But it was only when he saw the empty capsule box and realized just how much rapture-4 she'd taken this time, without him present to keep an eye on and moderate her consumption, that he realized the seriousness of the situation.

If he couldn't bring her down, she might never come out of it. Without her feet ever leaving the ground, she would just keep on floating, floating—until the life floated right out of her.

"Jena! Wake up! *Merde*, you stupid girl, stop stumbling around and listen to me!" Grabbing her by both arms, he began to shake her violently. When that didn't work, he started slapping her. Methodically, hard, back and forth right across the face. It had no effect. Jena fought weakly to pull away from him so she could continue dancing with the goddess, her smile blissful, her eyes focused on something he could not see.

"Confront death, my child," the goddess was urging her. "Accepting the eventuality of death will free you. I am your true mother. Accept me, and I will release you to act fully and freely, release you from the nasty, restraining constraints of pretense, practicality, and rationality." One of two left hands rose. It was missing its little finger. This reminded Jena of something, but she was too far gone to make the connection. "Accept me, serve me, and find my finger. I will be your mother, as I am mother to all. I will protect you."

"Yes," Jena murmured. "Yes, Mother. I will do it."

"Do what? You stupid bitch, do you *want* to OD? Wake *up*. Come out of it! I'm not taking you to the hospital! I can't risk getting arrested again."

An angry Jean-Paul smacked her again, harder than ever. Crimson began to trickle from one corner of her mouth. Reaching up, she touched the flow and gazed down at her red-stained fingertip with childlike wonder. Blood. Mother Kali would be pleased.

"I—I'm sorry, Jean-Paul." She shook her head, blinked, finally looked up at him and smiled faintly. "I'm all right now. It's moderating."

"Damn good thing, too." Roughly, he let go of her. "I thought I was going to lose you. Do you know how hard it is to get rid of a dead body in this town?"

"No." She put a reassuring hand on his arm. "Tell me. How is it done?"

Sudden uncertainty colored his expression as he looked back at her. "You really want to know?" Her eagerness seemed genuine, guileless. So he told her. It gave him yet another opportunity to play the big man, the knowledgeable one.

Later, they made love on the old mattress on the floor that served for a bed. Later, she killed him, wielding a kitchen knife with all her weight behind it, plunging it so deeply into his chest that the tip passed between two ribs to emerge from his back. She dedicated the slaying, the first of what she hoped would be many such sacrifices, to Mother Kali, who had finally shown her the Way. The next day she made arrangements for the disposal of his corpse, scrupulously following the directions he himself had described to her the previous afternoon. Then she sold what she could, packed a single suitcase, and bought a one-way ticket to India. To Sagramanda, where the most prominent temple of Kali in the entire country was located. It seemed the logical place to begin looking for the missing finger of a goddess.

She considered placing a farewell call to her parents. She had not spoken to her father for years, to her mother in months. But there was really no need, she assured herself. She was no longer part of their world.

Besides, she had a new mother now. One who would look after and protect her in ways she had never imagined.

She shook the last of the old thoughts out of her mind as she approached the museum. She had visited here many times before, searching the corridors, the less-visited rooms, for signs of the Mother's missing digit. Always without success. The ticket-taker recognized her as a regular and did not even ask to see the annual pass she had bought. Neatly, even primly, dressed, she attracted no more than the usual attention. Years living beneath Sagramanda's sun had turned her skin the color of weak tea. Youth kept it free of blemishes. In her lean, tall, almost model-like slenderness, she was moderately attractive without being eye-catching. Her height alone was enough to draw the attention of those local men brave enough to approach her. Whenever she felt too many native eyes on her, she would don large, ugly glasses.

Maybe it was the bookish look that drew the young couple to her. They appeared to be about her age, certainly no older. The man smiled hopefully and addressed her in English. When she had first arrived in Sagramanda, Jena had spoken only a few words of that language. Now she was as fluent as the stockbroker from New York she had encountered several months earlier.

"Yes, I think I can help you," she told the man in response to his questions. He and his wife were Australian, but their accent was not impenetrable.

She ended up giving them a tour of the museum, whose contents were intimately familiar to her. By the end of the afternoon, the three of them were chatting together like old friends.

"I'll tell you what you should do," she told them over iced coffee in the museum's café, "Everyone sees Sagramanda from the land. But to really appreciate it, you need to see it from the water. From the river." Her hands traced architecture in the air between them. "From a boat you get an unobstructed view of everything: new buildings, old warehouses, ghats, the itinerant sadhus trolling for contributions along the riverfront walkway."

The young woman eyed her husband. "Sounds romantic as well as educational. Where do we find a tour boat?"

Jena smiled knowingly, as if conveying some intimate secret. "That's why so few people see the city from the water. Believe it or not, there aren't any tour boats. But you can rent small electric watercraft by the hour."

The husband looked unsure. "We're from Newcastle, and pretty much at home on the water. But taking a boat out here, with all this commercial river traffic—I don't know. . . ."

"Tell you what." Jena leaned forward. "You pay for it, and a take-away dinner, and I'll give you the tour. Even the small boats have collision-avoidance electronics built into them. At least, the one we'll use will."

They were delighted by the suggestion and immediately agreed to her offer. At minimal cost they were acquiring a boat driver and a knowledgeable guide all in one.

"Meet me at the Hooghly South private slips, number twenty-four. Seven o'clock. Any taxi driver will know where it is."

Though they arrived before the scheduled departure time, Jena was earlier still. The small, slightly tubby craft's batteries were fully charged and waiting for them. The sheila was surprised to see Jena wearing a veil.

"As the sun goes down, the men here grow bolder," she explained to the other woman as she removed the face covering, folded it neatly, and placed it inside a long shoulder bag resting on a bench seat. With a nod in the husband's direction she added, "I don't have a mate to shoo away the obnoxious. They're worse than flies." Seeing a troubled look cross the woman's face in response to her suddenly threatening tone, Jena added serenely, "I won't need one now. We have your man to protect us." The Aussie had the grace to blush.

Under her practiced hands the boat backed out of the slip and spun away from the docks, humming smoothly upriver as its driver accelerated. Along the way she pointed out one sight of interest after another. Ensconced in the padded double seat situated forward of the wheel, husband and wife relaxed in each other's arms, content to let Jena do all the driving and most of the talking.

They stopped in midriver to enjoy a late supper, unpacking the takeaway meals just before nine o'clock. Around them, river traffic had slowed out of respect for the darkness. The Hooghly was still a highway for traditional boatmen who could not afford running lights, not even solar-powered LEDs, and who were reluctant to venture out into the busy watercourse after the sun went to sleep. It was also much cooler out in the middle of the river, a partial respite from the day's heat if not from the omnipresent humidity.

"So, what do you do?" Completely relaxed, utterly contented, the woman peered over at Jena. Their guide was busying herself with the contents of an open storage container beneath the driver's chair. "Are you a professional guide?"

Jena had to laugh. It was a musical sound, but one with a hard edge. "I'm the one who needs a guide. I can't find what I'm looking for."

"What might that be?" the husband asked casually, cold brew in hand.

"Enlightenment. Release from the cycle of karma. I have been promised that."

The woman was unsure whether to smile or frown. Having consumed several beers, she decided on the former. "I'm not even bloody
sure what that is, but anyway, who promised it?"

"The Mother Goddess. Kali." Reaching up with her right hand,
Jena pressed a sequence of small buttons that rimmed the device concealed beneath her blouse. Instantly responsive, the braceletlike pressure syringe resting there obediently slammed a stream of rapture-4
directly into her bloodstream. It was very clean, very pure, very clear
stuff. Full-on Shakti. For all that she was used to it, it never failed to
have the desired effect. She welcomed the dreamlike contentment that
rolled over her mind and surged through her body, lowering her blood
pressure, elevating her spirits, and lifting her soul. Exactly as Mother
Kali would have approved.

Maybe if he'd had a beer or two fewer, maybe if he'd been a little
less relaxed, the husband might have found the sudden shift in their
new friend's choice of conversation off-putting. Maybe he would have
thought the way she now began to sway slightly from side to side
unsettling. But the open boat was drifting lazily downstream on
autopilot, they were heading back, and in an hour or so he and his wife
would be back in the familiar confines of their comfortable mid-price
range-hotel. Tomorrow would see them off to Mumbai. Meanwhile,
their charming if suddenly sloe-eyed hostess was doing nothing to
generate suspicion. Anyway, she was alone, and he was much bigger
than she was.

Or at least he was until she cut him in half.

In a single flowing, almost dancelike movement, she drew the
sword from its place of concealment among the boat's tools and equipment and struck with it, making sure to guide it with her left hand.
Honed to extreme sharpness and wielded with both hands, it cut
through flesh and bone in equal measure, only slowing to a halt somewhere in the vicinity of the man's spleen. The look on his face rendered
shock passé. Never wavering, his eyes were still locked on her as he fell

over sideways in his seat, the beer falling from his hands, the bottle rolling across the deck of the small boat, blood gushing everywhere.

There was just enough time for the dead man's wife to let out a single scream. It went on and on, until Jena cut off her head. The head flew into the river, which was dangerous, but Jena did not want to take the time to look for it. Anyway, there were voracious fish in the depths of the great waterway that would make short work of the unexpected bounty.

Hands upraised, head back, she chanted over the two bodies as blood filled the bottom of the boat, until the deck was awash with red. Regrettably, none of the four still, limp hands she inspected boasted a finger that might serve to replace the one Mother Kali was missing. But she knew that the goddess would be pleased by the sacrifice. When she had finished her prayers, she weighted the two bodies with what she could find and wrestled them over the gunwale, a gift to the fish and the crocodiles. Then she opened the appropriate valves. As the rental craft began to sink, she inflated the small lifeboat and pushed it over the side. By the time the boat went down, she was paddling toward the near shore.

While serving Mother Kali was an endless pleasure, finding the goddess's missing finger was a task difficult enough to take even a dedicated servant a lifetime. Jena felt certain she was up to the challenge. It was only a matter of time.

Rapture-4 coursed through her body, filling her with chemicals as well as visions. Tickling her neurons and inflaming her thoughts. In the course of her searching and servitude there would be more such sacrifices, she knew.

There had already been many.

Today was Friday. Fridays were always difficult, he knew. There were families trying to get out of the city for the weekend, businesspeople fighting to finalize deals, couples arguing over how they were going to relax. He usually chose to work through the weekend. For one thing, it endeared him to his colleagues. For another, crimes committed on weekends often tended to differ from those committed during the week. Having been a cop for thirty years, Keshu Jamail Singh had learned to seek variety wherever he could.

He was a senior investigator, head of a department—but not *the* head of the department. In a city of a hundred million, there could be no single heads of anything. Oh, there was Commander-in-Chief Mukherjee, but his was largely a ceremonial position. Mukherjee was the public voice of the Sagramanda police force. With his Bollywood-star looks and sonorous voice, he was the perfect choice to intercede between the city government and the public. And, more importantly, the media. He quite fancied himself the knowledgeable investigator. Keshu and his hundred fellow senior investigators kept their opinions of Chief Mukherjee's abilities to themselves. They recognized his value to the department, and his uses, and knew that none of them could have smiled so fatuously at so many politicians, or presented requests for budgetary overrides with such oratorical skill. They needed Chief Mukherjee to facilitate actual police work. But not one of them would trust him to find his ass with his own hands in a darkened room.

Keshu Singh was responsible for supervising the investigation of the most serious crimes in the district known as Parganas Southeast. Six million people, more or less, fell under his jurisdiction. More or less, because it was impossible to maintain an accurate count of the surging, swelling, shifting population of Sagramanda. And that six million didn't even try to take into account the vast number of illegals who swarmed into the city seeking work: impoverished Bangladeshis, hopeful Burmese, resolute Nepalis, displaced Tibetans—all sought the promise of success in Sagramanda. For all but a very few, it remained nothing more tangible than a promise.

It was Keshu's job, and that of his fellow senior investigators, to keep citizens and supplicants from each other's throats and, failing that, to punish those who stormed egregiously over the top of what was deemed legal.

It was still pitch dark as the chopper began to descend toward the lights of the city. It was an hour before dawn; the ambrosial time when it was appropriate for one of his faith to rise. He had already been up for two hours; recited the Japji, the Jaapu, and the Ten Sawayyyas; had breakfast; read all of the morning news and relevant reports on the Net; and bade farewell to his wife. After slightly adjusting the dastar, or turban, that covered his head, he absently fingered the kara that encircled his wrist. It was steel, of course. Next to it was a second bracelet. Similar in design to the first, its composition and function were completely different and decidedly untraditional. It allowed him to communicate directly with his headquarters, to receive as well as send information, and generally to bypass the need for a full-service communicator. It was also quite decorative, even if it was not true steel.

Though of average height, Keshu was powerfully built. As both Sikh and one-time university wrestler, he looked more like a squat, bearded, turbaned bear than the average cop. His colleagues had a way of mitigating their superior's sometimes intimidating appearance. On introducing him, someone would invariably add "gesundheit" or the Hindi, or Bengali, or English equivalent. By now, the joke was old enough to have become fossilized. But it still had its intended effect on those who had not met the inspector previously.

Keshu still wrestled on an amateur level, though there were not many competitors in his age group. Too much chance of tearing a muscle or breaking a bone. Such risks seemed minor in comparison to the everyday dangers faced by someone in his position, but not to those who were businessmen, or teachers, or doctors. There were no politicians in his gym group. Politicians tended to shy away from any kind of rough physical contact. He knew. In the course of his career he had been called upon to arrest a number of them.

A government shuttle chopper was the favored means of transportation for senior officials. While the underground and the maglev were fast and reasonably efficient, nothing beat flying over the traffic to be dropped off on the roof of your office. Dozens of the compact, silent, fuel-efficient craft plied the skies above cities like Sagramanda like so many worker bees, ably shedding themselves every morning of bureaucrats, technocrats, plutocrats, elected officials, and the occasional very wealthy housewife. Larger lifters served as express delivery vehicles, while a few even transported the offspring of the especially privileged to their gated, guarded, exclusive private schools.

Keshu was well aware of the status he had acquired as he stepped out of the chopper and grunted a good-bye to its pilot. There had been some outcry when the shuttle service had first been proposed, until the rice-counters had shown that the increase in efficiency in terms of man-hours worked more than compensated for the cost of the transport. All Keshu knew was that it saved him from having to deal twice daily with city streets. It was a perk for which he had worked hard, and was appropriately grateful.

His cubicle was on the fifth floor of the Haradna East headquarters building. As senior inspector, he was entitled to a corner office. The room responded to his arrival by lowering the air-conditioning setting and darkening the windows. Settling himself into his chair, which promptly molded itself to his stout frame, he pursed his lower lip at the projection unit built into the desk. Before switching it on to contemplate the morning's litany of outrages, he swiveled in his seat to eye the right-angled intersection of Chittragout and Sabhagar streets.

This early in the morning the flow of traffic was slow but steady. Looking out his windows, he could see five centuries. Modern Marutis vied for lane space with imported cars and small delivery trucks. They kept to their lanes lest they encounter one of the millions of dischargers that had been placed in the city's sidewalks over the past fifty years. Prior to the installation of the dischargers, frustrated drivers had simply used the sidewalks to try and drive around traffic jams. The installation of the dischargers put an end to that practice. Drive over one, and it would fry a vehicle's electrical system, simultaneously setting off an alarm. The immobilized driver could only wait for the traffic police to arrive, issue a fine on the spot, and impound the disabled vehicle. Initially, the number of immobilized vehicles slowed traffic until they could be removed. But word about the efficiency of the dischargers spread quickly. People stopped trying to turn the sidewalks of Sagramanda into extra driving lanes, and the flow of foot traffic improved markedly. Drivers caught with illegally installed discharger shields had their fines quintupled and their vehicles confiscated.

Of course, the absence of vehicles on the sidewalks only opened them up to more residents and immigrants as potential dwelling sites and places of business, but at least feet and bodies were easier on the pavement than tires.

A camel cart was making its way down the street, its pair of huge wheels fashioned of plastic instead of wood. Plastic wore much better and did not suffer ill effects from the rain and the sun. The camel needed no fuel and in much of the densely packed city made as good time as a truck. Gazing out his own private portal onto India, Keshu also saw overburdened Tata trucks and buses, heavily laden donkeys, and a plethora of powered tri-wheeled rickshaws. The last of the latter had been converted to battery or fuel-cell power about twelve years ago, with concomitant improvements to the quality of the city's atmosphere both in terms of breathability and noise pollution.

What a country, Keshu mused. What a city. His city. Nobody paid much attention to population projections anymore. Not since the municipality's population count had passed seventy million. They were invariably inaccurate, anyway. With a sigh, he activated the desk and watched as the built-in box generated images and statistics in the air before him. There were no surprises.

With a hundred million human beings crammed into one corner

of the planet, there were bound to be quite a few who were desperate, despairing, or just plain bad.

There was a riot of some significance starting up off to the south, centered on the Mayapur roundabout. Preliminary reports suggested a protest against the granting of a major commercial concession to a large Chinese consortium. Harsh words were being bandied about concerning runaway production and lost jobs. The usual anarchic, opportunistic elements had appeared out of nowhere to join in and send the original demonstration spiraling out of control. Shops were being looted, pedestrians assaulted, vehicles overturned and burned.

Nothing out of the ordinary. A minor episode. His presence would not be required.

Before diving back into the interminable scroll of ongoing unsolved cases he skimmed through the litany of the previous twelve hours. Only nine murders, including one domestic dispute that by itself had resulted in four dead. Suspects already picked up in half the cases, not counting the family fight in which all the protagonists died. A good night, in that respect. He read on. To an outsider the long list of dreadful happenings would have bordered on the monstrous. In contrast, Keshu was not depressed. He had seen worse. Much worse.

As he was reading, the electricity failed in half of Haradna East. His readout did not die. Essential city services such as police, fire, and traffic stations were equipped with their own proprietary backup power, as were hospitals, most major businesses, and the better hotels. The system of interlocking power grids and cables was so complex that it required thousands of gigabytes of storage space just to monitor the important junctions.

Four major fires were burning across the city. Two substantial riots were in progress. It gave him much pleasure to note that none of these were taking place in his district. Within the past hour the city had recorded fifteen rapes, twenty-two robberies, eight cases of arson, and forty-four of serious vandalism. Those were the major crimes. He had no time to read about, much less deal with, the hundreds of minor ones. One hour, one crime at a time, he told himself imperturbably.

Especially at the start of such a calm day in the city.

His desk brewed tea. He contemplated spending the day doing a follow-up on the kidnapping of Bira Gumbadi. Mr. Gumbadi, senior vice president of the Bank of Bengal, Sagramanda section, had been kidnapped three weeks ago by a gang of dacoits who had disabled his limousine as it was whisking him home from an important speaking engagement. Using a small laser, they had proceeded to crack the sealed, airtight vehicle and whisk the protesting Mr. Gumbadi away before the car's automatic alarm and location system could draw private security to his aid. It had been very embarrassing for the security firm in question. Keshu felt bad for the company management, not least because it was comprised largely of ex-cops. That was one advantage to his job. Maybe he did not make as much as he would have in private practice, but on the other hand, when there was a major cock-up, he didn't find his picture plastered all over the evening news, either.

The kidnappers wanted fifty million rupees to free Mr. Gumbadi. Not an outrageous sum for one in his position, but substantial enough to give his family pause. Bargaining was ongoing. If, in the meantime, the inspector and his people could find and free the banker, gratitude would be liberally forthcoming, like dung spread across a newly planted field.

The darkened, bullet-proof transparency that was the door to his office changed color, attracting his attention. Issuing an oral command, he bade it rise into the ceiling.

Into the room came a small, dark man deferential in manner and afflicted with a pair of glasses that ought to be put out of their misery by a vision-correcting laser. After said instrument had corrected the style-blind owner's deficient eyesight, of course. That this procedure had not yet been performed was most likely due to an insufficiency of funds rather than an unawareness of the relevant medical technique.

Keshu made it a point not to stare. The financial compensation, or lack thereof, of others who worked in the department was not his concern.

"Excuse me, Inspector," the man said by way of introduction, "but might I have a moment of your time? I am Subrata, from downstairs."

Sitting up straight, Keshu beckoned for the man to enter. "Something I can do for you, my friend?"

The much smaller man placed a hardcopy on the chief inspector's desk. "I would not bother you, sir, if I did not think this a matter of some importance."

"I'm sure you wouldn't," Keshu concurred. No one would, who knew the chief inspector's reputation. Keshu Jamail Singh could tolerate the wasting of most anything but time.

"You know how we are all trained to search for patterns in columns of crimes. Robberies, rapes, extortion, kidnappings—everything and anything." Keshu saw no reason to comment. He was impatient to get back to his reading. "I have been working homicide, and I think I have found something that should be brought to your attention."

The chief inspector's beard rose and fell as he nodded. "Don't keep me in suspense, Mr. Subrata."

"No sir." The smaller man continued hastily, gesturing at the printout as he proceeded. "I have been working on this with several people down in Forensics, and we are all agreed on the conclusions. As you know, the most common method of committing murder in our wonderful city is by knife, which is cheap and easy. Even if unrecovered, the type of knife employed in a killing can frequently be determined by analyzing the nature of the inflicted wound or wounds: their depth, width, angle of penetration, and so on." Adjusting his glasses, he scanned a duplicate copy of the printout he had passed to his superior.

"The past year has seen many dozens of such killings. However, research and follow-up by myself and those people in Forensics seem to indicate that a small number exhibit enough unusual similarities so as to mark them as distinct."

Keshu was still not intrigued, but neither did the level rise on his built-in irritation meter. "Unusual in what way?"

"The blade utilized in these particular killings appears to be unusually large. The lethal wounds were much greater in extent than would have been caused by even a fairly large kitchen knife. A number of the killings included full decapitations, suggesting either an extremely sharp blade, a most powerful assailant, or a combination of both. Additional study ruled out the use, in these particular instances, of axes. Though a large machete remains a possibility, it is the consensus of myself and the people in Forensics that at least twenty-four of these studied murders were committed by someone wielding a sword."

Now Keshu was involved. "A sword? You say you are all reasonably sure of this?"

The smaller man was nodding vigorously. "Not just 'a' sword, sir. The same sword. Detailed analysis of the lacerations point to the same weapon being utilized in each instance. The killings were committed by a large, sharp blade with a smooth, unserrated edge. We feel confident that we have a forensics match for twenty-four." He shrugged diffidently. "There may, of course, be more. The bodies of a number of the victims studied were found in various stages of decomposition."

"Possible serial killer." Keshu was perusing the printout with his full faculties. "Why wasn't this brought to my attention before now?"

Again, Subrata shrugged. "Those of us who have been working on this wanted to be certain, knowing that the consequences would inevitably lead to certain conclusions."

From beneath bushy eyebrows the chief inspector's gaze rose, unblinking. "And you are certain?"

"Sufficient for prosecution, should the perpetrator be found," the other man replied. "It was decided to bring this to you now because of the most recent instances. Two people, a man and a woman, who were fished out of the Hooghly only two days ago. Both bodies came up entangled in a fisherman's net. Before the crocodiles could get to them.

Their wounds proved quite consistent with the other twenty-two unsolved cases." He added, almost apologetically, "Australian tourists."

Now his visitor *really* had the chief inspector's attention. "That's very bad. I don't recall seeing anything about it in yesterday's news, or this morning's."

Subrata allowed himself a thin smile. "Public Relations has been working overtime to keep this one in-house for as long as possible."

Keshu nodded to himself. "Sword-wielding Serial Killer on the Loose in Sagramanda!" was not a headline the municipal authorities would be likely to look forward to seeing splashed all over the front of their morning news report. How long his department could keep such a revelation quiet depended on the reaction of the Australian consulate. Clearly, they were not yet fully in the know. Perhaps his people could keep them in the dark a while longer yet. At least until the unfortunate tourists' friends and relations began to wonder about why they were not hearing from their vacationing friends, and started to make inquiries.

The disclosure prompted another, obvious follow-up question. "And the other twenty-two killings this is related to? Not all tourists, I presume?"

"Only three others. One elderly German gentleman, and an Indonesian couple from Sulawesi. Also two Bangladeshis and a Bhutanese who were not tourists, but illegal workers. The rest all Indian." Subrata gestured with the printout. "There is no pattern to it, sir. Men and women, a number of teenagers, but no children under the age of fifteen. There are victims from every caste, and every walk of life. Rich, poor, middle-class. Dark, light, long and short hair. Nothing to link them except the methodology behind their murders."

"Not just a serial killer, then," Keshu brooded. "One content to choose victims apparently at random. Unless we can establish some additional connection between victims, it suggests our quarry holds no specific grudge against any class or kind of people; only against humanity in general. A nondiscriminatory fanatic."

"That was our conclusion, too, sir." Subrata waited patiently.

Keshu was silent for several moments before he looked up anew. "Thank you for bringing this to my attention, Mr. Subrata. Please keep on it, give it all the attention it needs, and relay that request to your coworkers in Forensics. I want to be informed the moment anything relevant, including possible additional victims of this person or persons, is discovered. Use my personal contact number."

"Yes sir." The researcher turned to go, hesitated. "Will there be anything else, sir?"

"Just two things." The chief inspector stared at the other man through the space between them. "Hope that this individual or individuals makes a mistake. Otherwise they are going to be very hard to catch. And—pray that he or they do not kill any more foreign tourists, or there will be hell to pay for all of us."

"I assure you that my friends and I have already ascertained that possibility, sir." Subrata waited for the door to reascend, then exited through the open portal.

Keshu returned to the study of the morning's readouts, the subordinate's printout looming ominously on his desk. The Mayapur riot was winding down as a pair of rapid-response tactical squads squeezed it from two sides. Another disturbance threatened to flare up farther to the east. Near the zoo, of all places. He allowed himself a slight smile. Perhaps the city monkeys were trying to liberate their caged cousins. Or one of a number of international and/or local animal rights groups might be involved.

Six rape reports had come in since his arrival. Two arson attempts, one successful, the other quenched in the bud by automatic snuffers built into the infrastructure of the attacked building. One attempted bank holdup, unsuccessful, with both would-be robbers stunned by automated security and their getaway vehicle successfully immobilized. Violent confrontation at a private college campus between sit-in demonstrators and campus security guards. Assorted muggings, purse-

snatchings, and pickpocketings. Child-beatings, wife-beatings, hus-
band-beatings, beatings of household pets. Vandalism and car break-
ins. Arrests for graffiti, extortion, theft of utilities, public defecation.

A normal morning.

Except for the efficient Mr. Subrata's report.

With a sigh, the chief inspector rested his elbows on his desk and
rubbed at his eyes with the heels of both hands. On top of everything,
his wife had been nagging him mercilessly for the past week about the
vacation they were supposed to have taken last month that he continued
to put off. She would wave the reservation forms for the Maldives resort
in his face at every opportunity. Smiling encouragingly, touching him
affectionately while doing so, but it still counted as nagging.

What a job, he told himself. What a life. He wouldn't have traded
it for anything.

Better to have a wife ragging on you than a serial killer, he told himself. Using a curt voice command to halt the heads-up readout from the
box, he slipped the fingers of his right hand into the controller glove and
dove physically as well as mentally into the morning's work.

chapter iv

Chalcedony Schneemann hated Sagramanda.
For that matter, he hated India, even though he was half Indian. His mother had been born in Belgaum, in the southwest, and had grown up working in the tourist hotspot of Goa. That was where she had met his father, a German-American executive on holiday. They had fallen in love, she had become instantly pregnant, and he had taken her back with him to New York. But his mother had never forgotten her heritage. Growing up, he had been compelled to learn Hindi and Marathi as well as English and German.

For a corporate fixer whose job category supposedly did not exist, and who was paid in cash and under the table, Chal Schneemann was very well spoken.

Everyone who knew him called him Chal. He preferred it, and it worked out well, since nobody could pronounce his full first name properly anyway (he had been named after his mother's favorite semi-precious gemstone). He had been in Sagramanda for six months now and was no closer to finding his quarry than he was to developing a fondness for the gigantic, seething, steaming metropolis. He missed New York badly; its comparative cleanliness, its museums and concerts, its cultured women who could converse intelligently even when they were being screwed into the floor. Even the Indian food was better there, he grumbled to himself, and you didn't have to conduct a minute inspection of the restaurant's toilet before voiding your bowels.

An impartial observer might have commented gently that Chal was not permitting himself to be open to the experience, was not allowing the charms of the great city to infuse and inform him with its multifarious delights. By way of response, Chal most likely would have beat the crap out of said impartial observer, if not for the fact that it was critical to his work that he pass everywhere unnoticed. Officially, he was in Sagramanda to advise one executive at one branch of the well-known multinational company that paid him handsomely (and under the table) to travel around the world (though most often to the subcontinent) to solve otherwise intractable corporate problems.

Less officially, he was there to find another man. A renegade employee who had disappeared in the possession of valuable company property but who was believed to still be hiding somewhere in the city. A researcher who had stumbled across a discovery potentially worth billions, if not trillions. Of dollars, not rupees. An imprudent local employee who needed to be brought back into the corporate fold before he might misguidedly pass the sensitive information he had absconded with on to another competing multinational.

How Chal went about his business was not of particular concern to his corporate masters. Were he to be caught or challenged while performing his duty, any knowledge of him would be disowned by the same people who saw to it that he was so well compensated. They were interested only in results, not in methodology. Chal had complete freedom to do what was necessary. The cutthroat world of global competition demanded it, even encouraged it.

Personally, Chal had nothing against the researcher who had gone astray. He would prefer not to have to kill him, or torture him to reveal the whereabouts of what he had taken. Chal was perfectly prepared to do either, or both, as the occasion demanded. What he really wanted was to get back to New York. As always, he would do anything that would expedite his departure from the homeland of his mother. His life would have been easier had he simply based himself in Delhi or Mumbai. He categorically refused, preferring to endure the occasional monumental commute. New York was his home, America and Europe his playground. Not India.

Thus far he had been reduced to little more than following blind leads and asking endless questions. No, that was not quite true. One coworker of the missing researcher had been obstinate and had refused to answer any questions at all. Chal, who was of more than average height and weight and physically intimidating, had been forced to administer encouragement. Informing the pigheaded one that he was only doing his job, he had proceeded accordingly. Then he had been compelled to wait until the dazed, chastised coworker, remorselessly hammered down to the corridor floor, finished spitting out blood and teeth and struggled to talk again.

Yes, the bloodied, sobbing, and now fully compliant worker knew Taneer Buthlahee. No, she hadn't seen, heard from, or had any contact with the absent researcher in something like five months. No, she had no idea where he had gone, what he was doing, or what his immediate plans were.

Chal had thanked her calmly, turned to depart down the office corridor that was empty save for the two of them, then by way of farewell and a final object lesson kicked her in her already ruined mouth one last time, breaking her lower jaw. It ensured she would keep quiet until he was out of the building. In the course of his work he had been forced to beat on many people. He had never discriminated between subjects. He knew he had a bad habit of giving in to impatience, but when he required answers, he wanted answers. His life was not a movie, and he had neither the time nor the inclination to coddle the recalcitrant among those with whom he dealt.

Certainly he liked his job, though not every aspect of it. Take the travel, for example. When the company sent him to fix problems in places like London or Frankfurt, he delighted in the opportunity. Because of his background and his specialized knowledge of his mother's homeland, however, the majority of overseas assignments tended to see him working the streets and byways of Bangalore and Mangalore more often than Berlin or Milan.

He was very good at his work and prided himself on never having failed to successfully complete an assignment. The company paid him well, albeit surreptitiously. He stayed in the best hotels, always under a fictitious name that matched one of the several fictitious passports he always carried with him. Multinational corporations were even more skillful at obtaining such useful documents than were international terrorists.

Another employee might have spent as much time as possible at the five-star hotel he had chosen for his base of operations, availing himself of its programmable air-conditioning, fine restaurants, box connections, swimming pool, bakery, and direct-dial call girl service. Chal was far too conscientious for that. He would enjoy himself on his free time. There would be no idle idylls until he had completed his assignment.

His employers preferably wanted Mr. Taneer Buthlahee returned to the fold alive, or at the very least in sufficient condition to converse. At least for a few days. After that . . . If matters grew strained, Chal had been instructed to secure only the information that had been illegally appropriated by the wayward Mr. Buthlahee, and his employers would manage without questioning him. It was important this be accomplished as swiftly as possible, lest the missing researcher have the opportunity to solicit a large monetary offer from one or more of their mutual employer's rapacious competitors.

In addition to the considerable resources the company placed at his disposal, Chal had his own, private network of connections and informers. If such an offer as the company was worried about were to be floated, Chal was as likely as the vagrant researcher to hear about any legitimate response. This would put him in position to intercept both the errant scientist and the offer. It was likely that those putting forth such an offer would object to the visiting Mr. Schneemann's intrusion. That would present a problem. Chal did not worry about such a possibility. He had handled "problems" before. Some of them were even still alive.

If the pressures of work, or simply of dealing with Sagramanda, became too much for him, Chal knew where to go to simmer down for a day or two. Kanha National Park was a short charter flight from the city but a world away from the urban chaos of the enormous metropolis. It was where Kipling had found the inspiration for his *Jungle Book* stories. A hilly, ferociously protected segment of old India, it was home to leopards and tigers, sambar and the rare barasingha. There was a little lodge where one would not be noticed, away from the more popular tourist venues, where he could relax and drink tea and nibble homemade pakoras. . . .

He dragged himself back to the moment. The verdant tranquility of Kanha was far away.

As he stepped out of the air-conditioned taxi, the heat and humidity smacked him in the face like the hot towels thrown by the attendant who worked in the hotel sauna. It had always amused him that the posh hotel boasted a sauna, when often it seemed no less hot and humid right outside that establishment's climate-sealed front door. He had less than a block to walk. In that time he encountered perhaps forty people making their home on the older street. A few had raised the crudest of lean-tos of found cardboard and wood against the stone and concrete walls of the permanent buildings. They were well-off compared to the families that were living in the gutter. Hands and voices were raised in his direction as he approached. Both fell quickly when those doing the imploring got a good look at the face of the well-dressed, comparatively light-skinned pedestrian. Poor does not necessarily mean ignorant, much less stupid.

Chal entered the building, cleared security, and took a lift to the twenty-first floor. At the end of the surprisingly clean and neat hallway was a wall and door of transparent polycarbonate. Glowing letters floating about a centimeter in front of the unshatterable material declared that the rooms beyond housed the offices of Purkhasee Financial, Ltd.

He announced himself to the door. Someone within cleared him, a hidden buzzer sounded, and he pushed his way through. Ignoring the receptionist before she could so much as open her mouth, he turned to his left and walked all the way down to the last office. He had been here before.

Mushtaq was waiting for him. A man perhaps too fond of the worldly pleasures that had left him resembling a dissolute Buddha, the advisor was sitting in an elevated pool of warm saltwater, naked except for the briefest of swimsuits. Outside such pools his great weight combined with his weakened heart and circulatory system to place him in grave danger. Floating, he was able to function more or less normally. Both the temperature and saline content of the pool water were rigorously monitored. The view from the pool of the sweltering cityscape outside was impressive.

"Namaste, Chal! How are you? It has been some long time." Drifting over to the side of the pool, Mushtaq extended a hand from which protruded fingers that resembled the sausages Chal saw in butcher shop windows during his sojourns in Germany. He shook hands firmly with his host. The moist fingers seemed to envelop his own, as if he had dipped his hand into a mass of damp, clinging gelatin.

"The same," Chal replied noncommittally. He did not especially like Mushtaq, but he respected the man's business acumen. A devoted

Muslim, his host had one corner of the pool decked out for prayer, complete to a small but priceless antique rug where he could touch his head while inclining toward Mecca. "How are things in the savings and loan business?"

Mushtaq shrugged. The shrug rippled through his upper body as if his head were a stone that had just been cast into a flesh-colored pool. "Collections are down. You know how it is. People are happy to take your money but not to give it back. Then there are those who do not understand that I am not charging interest, but merely asking for some expression of gratefulness in return for my assistance."

Chal helped himself to one of several available chairs, sitting down with his back neither to the wide, sweeping windows nor to the door, but facing a solid wall. "You don't look like you're suffering."

Water sloshed out onto the overflow ditch that rimmed the pool as its occupant let loose with a rolling, heaving guffaw. "I suffer every day, my friend, but since it is my own choice, I can only complain to visitors who are sympathetic enough to lend a kind ear to my miseries. I don't expect that from such as you."

Chal was not offended by the scarcely veiled affront. He was never offended by the truth. "I need your help."

"Of course you do." Easing over to a platter heaped high with fruits and chocolates, Mushtaq settled on an El Rey mango bar and began peeling off the chilling, enclosing foil. "Nobody ever comes here just to visit." A sonorous belch escaped the loan shark's corpulent depths, rumbling up from regions even understanding doctors did not like to visit. "Someone has not paid a debt? I wouldn't think you'd need my help to deal with that."

"True enough." A glint of light beyond the window caught Chal's eye. It was only a reflection of the sun off the antenna on the roof of the building opposite. He relaxed again. "I'm looking for a man who quit his job without notice. When he left, he took something that was of value to the company he had been working for."

"Nothing so simple as a box terminal, I will wager." Chocolate smeared Mushtaq's face like misapplied dark brown lipstick.

"Information. Formulae. You don't need to know more than that."

"No, I don't." His host grunted. "What can I do?"

"Pass the word along your fingers, of which I know you have many more than ten, with many of them in this disreputable curry or the other." Chal leaned forward in the chair. "It is highly likely the man will try to sell the information he has stolen to the highest bidder." .

Pausing with chocolate halfway to gaping mouth, Mushtaq looked slightly alarmed. "This doesn't involve anything lethal, does it? Ever since the Americans dove wholeheartedly into the business of anti-terrorism, I have found it an area of commerce fiscally irresponsible to be involved with."

"I am told that the stolen information is scientifically explosive, but not inherently so. You can be assured of that. It involves a practical matter the discovery of which the missing researcher was intimately involved with." He smiled thinly. "Something to do with vegetables, I believe."

Mushtaq stared at him, saw his guest was not joking, started to laugh anyway, then thought better of it. Anything serious enough to require the personal attention of Chalcedony Schneemann was no laughing matter.

"You want to find this person before he can hold his private little auction."

Chal nodded. "As quickly as possible. My employers are most anxious. You have access to and utilize financial resources that do not operate through recognized banking channels. I know you. If an exceptionally large amount of money is about to change hands under less than suitably regulated circumstances, you will know about it." Rising from the chair, he removed a small mollysphere from his shirt pocket and placed it on the platter among his host's endless parade of snacks.

"Everything you need to know is there. The usual retainer for your services will be deposited into the appropriate account." He met the other man's deep-set eyes squarely. "If information supplied by you leads to the successful recovery of the absent gentleman, I believe even you will be startled by the size of the finder's fee you will receive."

Sliding over along the edge of the pool, pushing faintly perfumed saltwater out of his way, Mushtaq dried his fingers and picked up the molly. Pinched between fat thumb and forefinger, it gleamed like a silver pearl.

"Vegetables," he murmured as he stared at it. His gaze flicked sharply back to scan his visitor's face. It was, as usual, impassive. "I can supply all manner of fruits and vegetables, but I suspect not the kind your employers seek."

"No," Chal agreed. "Apparently only one man can do that, and he doesn't want to be found."

"He will be." Carefully setting the mollysphere aside, Mushtaq pushed away from the pool wall and drifted out into the middle of the twenty-first-floor raised pool, his bulbous body an outré silhouette against the floor-to-ceiling window behind him. "Alive?" he queried.

"Preferably." Chal prepared to take his leave. "At least long enough for me to have a chat with him."

Anil Buthlahee had come to Sagramanda to kill his son. Also the slut who had not merely seduced him, which was bad enough, but who had somehow managed to corrupt his mind.

The senior Buthlahee was a traditionalist in the best and worst sense. To him, for a male relative to sleep with a Dalit girl was bad enough. For it to have been his firstborn son was horrific. That Taneer thought so little of his family to even contemplate marrying the woman, whose name shall not be mentioned, was so far beyond any affront Anil had ever experienced that even now he could scarce believe it. Just as he could hardly accept the presence of the gun resting in his pants' pocket, its compact, unyielding shape bumping and grinding against the outer part of his right thigh like some obscene cold-blooded parasite. It held only four small-caliber bullets, each equipped with an explosive head.

That was twice as many as he would need, he felt.

Wandering the busy shopping street, Anil found it difficult to concentrate. How could Taneer have done such a thing? He had always been such a good boy. A good boy who had turned into a fine young man. The pride of his family, he had been the first not only to go to university, but to graduate. And then, to be hired by such an important company, and to rise so rapidly within.

And for what? To throw it all away on some stupid twat? If a man was in desperate need, one who belonged to the venerable VyMohans caste rented such creatures. One did not *marry* them. One did not bring them into a respectable family such as the Buthlahees.

Taneer would not do so. It would not be permitted. He, Anil Buthlahee, would not allow it. He had worked too hard. Next year he would turn fifty. Half a century of striving, of seven-day weeks and endless long hours and hard work, and for what? To preside over the wedding of a son to an Untouchable? Was that what his own sainted father and mother had worked so hard for, building up their one small store in Puri, slaving from before sunrise until late into the night to give him, Anil, the base from which to finally obtain a proper loan so he could begin to expand the family business?

He could not look his aged father in the face until this matter was appropriately resolved.

Using the family business as collateral, Anil had obtained money that had allowed him to expand one store at a time. Now the Buthlahee family owned twelve such stores, the smallest being larger than his parents' original enterprise. The stores were scattered up and down the coast, following the main north-south road. They managed to compete with the big city stores on their own terms. As a student, the brilliant Taneer had helped his father and cousins set up a proprietary wireless system for controlling real-time inventory that had allowed them to stay one step ahead of their competitors. They served local people seeking food and household goods as well as tourists traveling down the coast and the eight thousand priests of Jagannath Temple, Vishnu be praised. The Buthlahees operated the second-biggest store on Puri's main street, Bada Danda, where they sold everything from sunblock to computer and box accessories.

All for nothing, if the disgraceful prospect Taneer had chosen for himself was allowed to come to fruition.

Via email and vit, Anil and his wife and Taneer's cousins had pleaded and argued, threatened and screamed at him to break off the relationship. All to no avail. Taneer had declared defiantly that not only was he going to remain with the Untouchable woman-thing, he fully intended to make her his wife. Finally, forced to an extreme no decent VyMohans father should be expected to endure, that was the moment when Anil had disowned him. It was the last time father and son had spoken.

But disowning him was not enough, Anil knew. He had talked to his own father, and to his own cousins, as well as to Chautara, the esteemed senior uncle of the family. Sorrowfully, the conclusion was the same among all. Taneer could not be allowed to bring the entire family into permanent disgrace.

More than one male cousin had offered to perform the necessary duty. A grim-visaged Anil had turned them all down. It was his son who was the offender. Therefore it was his, Anil's, responsibility to see to the cleansing of the family name.

Hands brushed at his lower limbs. Some of the beggars imploring him had no legs. Some had been ravaged by HIV-connected diseases. The face of one girl of about sixteen, who had clearly been born beautiful, was covered with open, running sores. Whitened cankers clung to her full lips. Her eyes were already vacant, dead; the rest of her body would follow soon enough. He ignored them all. He did not want to start a riot by handing out rupees.

Dominating the horizon above the crowded, busy street was the Harap Jain temple. Encrusted with tens of thousands of shards of lovingly hand applied, electric hued, dichrotic glass, its five hundred meter-tall tower dazzled all who raised their eyes to drink in its simple yet spectacular beauty. The full length of the glass-encrusted spire was visible for only five minutes each hour. The rest of the time it was shrouded, as the computer-driven mosaic glass panels rotated inward. Otherwise, the drivers of too many vehicles on the streets below would find themselves blinded by the thousands of individual reflections as the sun changed its position in the sky. Not to mention the pilots of small choppers and other commuter craft that made use of the skyways above the city streets. Like every other religion, the Jains had been compelled to adapt their tenets to the needs of the greater city.

Inquiries at the company where Taneer had worked had brought a faster response than Anil could have hoped for. It appeared that those who had employed his son were as anxious to find him as the father. Utilizing skills born of a life spent engaged in bargaining and business, Anil assured those with whom he spoke that he would be pleased to inform them should he manage to reestablish contact with his son. He did not tell them it would be after he had shot dead his offspring and the whore.

Sagramanda did not frighten him. Business had required that he visit suppliers in the great metropolis several times a year. He felt that he knew the city as well as any nonresident. The delight of the city's chronically overwhelmed administration, public transportation was its pride and joy. The subway and maglev, the fuel-cell-powered buses and electric rickshaws, made it easy even for someone who was not rich to get around with a modicum of efficiency. Having more resources at his disposal than the average visitor, Anil managed quite well.

Finding his son and his son's whore, however, was another matter entirely. For one thing, he had no idea what the trollop looked like.

Before he had ceased communicating with his family Taneer could not stop from going on and on about her purported beauty. A bottle of mercury was also beautiful, Anil knew, and equally lethal if swallowed whole. The woman-thing was incidental to his search. Find Taneer, and he would find them both.

He had already posted his son's most recent picture, together with a substantial reward for information. The Net was a beautiful thing. For years now it had extended its reach even into the poorest villages. Illiterate farmers had learned how to use touch-screens to check the buying prices of various commodities. People who could not read could match portraits to memories, and vote. Sagramanda was home to many millions of technologically sophisticated people. Anil felt that if anyone saw his notice and reward offer and then caught a glimpse of Taneer on a city street, they would know how to respond.

So far, the communicator in his pocket had been silent on that score. He had programmed in a special ring for the line that would connect him to anyone having the information he sought. The device also enabled him to stay on top of business matters back home.

People in their hundreds swirled around him as he stopped outside a small food stall. It was one of dozens that lined the shady side of a wide sidewalk near the small but clean businessman's hotel where he was staying. Fragrant smoke filled the air as various kinds of meat and vegetables were rapidly turned on open gas and charcoal grills whose metal bars were burnt black from decades of charring thousands of meals. He had asked around before settling on this one as a regular hangout. Though he could afford much fancier food than roti and dal, that was the traditional fare he had grown up eating every day. It would not feel right to have anything else for his midday meal.

Gripping the insulated paper wrap that made it possible for him to hold the hot unleavened bread with its load of lentil puree (and a little chicken—he was particularly hungry today) in the thick fingers of his left hand, he seasoned it with some ambal and took a big bite as he turned up the street. He had several people to meet today. One worked for a private investigation agency that had been highly recommended to him by a fellow businessman back home. No avenue would be left unexplored in the search for his renegade offspring. The honor of the entire Buthlahee family was at stake and, as the family patriarch, everyone was relying on him to do the right thing.

Not for the first time, and in spite of himself, he found himself wondering just how this Dalit girl had managed to enchant his son. Taneer was intelligent, sharp, educated, and for a young man not yet thirty, quite sophisticated in the ways of the world. Yet he had thrown away everything, everything—future, family, honor—for this Untouchable woman. Perhaps hypnotism was involved, though Anil was not sure he believed in that. Considering himself a modern man, he did not lend much countenance to sorcery, either. Drugs seemed more likely. Had this mercenary whore turned his son into some kind of addict? When they had last spoken, and argued, Taneer had been angry. But he had not sounded drugged.

Could it just be natural attraction, then? Or rather, unnatural attraction. Could she be that beautiful, that seductive? Trying to imagine himself lying with an outcaste girl, he shuddered. It nearly put him off his lunch. He found himself eyeing other women on the street; some in Western dress, some in saris, others in the amalgamation attire that had recently become popular.

Get a hold of yourself, he thought firmly. You have a good wife, and other children. You are not here on holiday. Resolutely, he refocused his gaze on both the task and the street ahead. An overloaded donkey treading a fine line between sidewalk and motorized traffic was complaining about its load of electronic components. Past and future, Anil ruminated as he eyed the ancient beast of burden. Then the donkey let loose a flood of urine, and the determinedly homicidal businessman from Puri had to sidestep like an odissi dancer to avoid having his shoes drenched.

chapter v

Sanjay could hardly believe his luck. First, he had
escaped the unexpected late monsoon downpour simply by
being aboard the transfer bus when the storm had struck. Then, it had
let up just long enough for a silent electric transport to disgorge its
load of tourists in front of the long line of shops of which his was one.
When the intermittent storm had returned with full force the
steaming, soaking gray downpour had driven the ill-prepared visitors
into the shops, whose proprietors waited to greet them with open
arms, wide smiles, hot tea, and hastily inflated prices.

Sanjay made out as well as any of his neighbor merchants. With
so much tourist largesse to spread around, there was none of the
occasional acrimony that bubbled up when one lucky shopkeeper
succeeded in monopolizing the clientele. Not for the first time,
Sanjay thought he should add some T-shirts to his inventory. It took

a lot of space to display them properly, but the profit margin was substantial.

It was while he was contemplating this potential expansion of his stock that a local gentleman entered. Sanjay sized him up swiftly. About his own age, the visitor was dressed modestly but was exceedingly well groomed. It was almost as if he was deliberately dressing down. For what reason someone might do this, Sanjay could not imagine. In contemporary India, the style was to flaunt it if you had it. Sanjay himself had no compunctions about showing off his fine wrist communicator or designer running shoes. Perhaps this gentleman's better clothes were all with his laundry-wallah.

Though he pretended to inspect the shop's offerings, it was clear from the moment the man entered that he was no tourist. Feigning disinterest, Sanjay missed nothing as he followed the visitor's movements. Occasionally he would find himself diverted to attend to another potential customer. Interestingly, and strangely, each time someone else entered, it seemed to unsettle the man.

Shit or get off the pot, Sanjay thought, employing a favorite metaphor an American tourist lady had once explained to him in her careful English. If the man was too uneasy to approach him . . .

"Excuse me," he said with a smile, "may I help you, sir? Are you looking possibly for something in particular? For a lady, perhaps?"

Unexpectedly, the man looked alarmed. "What makes you say that?" From his tone Sanjay could tell that this odd caller was an educated person.

"Is it such an unusual thing to ask, when a man looks at silver and amber jewelry for almost an hour without inquiring about anything?"

Sanjay had a smile that was all the more winning for being genuine, instead of manufactured like that of some of his fellow shop owners. It relaxed his edgy visitor—a little.

"No, I suppose it is not. I am not here shopping for a woman. I am, in a way, shopping for myself." He glanced significantly at the door. "Would it be possible for us to have some privacy?"

Sanjay hesitated only briefly. He had owned his business long enough to recognize a potential robber on sight, and this peculiar visitor was not one. The man's look, his voice, even his clothing were all wrong. Sliding his fingertips over the appropriate contacts on his gold bracelet, Sanjay locked the door, darkened the windows, and activated the shop's security bubble.

"There," he announced when he was done. "No one can see us; no one can hear us." He indicated the window. "We are safe from infrared scopes, directional microphones, and all manner of eavesdropping equipment. Is that enough privacy for you?"

Tension leached out of the man like steam from a safety valve. "My friend was right. You are as vigilant as he claimed."

"Please, have a seat." Directing his guest to the chair opposite, Sanjay sat down behind his counter. Without thinking and despite his preliminary appraisal of the visitor, he made sure that the safety was off on the drawer that concealed the loaded pop-up gun. "What friend was that?"

"No need to bring his name into this." Taneer had to fight not to keep glancing in the direction of the door. The shop owner's assurances notwithstanding, the street, after all, was still very close. "Or mine."

Sanjay shrugged. Whatever game his visitor was playing, the rules would no doubt eventually be spelled out. "As you wish. What shall I call you?"

"'Mohan' will do."

Sanjay had a quick response. "But you're not, are you?"

It brought the first hint of a smile, which did not linger long. "My friend told me that you have many interesting contacts on the street, and that you sometimes deal in items not usually found in tourist gift shops." When Sanjay started to reach for the relevant hidden sample drawer, Taneer raised a hand. "That's not what I'm interested in. I need an intermediary. An honest broker." The intensity in his voice matched that of his stare. "The most important thing is, my friend said you were discreet and reliable."

"I am very much flattered, sir. I come from a small, poor village where sometimes all a man has to offer are such intangibles." He indicated their surroundings. "I am convinced it has helped me to get where I am today. So. I take it, then, that you are not here to buy, but that you have something you wish to sell?"

Taneer nodded.

"Can I see it?" Sanjay prompted him. "What is it? Gold? Jewels? Pre-nineteenth-century artifacts? Please be at ease. I assure you that I can be most conveniently ambivalent where provenance is concerned." He hesitated only momentarily. "Drugs? Restricted pornography?"

His visitor took a deep breath. Bending over in the chair, he reached down and removed his right shoe. The heel, interestingly, rotated sideways beneath his fingers to reveal a hidden compartment from which "Mohan" withdrew a tiny metal case. Utilizing his own control bracelet, he entered a combination that unlocked this. It contained a single molly-sphere. A small one, no bigger in diameter than the tip of Sanjay's little finger. The man handled it as if it were a flawless hot pink diamond.

"That tells me nothing." When it came to business, Sanjay could be disarmingly direct. "I surmise it most probably contains information you desire to sell." His visitor nodded confirmation. "I am sure you will tell me how and to whom you want it offered. But first you must tell me what you want for it. Your asking price."

Taneer held out the molly. "Before we get to that, you need to know that this is a copy. Not to insult you, but without periodic electronic reactivation by me, the information it contains will simply evaporate. So there's no point in anyone trying to take it by force. As to potential buyers, I'll give you the names of several companies with offices or representatives in the city who I think will be interested in what I am offering.

"Your task will be to find a safe and respected means of engaging them through a third party. You will act as my primary agent in this. No one else is to be involved except yourself and whoever you choose to use as your own intermediary. That way, you will be in contact with me and this other individual, while they will have contact only with you and the eventual buyer. As I will never have any dealings with this third party, they will not be able to identify me to anyone else who might be looking for me. While I realize this arrangement is slightly cumbersome, it will put another level of separation between myself and the final purchaser. It will be more time-consuming, and will cost me more because two commissions will have to be paid, but the added distance provides a necessary additional level of safety." Changing tack, he scanned the area behind the counter.

"Do you have an old-style, free-standing calculator? One with a simple built-in readout and no integrated projection unit?"

Removing the requested device from a drawer, Sanjay pushed it across the countertop. His visitor tapped on it briefly, then slid it back. "The information I have for sale will be sold by single bid, one chance only. No negotiations, no auction. The bids are to be submitted in a format and at a time I will specify later." He tapped the calculator's faded readout screen. "This is the figure I expect to sell at. Your commission, if all goes as well as I hope, will be one percent."

Sanjay almost rose angrily from his chair. What a waste of time this had been! he thought. An imposition on his hospitality and his good nature! Then he saw the figure the man had entered.

It nearly did not fit on the calculator's readout.

He sat back down, scowled at the figure. "There is a mistake. Your finger must have weighed too long on the zero."

"No." Taneer spoke quietly, folding his arms in front of him. "There is no mistake. That is the correct figure. In U.S. dollars."

Now Sanjay knew it had to be a mistake. Either that, or his visitor was an exceptionally well-dressed escapee from one of the city's many asylums. The smile he had been wearing ever since the other man had entered was in danger of disappearing permanently. "You are most unkindly playing some kind of game with me. This is a joke."

Taneer shook his head slowly from side to side. His expression was completely sober, dead serious. "Am I smiling? Have I been acting like someone with nothing better to do than spend my afternoons playing bad jokes on people I've never met before? Do you think I have spent as much time in this shop as I have already in order to leave with nothing more than a smile?"

Sanjay's mind was racing furiously. Though he was good with figures, he knew he was not a fast thinker, or a deep one. He was smart enough to know his limitations. What this stranger was proposing, if it indeed was not all part of some elaborate joke being played on him by a friend or acquaintance, or a reality vit show being recorded by a hidden camera, was so far beyond anything he had dealt with previously, even in his business with Bindar, as to border on the inconceivable.

So, in his usual direct manner, he said as much.

"That's why I'm here, presenting this proposition to you now," his visitor explained. "There are others who were recommended to me that I could have gone to; more sophisticated, more knowledgeable, with access to more extensive resources than you and your little business." Sanjay took no offense at these words. He had never regarded the truth as insulting. "But they are also much more likely to be watched, to be under observation."

No fool, Sanjay asked, "Watched by who?"

Having not come to an agreement, Taneer continued to hold back everything that was not necessary. "Those who would rather steal than purchase. I'm sure even in your business you've had to deal with such people."

Glad of the commonality, however tenuous, Sanjay nodded knowingly. "Truly, the world is full of thieves. People who make it difficult for someone to make an honest living." He did not add that he was still very much unsure as to which of those two groups his visitor belonged. That, however, need not prevent the doing of business.

"There is some possible danger attached to this dealing, then?"

Taneer nodded brusquely. "With this kind of money involved, how could it be otherwise? I assure you that I'm running a much bigger risk than you, though. It's this they're after." He rolled the small, spherical storage device around in his palm. "And me. Are you still interested?"

Sanjay had already made up his mind. The risks in agreeing to deal with this stranger were unknown. The reward, if his visitor was being truthful, was potentially enormous. He could have everything he had ever dreamed of. Everyone he *knew* could have everything they had ever dreamed of. Silently, he converted the figure his guest had entered into the calculator from American dollars to Indian rupees. The number was so high he did not even have a proper name for it.

His one percent commission would not be so insignificant after all.

"Five percent," he replied gruffly. He could not help it. It was in his blood.

For the first time since he had entered the shop, Taneer chuckled. "Two."

"Four," Sanjay countered.

"Two." Taneer started to rise.

"Three," Sanjay countered again, perhaps a bit too anxiously.

Shaking his head with amusement, Taneer resumed his seat. "All right, my friend. I don't want to appear greedy."

Sanjay smiled back. He was starting to like this fellow. He would have to watch that. "Then why not give me five?"

"Three percent. Say yes now, or I walk out that door and you'll never see me again."

"I think if that happens, my life will become dull once more. Three percent."

They shook hands on it. Then Sanjay settled back in his chair and asked, "It might be useful for me to know what it is that I am selling." He indicated the mollysphere shifting back and forth in Sanjay's hand. "Information, that much you have confirmed. But information about what?"

Taneer's smile evaporated faster than vodka at a Russian wedding. "Better that you don't know. You wouldn't understand the particulars. There are not many people in the world who will. But there are enough." Ceremoniously, he placed the storage device on the desktop. "This is not a complete rendering of what it is I have to sell. But there is more than enough here to convince anyone sufficiently knowledge-able who delves into the details to prove to them that I can deliver what is promised. The rest of the relevant material can and will be sup-plied when the final details of the sale are worked out." His eyes met those of the shopkeeper. "I am telling the truth when I say to you that the less you know of it, the better. For both of us."

Sanjay shrugged as if he dealt with this level of commerce every day. "I am only to be your middleman. I must accept your instructions. You strike me as a truthful person."

Taneer rose from his seat. "I have ninety-seven percent of that figure at risk. I can afford to be." He nodded in the direction of the remote that controlled the shopkeeper's box. "May I access that?"

Sanjay hesitated. He disliked the idea of anyone else poking around in his personal system. Of course, if he was looking over the visitor's shoulder while the man worked . . .

"Certainly," he said graciously, as if it had never crossed his mind to refuse the request.

It was an education to watch his guest manipulate the familiar multiple floating projections. The man had the skill of a technician and the technique of an artist. Images and figures, schematics and solids appeared and dissolved within the hovering tunnel above his modest counter in a dizzying succession of colors and forms. When his visitor was finished, Sanjay was not even entirely sure what had been done, even though every bit of it had transpired before his eyes, on his own equipment.

Taneer explained it to him. "I've entered the necessary information into your secure database."

Eyeing him in disbelief, the shopkeeper checked the relevant file. The new material was there, just as his visitor claimed. It should not have been, but it was.

"How did you do that? Those files are personal, protected, and guarded."

Taneer just smiled. "Maybe one day I'll explain it to you, though it's not something you need to know. When our business together is finished, you won't need to know such things because you'll be able to hire someone like myself to do them for you."

"That is so," Sanjay realized. He studied the readout floating in the air before him. "When do you want me to start making inquiries?"

"Right away. The sooner a buyer is agreed upon, the better it will be for everyone concerned." Raising his left foot off the ground, Taneer indicated the heel of his shoe. "It may not appear so, but what I have been carrying around in my shoe is surprisingly heavy, and grows heavier by the day."

Sanjay dipped his head. "I will do my job, sir, and not fail you. Soon the only burden you will bow beneath is the weight of too much money."

They shook hands again. As Taneer was going out the door, he turned to leave one last thought in his wake. It should not have been necessary to say it, but even at his comparatively young age, he was not one to leave important matters unspoken.

"You'll mention this to no one else, of course. No one," he finished solemnly.

Sanjay's nod was brisk. "Not even to my most beloved wife. I know that it is difficult for a man to keep his wits about him if his head is removed from his shoulders."

"If the wrong people learn about this, they won't start with your head." Leaving that final warning hanging in the air, Taneer stepped back out into the heat and glare of midday. The usual afternoon mix of pedestrian and vehicular traffic soon swallowed him up.

Returning to his counter, Sanjay did not reactivate the "Open" sign on his shop front door, nor did he lighten his windows so passersby could look in and once more view his stock. Instead, he called up the information his visitor had somehow magically inserted into his personal files. None of the names were known to him. For the most part, the street addresses were equally unfamiliar. They lay in parts of the city that were alien to him: very high-rent commercial districts and blocks. Well, they would be known to him soon, he realized. Or at least to whomever he would engage to make the necessary representations. His own contact. The second intermediary, whose participation would provide the extra level of security his just-departed guest demanded.

No boxwork, Taneer had warned him. Nothing online to be traced. Everything had to be done in person. The old-fashioned way. Step back in time a couple of centuries, and then proceed.

Sitting behind his simple counter, visions of wealth and freedom dancing tantalizingly at the edge of his thoughts, Sanjay Ghosh set to work.

Depahli's gaze kept returning to the dancing, swaying numbers on the time-designated portion of the wall that had been implanted with the clock. It was as if they were following her around the apartment. They *would* have followed her around except that they had been programmed to remain in one place.

The men she was waiting for were late. That was not unexpected. Riots that sprang up like weeds, equipment failure, traffic jams in unexpected places, animals on the road, the loud and often violent settling of personal vendettas: all could and often did combine to slow the delivery of materials. In the case of her order, she had placed it in person, which was supposed to expedite such matters. Though she had lived with Taneer for nearly a year and paid close attention to his instructions, she was still comparatively new to working the box. She tended to look away from its scanner and not speak clearly in the direction of the vorec. It would take a while before she was as comfortable talking to a device as she was to another person.

The sensitive nature of her order had not intimidated her from shopping for it, or from dealing with the understanding female clerk at the other end of the connection. She could have placed it over her personal communicator as well as directly via the apartment box. But it was useful to be able to talk to someone knowledgeable about what she was buying. Receiving an explanation from another woman who had used it herself was better than reading about it on the box, or even viewing a full holo demonstration.

But if the delivery people didn't hurry, they would not be able to complete the installation in time, before she expected Taneer home. Everything would still function, but the surprise would be lost.

Though she was a naturally fast learner, the totality of her ignorance concerning things technological when she had first met Taneer had frequently left them both gasping with laughter. In truth, he had enjoyed teaching her as much as she had enjoyed being taught. Now, she could work everything in the unassuming apartment: the vit, the built-in kitchen, the mobile small appliances scattered throughout the four rooms, and she was learning more and more about how to operate the box. Circumscribed as her physical movements were, it was the safest window to the rest of the world. When she had successfully placed her first order, using the alternative, secured cash account Taneer had set up exclusively for her use, she had insisted on celebrating. Her man had found it amusing that she could get so excited over doing something that had been second-nature to him as a child.

He had not grown up a Dalit child, she had reminded him firmly.

A pleasant male voice broke into her reverie to announce that there was someone at the door. As she hoped, it was a pair of installers with her order. After verifying their identities, the building admitted them.

A second security check in the hallway proved equally routine. Moments later they were on the tenth floor and querying her door in person.

Though not Muslim, she wore a veil and modified abaya. With her beauty effectively concealed, she would not be a distraction to the two men. Not being Muslim themselves, neither thought to comment on the contradiction of a Muslim woman admitting two strange men into her home. Or perhaps they assumed that the male resident was close by.

They set about their work with a professionalism that put her at ease. Other than to query her about where she wished a certain component to be installed, or how she wanted another positioned, they went about their business in silence. Neither commented on the sensitive nature of the system she had purchased. No doubt they had performed dozens, perhaps hundreds, of such installations and it was all strictly business to them.

When they had finished, they ran several of the system's embedded programs to make sure it was functioning properly. Watching these, Depahli found herself blushing beneath the veil. They paid not the slightest attention to her. It struck her then that perhaps they were eunuchs, or gay, and had no interest whatsoever in the details. Business, after all, was business.

The senior of the two workmen turned the system vorec over to her, spent a few moments instructing her on how to program it to recognize her voice, had her peer briefly into the unit that imprinted her retinal pattern onto the receipt, and bid her good day as he and his companion took their leave.

She experimented with the installation for the next hour, gradually becoming more comfortable with its individual eccentricities, learning how to customize it to her tastes. Taneer would do the same, of course—if she could just get him to relax. That was becoming harder and harder as the time for reestablishing contact with the outside world drew near. It was why she had purchased the system. If it couldn't relax him, it was likely nothing could.

When he finally arrived just before dark, after taking the usual random, circuitous route back to the apartment, he was tired but elated.

"I think we're on our way at last, Depa." Smiling, he put his arms around her and hugged her tight. "I think I've found just the right person to move this along."

"Finally!" For all her physical perfection, she still had to stand on tiptoes to kiss him. "I have a surprise for you."

His smile metamorphosed into a grin. "I know that smile, you little vixen, you. What have you been cooking up while I've been gone?"

Taking his hand, she drew him toward the kitchen. "Dinner first. After you've had your fill of my cooking, you'll see what I've been cooking up."

She had become adept at programming the kitchen, and providing it with the ingredients necessary for it to perform its magic. As befitted the occasion of the installation she had prepared a special, though not overbearing, meal. Her own special mulligatawny soup to start, then malai chingri—prawns in coconut milk. There was onion kulcha, or flat bread, on the side; a nice selection of ghonto—mixed vegetables; and a delightful assortment of momos—stuffed and steamed dumplings from Mizoram. For dessert, it had to be rosogulla—cottage cheese balls in pure sugar syrup.

They ate by simulated candlelight, Depahli having programmed the little kitchen's illumination unit accordingly.

Taneer drained the last of his iced tea, set the glass down on the simulated marble table with its slowly shifting patterns that simulated pietra dura, or inlaid semiprecious stone, and shook his head slowly as he gazed across at her.

"What a marvel you are. If only I could find a way to make my family see that."

"Your family will roll in camel dung before they acknowledge me. I care nothing for their approval, but I wish that they would do so if only for your sake, to settle your mind," she shot back at him.

Rising, he came around the table and took her hand in his, easing her up from her chair. "My mind was long since settled on this matter," he murmured decisively. Then he kissed her. "When this is all over . . ."

Surprisingly, she pulled away from him, grinning wickedly. "Before it is over, you are going to have to learn to relax, or you'll have a heart attack before you can enjoy your money. Come with me."

She led him into the bedroom. Smiling but uncertain, he followed. "I don't see anything. Am I supposed to see something?"

"Watch," she advised him. Moving to her right, she took the system vorec out of the drawer where she had concealed it and spoke commands.

The lights in the bedroom darkened. Traditional music—sensuous with sitar, pregnant with tabla drums—issued from unseen speakers. The delicious scent of roses and sandalwood tickled Taneer's nostrils. Concealed projection units came to life, their imaging converging on the large bed that occupied the far side of the room.

Out of the converging lights two figures coalesced, one male, one female. They were Indian, but they were not dressed like anyone Taneer had ever seen outside of a movie or vit special. Clad in the jewels and sparse but royal raiment of more than a thousand years ago, they knelt facing one another on the bed. As he watched, they began to disrobe. The man stared into the woman's eyes, and she into his. Their bodies were suffused with the gleam of the golden light of which they were composed.

Standing on tiptoes once again, a delighted Depahli whispered into her man's ear. "They're waiting for us."

Sophisticated in the ways of modern science Taneer might be, but there were zones of experience into which his expertise and knowledge had not delved. It was clear she had succeeded in surprising him. Her delight was complete, and there was more to come. Much more to come.

"I don't understand." He was still smiling, but clearly confused. "What are we supposed to do? Watch?"

"Silly man." Taking both of his hands in hers, she backed toward the bed, gently drawing him with her. "Don't you know by now that I don't care for spectator sports?" With a nod, she indicated the lambent figures kneeling on the bed. "They are special avatars, customized just for us. Don't you see that the man's dimensions match yours, and that of the woman mine?"

"I still don't understand," he confessed as she helped him remove his clothing.

"You cannot imagine how much it pleases me to have discovered something you don't understand, Mr. Taneer Buthlahee I-know-all." Giggling, she moved toward the still-motionless, three-dimensional, fully formed female image kneeling on the bed—and knelt within it. Not beside it—within it.

As the equipment recognized her incursion and the appropriate program reacted to her presence, the glow that now surrounded her intensified. It was as if she had suddenly taken up habitation within a ghost. While Taneer could see her clearly through the sculpted light, she wore around her as weightlessly as chiseled breath the image of the woman from ancient times, though no moisture was involved. When Depahli raised her hand to beckon to him, the ethereal figure she now occupied gestured simultaneously. It was as if, he thought, she had slipped into the most diaphanous of full body gloves.

Warily, he moved to join her on the bed. All giggles and smiles at his hesitation, she helped him to position his naked form within the image of the ancient warrior-king kneeling opposite her. As his eyes threatened to play tricks on him, he had to blink several times to get used to what he was seeing, which, of course, was the intent of the system's designers.

"I've seen installations of this kind in commercial use," he muttered uncertainly. "I didn't know they were available for home purchase."

"You would be surprised, my big darling, what is available for home purchase."

He leaned toward her. As he did so, the radiant, shimmering image of the ancient warrior-king he was "wearing" matched itself perfectly to his movements. "You have become quite the feisty little box cutter, haven't you?" Raising his right arm, he stared in fascination at the glow that enveloped it. It conformed perfectly to the shape of his arm.

"Watch this." She uttered a command in the direction of the vorec lying on the end table.

The diameter of the lustrous aura sheathing his arm expanded slightly, becoming instantly more muscular. Looking down, he saw that the rest of his radiant shell had taken on the build of a formidable athlete. And that wasn't all.

"You little minx!" he growled affectionately. "Do you want your new toy to give me a complex?"

"No, no!" Giggling, she rescinded the order, and his gently pulsing outer shell became once again more cloak than camouflage.

The slight tingling he felt was probably imaginary, he decided. The installation generated no heat, no stimulation of the nervous system. That, they would have to supply themselves. "What else can this devilish little plaything of yours do?"

"Oh, many things. I have been practicing religiously since the installers left. See?" She spoke another command.

He found himself looking down at the glowing image of none other than the goddess Parvati herself, from within whose many-armed façade the face of the woman for whom he had forsaken family and tradition stared back at him. Part of the amazing apparition, however, was obstructed by his trunk.

Looking down at himself, he saw glowing around his own body stumpy legs, a protuberant belly, tusks, and most impressively, a slowly waving, startlingly realistic trunk.

"Ganesh and Parvati. What a combination." He wagged a finger at her, since he had no control over the trunk. "Fun is fun, but don't be sacrilegious!"

"All right," she laughed. A quick command, and they were once more swathed in still-imposing but more straightforward maiden and king. "Get ready."

"Ready?" He tried not to sound alarmed. "Ready for what?"

"School is in session, my love, and I guarantee you are going to enjoy the homework."

This time she addressed a much more complicated command to the vorec. Taneer jerked slightly as his lambent avatar began to move. So did the one in front of him. Not only were they moving together, they were moving *together*. Slightly slack-jawed, he watched the performance unfold. Abruptly it halted, and the glowing shades returned to their original positions.

"You have to follow along," Depahli chided him. "The virtual sutra not only performs, it also instructs. If you don't stay inside the projections, the program reverts back to the beginning and waits for you to start over."

"I . . . see," he mumbled, a little weakly. "It's like one of the thousands of inhabitable virtual games you can download from your box to your vit."

"Yes," she told him. Her smile widened. "An instructional game. I can command it to run as a continuous loop, until we get it right."

"Get what right?" He swallowed hard.

"Third lotus position. Part of the installation's programming contains the entire *Kama Sutra* as virtuals. Also *The Ananga Ranga*, but I thought we should start with something simple. Try again." She spoke to the vorec.

It took him a moment to catch on. Whenever he moved a part of his body correctly, identical to the movement of his avatar, its glow intensified. When he made a misstep and part of him thrust outside his ethereal envelope, its movements slowed and its glow faded.

It was really quite simple, he decided as they progressed. All you had to do was follow the patient, guiding movements of your wraith-like self and physical adjustments that might previously have seemed impossible suddenly became simple and understandable. Enthusiasm quickly replaced hesitation. Any initial feelings of inadequacy disappeared. It was perfectly appropriate that such a system and its resident software should be available in India, he reflected through his exhaustion and his sweat. Did not the very word "avatar" descend from the Sanskrit?

Before the night was done, the radiance from their respective and untiring avatars blushed bright enough to read fine print by.

chapter vi

No one paid any particular attention to the tall, willowy foreign woman who slipped like a wind-borne twig through the narrow streets. This part of the city was used to being inundated with spurts of tourists. They came and went like sudden hailstorms, pelting the locals with questions and camera flashes and the smell of money, and then they went away.

So while it was somewhat uncommon to see a single tourist perambulating by herself, it was hardly unprecedented. Fifty years or so earlier, she would have been an easy target for pickpockets or muggers. But like every other tourist site in Sagramanda, the dense accumulation of shops and stores around the old temple was peppered with concealed monitors and camouflaged sensors. Perpetrators might successfully commit a crime in its vicinity, but they were unlikely to get away with it.

Those denizens of the immediate, overcrowded neighborhood who did happen to glance into the face of the long-legged visitor might have had second thoughts about her origin. Though her features were European, her skin was darker than that of many locals. Furthermore, she made her way with complete confidence, expressing no disgust or outrage at the lingering puddles of urine or accumulated piles of rubbish she effortlessly avoided. In the midst of filth, she showed no emotion whatsoever. That was unlike the typical tourist.

The small open area that fronted the temple, a miniature plaza nearly roofed over by the porches and overhangs of the buildings that surrounded it, was much cleaner. The priests kept it so, picking up any intruding trash and regularly sweeping the large squares of stained white paving stones. It was a tiny place, almost claustrophobic. Even though this was the principal temple to the goddess Kali in all of India, one could miss it by a single street without knowing it was there.

Neither was the building itself imposing. Wide white stone stairs led up to a single wraparound deck that in turn surrounded the inner temple. Clad in simple green and white tiles, the old dome overhead was no bigger than that of a country church in the south of France. Perhaps only the bright, bloodred paint that covered the external pillars hinted at the presence inside of the unusual.

From some locations on the diminutive square it was almost impossible to see the temple through the maze of fiber optic cables, power lines, illegal boxline taps, and other wires that crisscrossed the restricted open space. It was as if the temple had been encased in a gigantic web of brown and silver silk spun by unseen spiders. Vendors of fruit and flowers, incense, and small souvenirs for the faithful occupied every crack of an alcove, every semisheltered niche. Especially flowers, as these were bought to be cast to the image of the goddess during prayer. Red flowers were especially popular; natural color if possible, dyed if one could not afford the real thing. Even more than the constant babble in multiple languages, the clash of odors was stunning to the senses: stale urine and powerful disinfectant, fresh roses and decomposing offal.

None of it appeared to affect, much less faze, the woman dressed in the half sari and loose cotton pants. Approaching the temple, she touched a button on the haft of the umbrella that had been shielding her from both sun and rain, collapsing and automatically furling the portable protective canopy. The two short, dark men who had had their eyes on her ever since she had entered the temple square exchanged a few mumbled words and moved on. What had at first glance seemed a possible easy target was on reflection entirely too familiar with her surroundings. They decided to look elsewhere for a victim.

They never knew that was the best decision they were to make all day.

Ignoring the imploring, singsong din of the many vendors packed tighter than sardines along the alleyway, Jena climbed the temple steps as deliberately as she had many times before. At the top, she found herself confronted by a priest. A new man, one who did not know her. His smile was wide, inviting, and phony.

"Memsahib has come to see the temple of Kali?" Without waiting for a reply, he continued, "I am Nusad, and I would be happy to be your guide."

She started to brush him off, then had a wicked thought. She was in no hurry, and could use a little entertainment. Looking around, she saw no one she recognized, either in the temple or on the small square it fronted. That was not surprising. Like many temples, this one rotated priests and acolytes frequently. That suited her fine. She did not want anyone to recognize her, either.

So she said, in English, "Very nice to meet you, Nusad. Yes, you may show me the temple."

She took the standard tour. It was interesting to see what was shown to and what was kept hidden from the tourists these days. She overpaid for the devotional flowers at the shop the priest led her to, wondering what percentage comprised his personal kickback. She lis-

tened to his rehearsed history of Hindu mythology. The greatly con-
densed version, suitable for ignorant foreigners. Only when he led her
inside to the flower-draped, incense-surrounded statue of Mother Kali
did her attitude change.

The self-assured young priest did not notice the subtle shift. He
was too engrossed in his spiel. "This is how you pray," he was telling
her. "First you throw the flowers you are carrying to—"

She turned on him so sharply it broke his train of thought. "I know
how to pray," she informed him tautly. Turning away from him, she
approached the statue and reached toward it. No other priests or visitors were around.

"Here, memsahib, you can't do—"

She snapped at him. In Hindi. And again, for good measure, in
Bengali. The look on his face was priceless, worth having to endure the
preceding ten minutes of touristy babble. Turning back to the statue,
she did not throw but placed her offering at the goddess's feet.
Straightening, she steepled her hands together before her face, palms
together, fingers pointing upward, lowered her head, and began to
whisper in Hindi.

The stunned priest could only stand by, openmouthed, listening.
This was something he had never seen before. A white person who knew
the proper words. And there was more, much more, embedded in the
prayer. Indisputably, improbably, the foreign woman was praying in
earnest and not for show. Some of what she was saying would have made
the hair stand up on his head, were it not clean-shaven.

The words that he managed to catch had something to do with a
late-night commuter train. A businessman, traveling home. Him getting off at a commuter nexus in a well-off suburb. Being followed.
Somewhere between train and house being stabbed in the back, several
times, blood pouring out to darken his high-collared white coat.

Fantasy, of course. Homicidal make-believe. The shaken priest had
heard of such things but had never encountered it before in person.

Wish-fulfillment. The foreign woman had a fertile, if horrific, imagi-
nation. She had everything, in fact, to complete the illusion she was
trying so hard to craft except the requisite severed head of a demon
clutched in her right hand. He almost expected her to break into the
appropriate dance—and was half afraid that she might. If it was a certain, specific kind of dance, it might drop him to his knees. Thankfully, she did not commence anything so disconcerting.

Concluding her prayers, she turned to leave. Her eyes were
shining; some of it was due to devotion, some to the lingering effects
of a hefty morning dose of rapture-4. Taken together, it was enough to
cause the now thoroughly unsettled priest to step quickly out of her
way. He retreated until he was backed up against the temple wall. The
colors of her half-Western, half-Indian raiment had not registered on
him until now: black and red.

She turned to him in passing, her face alight, her eyes burning.
The two of them were alone on the isolated segment of wraparound
porch. "Thank you for the tour, priest. Aren't you going to harangue
me until, out of guilt or fear, I consent to contribute an excessive donation to 'the upkeep of the temple'?"

He shook his head slowly, unable to tear his eyes away from that
mesmerizing gaze.

She smiled. "Well, don't worry. I always make one." Reaching into
her shoulder bag and using her right hand, she removed not money,
but a small knife. It looked like a miniature Tibetan phurpa, but he
couldn't be sure. Still smiling at him, she extended the tiny but ultra-
sharp blade and drew the cutting edge across the back of her right
hand, deftly avoiding the tendons. Droplets of bright red blood began
to drip onto the temple floor. Reaching out, never taking her eyes from
his, she fingered up a fold of his robe and used it to wipe the blade
clean. Pressing the back of her hand to her mouth, she sucked at the
self-inflicted wound. It was then that the priest noticed the framing
network of scars. They covered the back of her hand and extended, like

the ghosts of worms, all the way up her forearm until they disappeared beneath the sleeve of her sari top.

"My donation," she whispered. Moving closer, she added, "Don't call me 'memsahib.' I am Devi Jena. And this is your Shakti for the day. May it inspire you in the faith." Then, before he could escape to either side, she kissed him, full on the mouth. Amid the hot pressure he tasted salt and blood.

Then she was gone, around the corner of the temple and down the stairs, a swirl of hair and silk that was swallowed up by the milling, noisy crowd.

He didn't tell anyone about the encounter. How could he? No one would believe him. To the end of his days, he never forgot it.

It would have been better for some still alive if he had been both more worldly and more secular, and had gone to the police.

It was not surprising that the air-conditioning in the museum always worked. Tourist dollars were irreplaceable. Tourism was not only a business whose benefits were spread among many, it was a comparatively clean industry. In a city like Sagramanda, locked in an eternal and it sometimes seemed eternally losing battle with every imaginable kind of pollution, that was important.

Even more important than ensuring that the air-conditioning functioned properly at major tourist sites, however, was ensuring that the tourists did. Finding murdered ones floating in the Hooghly and gnawed by the fishes was even worse for business than poor climate control.

Among the few effects found on the body of the waterlogged, dead Australian woman was a ticket stub. Though tourist sites had long since advanced beyond the need to issue such antiquated shards of admittance, they continued to do so because visitors insisted on receiving them. They made excellent mementos. To enhance their keepsake value, many years ago government as well as privately operated sites had taken to issuing permanent plastic souvenir tickets.

Though dirty and scratched, the one that had been extracted from a pocket of the dead tourist's pants indicated that she, at least, had visited the museum on a certain day and at a certain time. Ascertaining that several members of the museum staff who had been on duty the day of her visit were on duty today, Keshu had determined to pay a visit to the venerable old mausoleum himself. On this visit he was attended to and assisted by one Corporal Bubaneesaywayti. Americans, at least, would have been amused to know that the dour junior officer was usually referred to by friends and colleagues alike as Corporal Bubba: a regional reference as out of place in Sagramanda as saag bhaji would have been in St. Louis.

The outside of the massive pile of stone and concrete never failed to impress: an elaborate amalgamation of Victorian British design and Indian workmanship. The interior offered more of the same, though recent renovations tended to conceal the least practical aspects of nineteenth-century architectural design.

The museum boasted a wealth of artifacts relating to the history of the country. Glittering howdahs that had once borne magnificently mustachioed maharajahs from affairs of state to elaborate durbar dinners. Ornate costumes of silk and silver, gold thread and strung pearls—some even intended to be worn by women. Ranks of damascened spears, swords, knives, pikes, and other assorted martial cutlery. Armor for men, armor for horses, armor (most impressively of all) for war elephants. Exquisite miniatures of ivory and carved gemstone. The back side of one favored maharani's hand mirror that had been fashioned from a single slice of pale sapphire.

Wandering through the high-ceilinged halls, Keshu found himself more taken with the displays of artifacts from everyday life. Many of these were overlaid with virtuals, much as in the old days painted plastic overlays were used in books to teach everything from human anatomy to archeology. Nowadays layers of reality were cloaked in virtuals, which were not only more realistic and capable of movement but which could be changed with the touch of a finger on a control or the application of a suitable program.

Inspector and corporal passed by, and through, villagers working the massive brick kilns of ancient Mohenjo-daro. They questioned guides and guards as virtual laborers toiled to build the Taj Mahal beneath the sorrowful gaze of a virtual Shah Jahan. As they queried a ticket-taker for a special exhibition, carefully modulated concealed speakers accompanied the recycling and untiring charge of the invaders from the north who had given rise to the empire of the Mughals. The rampaging imagery was inspiring, though Keshu thought the volume needed to be turned up.

Corporal Bubba was more taken with the display that chronicled the history of Bollywood films; especially the enticing virtuals of famous stars of the past. Many who had never appeared on screen together sang and danced their favorite numbers in tandem. Through the magic of virtuals and programming, famous faces (and figures) from different eras of entertainment were able to interact seamlessly with one another.

So much history, Keshu thought as he and his assistant trudged onward, questioning every employee they encountered, even the temps. A world unto itself, India was. His world.

Once, he had attended a conference of his peers in Tokyo. Another world unto itself. The conference had been held in a hotel built in the shape of two giant half-moons that faced one another and were bound together by a network of stainless steel strands. At night, thousands of LEDs embedded in the cables lit up in a light show unlike anything he had ever seen before.

The hotel and conference center had been constructed on shallow land reclaimed from Tokyo Bay. On his last day, there had been an earthquake. A minor one, hardly strong enough to cause the hotel staff and his Japanese hosts to pause in their work. Boarding the sky cruiser for the supersonic trip back home, a shaken Keshu had vowed never to leave Sagramanda again. Or, at least, India. Some things that were homegrown simply could not be transplanted, he realized.

"*Haa*, I remember them."

"What?" His thoughts still on the terrifying moment when the Earth had shuddered beneath him, the inspector had to pull himself back to the moment.

Corporal Bubba leaned close. "He says he remembers them, sir."

Keshu refocused on the guard. The man was very old; perhaps as old as some of the static exhibits now relegated to the rear, less-visited corridors of the museum complex. But his memory of matters recent, it developed, was sharp and clear.

He was holding the display spindle Bubba had handed him. A third of a meter long and the thickness of the corporal's thumb, it was currently enveloped in a holoed projection of the two dead tourists. Its operation was simple enough for anyone to operate. Press the button at the top of the spindle to turn on and off, press one of two buttons on the bottom to zoom in or out. Rotating the spindle in one's fingers caused the projected image to rotate with it.

The old man pushed a finger into the face of the dead Australian man. While the images had been enhanced by forensics reconstructors, the program's effectiveness had been undermined by the fact that both bodies had been hauled out of the river in the first stages of decomposition.

"You're sure?" Keshu prompted the guard, all thoughts of distant and unstable Japan now banished from his mind.

The senior nodded. He had a long, somber face lined with more channels than the Brahmaputra, wide eyes that seemed on the verge of weeping, a nose sharp enough to cut nonsense, and a deferential manner. But he was certain of what he had seen.

"I have been a guard's assistant and full guard here for forty years," he declared formally. "I have a good eye for people and have caught many thieves." Once again he pushed an identifying finger into the holo, this time into the face of the dead woman. "I remember these two as clearly as I remember everyone."

An energized Keshu nodded approvingly. "Do you remember anything else about them? Anything they said, perhaps? Some indication of where the two of them might have been going after they finished here?"

"No." The guard shook his head. "I didn't hear what they were saying." He stiffened slightly. "I watch the visitors. I don't eavesdrop."

Keshu was not disappointed. It would have been foolish to hope for anything more, and he had been a cop long enough to learn not to expect it.

"You said 'the two of them.'" The guard's expression had not changed. "Don't you mean 'the three of them'?"

Corporal Bubba looked up from his recorder, exchanged a glance with his superior. Restraining himself, Keshu addressed the elderly guard cautiously. "We only know of the two." He gestured at the spindle the old man continued to finger. "You say you saw three? There was a third person with these two? *You're sure?*"

"Yes." The oldster was wonderfully positive. "Another woman. Also a foreigner, I think, though she was dressed like a local. I have seen her here before." He hesitated. "This is important?"

Keshu kept calm. "Yes, it is important. What can you tell us about this third person?" Next to him, Corporal Bubba was busy with his recorder. "Can you describe her to us? Height, hair length or color, body shape, distinguishing marks: anything you can tell us about her will be most helpful."

The old man proceeded to provide an account that, given the time that had passed since he had last seen the trio of visitors, would have done proud any officer in the force hoping for promotion to the rank of detective. When he had finished and Keshu was certain Bubba had it all down for entry into the department's reconstructor, the inspector thanked the guard from the bottom of his heart. He did not also have to press the pair of bills into the old man's hand, but he wanted to. Not only did he know what a break like this potentially might be worth, he had a pretty good idea what the old man received in the way of take-home pay after forty years of standing around watching tourists.

Leaving the museum and stepping back out into the appalling heat, Bubba commented as he put away his recorder. "Good to have a lead on this one, sir."

"Yes. We were going nowhere fast." Keshu headed for their car, secure in the no-parking zone at the base of the entry steps.

"Do you think if we find this other woman she might lead us not just to the murderer of these two unfortunate visitors, but to the serial killer himself that everyone in the department is talking about?"

Avoiding the visitors both ascending and descending the steps around them, Keshu paused halfway down the marble staircase. He ignored the effusive, recorded greetings being spoken by virtuals of the Mahatma and assorted other Gandhis to stare hard at the junior officer. "What makes you so sure, Corporal, that the third person is not the killer we seek? Do you not think a woman could commit these crimes? Or is it because the very informative old guard-wallah said he thought she might be white?"

Bubba was not afraid to meet his superior's gaze as they continued toward their car. "Neither one, sir. But the pictures from Forensics show very extreme wounds. It would take an exceptionally strong woman, of whatever background, to inflict those even with a very sharp weapon."

Raising his right arm toward his lips, Keshu uttered a terse command toward his bracelet pickup. The police cruiser unlocked, allowing them both to enter. The silent fuel-cell-powered electric engine started up instantly. Leaning on the accelerator, Corporal Bubba guided it toward the parking lot exit.

"We know nothing of the physical capabilities of this killer," Keshu made clear. "There are some physically very strong women in this world. There are also other ways of enhancing one's strength.

Steroids, vitamins. Banned substances. Of course," he added with a nod, "you may be perfectly correct. This third woman may only be a lead in the deaths of the two tourists. Or she may have nothing to do with it at all. But she is by far the best lead we have had so far."

"I believe she is the only lead we have, sir."

"Thanks for reminding me of that, Corporal," Keshu said dryly. He gestured to where his subordinate's recorder now rested in its charging slot in the console between them. "Thank Rama for the acuteness of the old man's memory. When we enter it all into the reconstructor, we'll at least have an image of someone to look for. And if this other woman is not directly connected to the killings, maybe she can supply us with additional useful information."

Without activating the car's siren or lights, Bubba pulled out onto a main street and slid over into the services lane, heading north. Effortlessly, he eased in between a garbage truck and a service transport carrying a team of power line technicians. The in-dash AI smoothly synchronized the cruiser's speed to that of the other vehicles. Overhead, the double-decked lanes of the same expressway vibrated slightly with the hum of southbound traffic.

"I think she should not be too difficult to locate, sir, if the reconstructor can re-create a reasonably accurate portrait. There are not that many Europeans who are resident in the city. I would think there would be very few tall European women."

Typically, Keshu was brooding again, always focused on the worst-case scenario. "She may not be resident in the city. Maybe she lives in Delhi, or Bangalore, and only comes here to visit. To kill—if she is our killer. Which reminds me that once we have an image, it must be disseminated to every police department in the country. So we have a country to search, not just Sagramanda."

"Yes sir." Bubba was clearly disheartened by his superior's coldly professional analysis.

"Furthermore," the inspector continued, "it is also possible that she lives outside the country and only visits to commit murder." He was deep in thought now, arguing with himself. "But I think that less likely, since it would be too easy to pick out such an individual at points of entry. No, I think our serial killer lives in the country, though not necessarily in the city. I am less certain the witness we seek is European. Perhaps she is mixed. That would extend the list of possible suspects into the many tens of thousands."

He sighed and leaned back against the cushioning seat. It had been designed and built by Maruti to comfort and protect a body at pursuit speeds up to 300k an hour. Given the population density within Sagramanda, however, chase speeds tended to be in the single digits.

"If our quarry is a woman," he went on, "it *would* go a long way toward explaining the killer's success. Most people would not expect from a woman the kind of violence on display in the official Forensics' recordings. And she might successfully slip in and out of places with a large knife or sword where local Security would immediately detect a gun." He could not keep from thinking of the ceremonial kirpan at his waist whose function was purely religious.

"She could be working with the actual killer," Bubba suggested as they dove off the expressway and back onto city streets. "Maybe she serves as the bait."

Keshu nodded slowly. "But to what end? None of the victims who have been slain in this manner, including our unlucky Australians, had anything missing from their person. So robbery is not a motive, either for a solo killer, a pair, or a group. Neither have any of the victims been sexually assaulted. They do not appear to be linked by anything: gender, age, ethnicity, caste—nothing. The only thing that ties them together is the method by which they were murdered." He looked over at the corporal. "We are faced with the worst kind of serial killer: one who slays arbitrarily, and generates no pattern."

"Well, at least now we have, if not a direct link to the killer, a potential witness, sir."

The corporal was being disingenuous, Keshu knew. Trying to offer a glimmer of hope to a senior inspector notorious for his pessimism. He ought to be grateful for the thought, but he was too depressed.

Instead of someone performing random acts of kindness they had someone, or several someones, at large in the city intent on carrying out random acts of murder. If resourceful in hiding their tracks and good at leaving no clues, such an individual would be difficult enough to track down in a town of ten thousand. In Sagramanda, such a task was more than daunting. It was also a challenge; something that had driven Keshu since before he had undergone the sacred Amrit ceremony. Whether the challenge would prove too great for him and for the entire department to handle remained to be seen. Meanwhile, he had already come to one certain conclusion about their killer or killers.

They were not going to stop killing of their own accord.

Motive, he thought furiously. If only they could come up with a motive. Even serial killers had reasons for the outrages they committed. What bound the blade-slain victims together? What link was he overlooking?

Corporal Bubba said nothing more during the remainder of the drive back to headquarters, addressing himself neither to the car's AI nor to its other human occupant.

He knew that both were deeply engaged in the business of processing information.

chapter vii

Chal was a patient man, but the lack of leads was beginning to irritate him. Never particularly fond of Indian food, he was also growing tired of eating at the numerous Western fast-food franchises that had extended their french-fried tentacles throughout the city. He could afford better, but preferred to avoid the fancier restaurants. For one thing, such destinations were among the few where despite his assiduous lifelong efforts to maintain his anonymity, he might be recognized. For another, he took an almost perverse delight in subjecting his body to the corruption fast food could engender. Lastly, the very act of eating wasted time. The dour tracker regarded eating as akin to putting fuel in a car: a necessity to ensure forward motion best completed in the least possible amount of time.

Yet it seemed as if the time thus saved was being wasted. None of

his contacts had brought him anything useful. That was the conun-
drum he was mulling over in his mind as he walked down Park Street.

It was natural that he would take his time; not only because he
enjoyed walking, but because he was on his way to report his lack of
progress to Mr. Nayari. It was from Mr. Nayari's company that the
much-sought-after researcher had taken his abrupt leave, and it was
from a sizable if surreptitious account that Mr. Nayari was personally
paying Chal for his services. Given the size of the daily retainer Chal
was charging the company, it was not unreasonable for the vice president to expect results. While Chal could not yet supply these, he felt
it incumbent on him to provide an explanation for his lack of progress
thus far. "Sagramanda is a big city," he knew, would not be accepted as
a sufficient excuse.

He was passing the old cemetery, with its stone monuments and
thick vegetation, when the weapon was pointed at him. Its appearance
was accompanied by a whisper.

"Step in here, please, sir, or I will have to shoot you where you
stand."

From off to one side, another young man materialized out of the
bushes to come up behind Schneemann. Eyeing the speaker and his
weapon, Chal nodded tersely, wiped several fingers over the left breast
pocket of his one-piece beige jumpsuit, raised his hands, and stepped
off the sidewalk and into the underbrush. Once out of public view, he
found himself confronted by three young men.

Defying the heat of midday, they wore long white leather pants
electrostatically charged to repel dirt. Two flaunted matching white
cotton tank tops while their companion, the one holding the weapon,
wore a T-shirt emblazoned with the dancing image of a popular singer.
All were shorter and considerably darker of skin than the larger,
mixed-race Chal. One had the sloe-eyed features of a Nepali. If pressed
by the police, they would smilingly insist that the stripes that streaked
their pants legs were only decoration. Among Sagramanda's gang cul-

ture, such stripes stood for the number of people the owner of each pair of pants had beaten up or robbed. Red stripes for male victims, green for women. One of the trio displayed an inordinate number of green stripes, of which he was no doubt proud.

Chal's attention remained concentrated on the single visible weapon. It was a wire shocker. He had to smile at the irony of it. Whatever hath that multitalented dead American Thomas Edison wrought? he mused to himself not for the first time. It was doubtful the famous inventor had ever envisioned anything as compactly diabolical as the wire shocker.

"Wallet," the young man nearest him demanded curtly. "Do not try to hide anything from us or it will go harsh with you."

Expertly feigning fear, Chal nodded again. "The decoy is in my breast pocket; the real, secured one is up inside my right pants' leg."

Seeing that their victim was going to cooperate, the youth holding the wire shocker relaxed slightly. His cronies advanced hastily, one kneeling to remove the outed security wallet from their impassive prey's pants' leg, the other reaching for Chal's top pocket. Being naturally anxious to conclude their mugging as quickly as possible, they worked fast and in tandem. Both made contact with their target at the same time. There was the sharp, crackling sound of a powerful electrical discharge. The two stunned gang members found themselves shocked backward, down, and out.

By lightly pressing his fingers in a particular pattern over his left breast pocket, Chal had activated the sealed superconductive wiring woven into the fabric of his jumpsuit. Fully powered up, the thin, flexible, lightweight batteries sewn into the back of his jumpsuit not only provided protection to his spine, they were also capable of delivering a charge of several hundred volts to anyone who touched him once the system had been activated. Their wearer was not affected because he was fully grounded through the soles of his special shoes, to which the jumpsuit's integrated defensive mechanism was linked.

Its effect was instructive. The youth who had reached for Chal's other top pocket was blown into a clump of bushes. Receiving a slightly bigger jolt, the kneeling Nepali now lay on his back. Several fingers on his clutching right hand were burned black. Smoke issued from the tips.

Motivated by a mixture of fear and fury, the third youth instinctively fired his weapon. Connected to its gun by a superthin conducting wire, the penetrating dart struck its target square in the stomach. Glancing down at where it had pierced his jumpsuit to embed itself in the Nanocarb-Kevlar undersuit he always wore, Chal eyed the dart with interest as its potentially lethal charge was dissipated by the combination of outer jumpsuit and inner defensive material. Had the dart packed an explosive instead of an electrical head, his unpretentious looking but very expensive clothing would have successfully dissipated its deadly effects as well.

Having shot his electronic wad, the wide-eyed surviving youth dropped his now-useless discharged weapon, turned, and ran. Chal could have shot him several times before he fled out of range, but there was no need. He had delivered a lesson that might or might not be absorbed. Whether it was or not was of no consequence to him. Sagramanda was home to thousands of such youths. Statistics showed that there were already enough who would not make it to adulthood. He saw no reason to add to the total.

Testing the wire that connected the dart in his belly to the gun lying on the ground, he made sure that it had spent its charge before yanking it out of his body armor. Without bothering to look down, he stepped over the supine body of the half-paralyzed Nepali. Gazing in unblinking shock at his burned fingers, the youth was already beginning to twitch spasmodically. In less than an hour he and his companion of the bushes would be back on their feet. Unsteady, in pain, but alive. Their delayed recovery would give them time to contemplate the ironic nature of their surroundings.

Emerging from the cemetery brush, an unperturbed Chal resumed his interrupted stroll up Park Street. From the time he had disappeared within until the time he had reemerged, his expression had not changed. None of the other pedestrians looked at him; no one glanced in his direction. What people did in the bushes was their own business.

Though clad in bronze-hued glass from New New Delhi and green marble from Rajasthan, the tower that housed the Sagramanda administrative offices of the company that had engaged his services had been designed to look like an ancient Chandela temple. Multiple smaller spires surrounded and supported the sixty-story main structure. Instead of the sculptures of sensuous apsaras, or celestial maidens, who decorated the real temples in places like distant Khajuraho, the office tower and its subsidiary spires boasted glowing virtuals that promoted the giant multinational's many divisions and diverse products. While the virtuals did not stray far from their projection units they gave the structure, especially at night, the appearance of being under assault by angels.

Heavenly commerce, Chal thought as he entered the first of several double-doored layers of building security. How Indian.

With his suit deactivated, he set off no immediate alarms. The ultrathin, concealed superconducting wires that were part of the weave were of course picked up by detectors, as were the twin flexible battery packs that were woven into the back of his jumpsuit. When a swift, professional analytic scan by building security revealed that they were connected to nothing explosive and that the batteries had fully discharged, he was allowed to proceed. The woman who accepted his weapons for safekeeping while he was on business within the building kept looking from the sophisticated devices, several of which were beyond her experience, to their owner. Clearly, she wanted to ask about them, and about him. He left her unsatisfied, with only a polite smile.

He did not feel naked or unarmed as he walked toward one of two express lifts. Not every lethal weapon had been checked with building security. For example, he still had his arms and legs.

The live receptionist on the fifty-ninth floor greeted her sinewy visitor with a pleasant "Soobden"—good day. Jaded as he was, Chal tended to look at people once, size them up, and file the information. On this occasion he was moved to look twice. Not because the woman was exceptionally beautiful in her early maturity, which she was. Not because the full-length sari she was wearing rippled of its own accord, programmed as it was with its own integrated flex-breeze, to alternately stand away from and cling to her supple body. No, he looked a second time because one glance was not enough to enable him to identify the long, slender gun she wore strapped to her long, slender left leg underneath the distractingly motile sari.

Though he could have put the question to her as a matter of mutual professional interest, it would have been impolitic to pry. Nothing in her demeanor suggested the presence of such an impressive weapon in such an intimate location. Doubtless if he acted in a threatening manner the device would present itself for closer inspection— probably by being thrust swiftly and efficiently in his direction.

Giving no indication that he was aware of its existence, he announced himself. Outward demureness ably masking her concealed aptitudes, she allowed as how he was expected, and that he should go in. Softly voicing a command (in perfect Etonian English, he noted), she caused a pair of security-camouflaged doors to appear in the wall behind her desk. A thousand years ago one would have assumed a Chaldean witch had performed sorcery. Today it was simply a matter of rearranging batches of preprogrammed photons. Flashing her a faint and oddly knowing smile, Chal eased around the reception desk and all of her concealed weapons. The doors opened as soon as he drew near enough.

Gautaum Nayari was standing by a wall staring down at Sagramanda. The wall was the window: completely transparent armor glass from floor to ceiling. When he did not immediately turn to greet his visitor, Chal contained his irritation and walked over to stand beside the executive.

"What do you see?" Nayari gestured with the home-rolled incense stick he was smoking.

Chal disliked games. In his profession, it was directness that was prized. But this was the man whose company was paying for his time. If Nayari could not buy his interest, he could at least rent his attention.

"City. People. Smog. Buildings, vehicles." Unsmiling, he turned to his right to regard his host. "Am I missing something?"

"Customers."

Nayari walked away from him, toward the small shrine built into the back of the office. Designed like a stupa lying on its side, it had the general shape of a fallen helmet, with the shrine to Ganesh at its apex. Figures of Ganesh, who promised prosperity and happiness, were everywhere in India, and Chal had seen thousands of them. This one was bronze and wore a patina of considerable age, its dull golden hue burnished with sooty black, its costume inlaid with jewels. The statue was an antique, and the rose-cut stones were not imitations.

The executive took his seat. Or rather, it took him, rolling up to meet his approach and gently nudging the backs of his knees. Wafting upward from the incense stick, hints of sandalwood and nutmeg tickled Chal's nostrils.

"People today need four things," Nayari declaimed importantly. "Food, shelter, entertainment, and energy. The company doesn't get involved with the first two. For one thing, the profit margins are insufficient. We are very big on the last two."

"I know," Chal responded. "I've read the annual report."

Nayari's eyebrows rose slightly. They were like the man; very thick and forward. Ruffs of white hair like mislaid cat fur framed a skull that was otherwise bald from front to back, as if someone had pushed a shovel down the middle of a snowbank, leaving high drifts on both sides. The executive was quite dark-skinned, though this was not necessarily reflective of caste. His eyes were those of someone twenty years younger, as was the mind behind them. The latter had to be, for him to occupy and maintain an important position in a company of such size and reach.

"Most of the men like yourself that I have met are not big readers."

Chal shrugged slightly. "'To stop learning is to start to die.' Erasmus, I believe. It's the same in any profession." A hint of a smile tweaked the corners of his mouth. "Before agreeing to any job, I like to know that my employer can afford my services."

The executive let out a guffaw of approval. Or maybe it was just a surprised grunt. "Given someone with your reputation for efficiency, I had expected to see results by now."

"This isn't some backward mud-and-dung village in southern Tamil Nadu." Chal's tone was curt, but not disrespectful. He could have severed this puffed-up, self-important windbag's throat before the man's finger could hit the alarm button that was no doubt built into his desk. Such actions were generally good for the soul but bad for the pocketbook. Schneemann never gave in to impulse. He continued conscientiously.

"I have sources who are devoting all their efforts to locating your missing individual. I have contacts who will inform me the instant anyone in officialdom receives information as to his whereabouts. Meanwhile, I am not waiting on them but am also pursuing specific information on my own." Afraid that his eyes might betray his feelings, he kept his gaze focused on the statue of Ganesh reposing in its shrine well back of the desk. The right hand of the elephant-headed god remained aloft, palm benevolently facing him.

Suddenly Nayari seemed to slump, some of the sturdy officiousness oozing out of him like accumulated gas. "I don't mean to belabor the same points, or to in any way belittle your efforts, Mr. Schneemann, but I am under a great deal of pressure to get this issue resolved." With a sweep of his hand he indicated his spare but elegant office. "It may appear to you that I am a powerful man. And I do exercise a certain amount of power, especially within this country. But there are those above me who are even more concerned, more impatient, to see this awkward matter swiftly brought to a conclusion."

Some sort of empathetic response seemed in order. "I'm doing the best I can, Mr. Nayari."

"I know, I know." Despite the perfectly controlled temperature and the genetically engineered antiperspirant he wore, the executive was starting to sweat. "Despite what the company is paying you for your current assignment, Mr. Schneemann, I am not certain you entirely understand what is at stake here."

Chal hardly ever lost his cool. "It might help if I had some idea what is at stake, besides 'information.' For a start, you might at least tell me which half of company interests this *does* involve: entertainment, or energy?"

Nayari looked up at him. He was not uncomfortable sitting at a lower level than his visitor. Someone occupying a less-powerful position might have been, would have stood or sought a dais on which to stand. Nayari was only frightened of real threats, not implied ones. "I wish I could give you more details. Believe me, I wish I could. But I *can* answer your question. It involves energy."

Chal nodded, noting the streak of slight discoloration in the thick carpet that semicircled around the executive's desk. No wonder Nayari wasn't afraid. The discoloration almost completely masked the presence of the charged conductor woven into the carpet. It was impossible to tell whether it was presently activated or not without crossing the line. It was a test he had no intention of taking.

"Considering what you are paying me, and how everyone inside the company I have come in contact with reacts when I mention what I am doing, I didn't think it had to do with some vit star's infidelities or a stolen story script for the next big soap opera. I know that billions are at stake." He spoke the word calmly, as if discussing last week's rent.

"Billions." Nayari nodded in agreement. "Careers. Entire companies. Not just subsidiaries. Whole companies. A significant portion of humanity's future."

"Then why put just me in charge?" There was no sarcasm underlying Chal's question. It was an honest inquiry.

The display of personal concern that had started to overcome the executive vanished. He was once more the cool, implacable, completely collected administrator. "Because within your idiosyncratic job description you were clearly the most trustworthy person in the company. Given what is at risk, that was deemed more important than any other considering factor. Also, it was decided that because you live outside India, you could bring an outsider's perspective to a sensitive situation."

Translation: he could act with impunity and if caught, the company could more easily disown one of his singular ilk than, say, half a dozen. He was not offended by the explanation. It was no less than what he expected.

"And," Nayari continued, not yet finished, "you have a reputation for discretion. The last thing the company wants is to attract attention to what everyone hopes will remain an internal matter."

Translation number two: if whatever the missing researcher Taneer Buthlahee had made off with got out onto the open market, heads would roll: perhaps literally. And one of them surely sat on the shoulders of the erstwhile powerbroker seated before him.

"I promise you, Mr. Nayari," he replied calmly, "that I understand the need to resolve this matter as quickly as possible. Rest assured I will do so."

Preoccupied now, the executive nodded absently. Chal had to prompt him. "Was there anything else, Mr. Nayari?"

"What? No, no. I don't want to hold you up any longer. I just wanted to"—he sighed—"reemphasize the importance of haste. If you come across anything to report, anything at all . . ." His voice was level, but his posture was pleading. Chal almost felt sorry for him. Almost.

"The instant I know anything, I promise that you'll know it too, Mr. Nayari."

"Good. Excellent. If you need more resources . . ."

Translation the last: find the son of a bitch and I'll personally see to it that you receive an ample bonus on top of the already promised remuneration.

"I have access to as much as I can appropriately supervise," Chal replied. "Wouldn't do to spread the word too far afield. As you say, that's exactly what the company doesn't want to happen."

"True, true," Nayari murmured. "Well then, I hope to hear from you soon."

"And I hope to speak to you soon. With news."

Exiting the impressive but aloof office, recovering his assortment of armament from the efficient and otherwise unresponsive receptionist, striding down the corridor toward the private, guarded lift, Chal was silently fuming. What did they expect him to do? Put a hundred million people in a giant chickpea sorter and sift out the one named Taneer Buthlahee? The man he was hunting might not be experienced at hiding, but an accomplished research technician and scientist was no fool. He was not going to walk around in plain sight, nor do anything to advertise his location. What part of that did Nayari and his breed not understand?

He entered the lift shaking his head. The guard/operator took one look at him and had sense enough to hold his tongue, since his solitary passenger wore the expression of someone capable of cutting it out at a moment's notice just because a comment or question had irritated him.

Together, the two men rode down in silence; both armed, both working for the same employer, but in matters of competency and experience as far apart as Delhi was from Dublin.

It was really quite interesting to observe the animals, Anil Buthlahee mused as he strolled through the zoo. There were no bars, no cages in the ancient sense. Movement of the exhibits was restricted by less medieval means such as moats, precisely sloped ground, and in the case of particularly agile specimens, varying levels of restrictive electronics such as beamed microwaves. The result was that visitors could get quite close to dangerous creatures like cobras and lions without fear of being killed.

People were much more dangerous, Anil knew. Take the device resting inside his shirt pocket. Anil was no marksman. When he had gone looking for a tool with which to commit the necessary deed, he had deliberately sought out one that need not be especially accurate to carry out its task.

The Dalit bitch, now—he would prefer that she die slowly, for having forever corrupted his son and permanently sullied the family honor. But in lieu of carrying around multiple weapons, he would have to be satisfied with her ordinary death.

Animals had castes of their own, as was only proper. Was that not the true way of things? Did not the gorillas lord it over the chimpanzees, and the chimpanzees over the lesser simians? Were not lions and tigers superior to the leopard, and the leopard to the ocelot and margay? Even among the insects there was a natural hierarchy that all parties respected. Therefore it was nothing unusual to find a similar arrangement among humans, or at least those who were part of a successful civilization that stretched thousands of years into antiquity. Brahmins did not marry Kshatriyas, Shudras did not marry Brahmins. And VyMohans, of which the Buthlahee clan was a noble and respected part, most assuredly did not marry Dalits.

He wiped his hands down the front of his lightweight cotton shirt, smoothing out the wrinkles. It was brown, proudly reflecting his caste. A traditionalist to the core of his being, Anil was not shy about revealing the truth about himself to any who might care to look. Why try to pretend he was Brahmin, or something else he was not? He was a merchant, albeit a very successful one. Adhering to his true nature had been at the core of his success. If only his eldest son had been content with that.

But no—he had to go and fall in *love*.

As if love had anything to do with a successful marriage. Likability, yes. But love? At the age of fifteen, Anil had been betrothed to a girl of twelve from across town. Their families had known one another off and on for years. Now, more than thirty years later, he was still happily married to the same woman. There were no problems of religion, no problems of caste. They had been, and still were, hardworking, mutually supportive, and content. Which was one reason why his heartbroken wife did not try to keep her husband from doing what had to be done. That did not mean she was happy about it.

Neither was he happy about it. But he intended to do it, nonetheless. At least the wretchedness and despair of having to kill his eldest son would be mitigated somewhat by the joy he would take in executing the female creature responsible for their collective disgrace.

He was standing and watching the barasingha feed. Only their antlers showed above water as they browsed on plants growing out of the mud, their heads otherwise completely submerged. No wonder they were commonly called swamp deer. As he studied their sleek, elegant forms, unique to one small part of his country, the Rat sidled up alongside him.

It was a name the little man had taken for his own. What his previous name was, or his caste, or religion, Anil did not know. But the Rat had performed certain services for a fellow businessman, and was a friend to many in the city. There was nothing demeaning about the name he had chosen, Anil knew. Rats were to be admired. They were tough, clever, and if you fed them, quite friendly. Also quite tasty, if properly prepared. The Rat spoke often about his visit to the temple of Durga in far distant Deshnok, on the other side of India, where temple priests fed milk to thousands upon thousands of rats. As a visitor, one was expected to remove one's shoes and go barefoot among them, which the Rat had done frequently and in perfect safety. Rats had swarmed all over his naked feet, and he had never been so much as nipped. On one especially fortuitous afternoon, he had even espied a white rat, a sign of special good fortune.

"I have news," the Rat murmured as he pretended to watch the barasingha.

"Of my son and his whore?" Despite its small size, the weight of the gun was heavy against his chest.

Squinting into the sun, the Rat glanced over and up at him. "Indirectly, one might say. It seems that others are also interested in finding your offspring."

Anil frowned. "Others?"

"The company he worked for is most interested in learning his present whereabouts. For what reason I do not know and therefore cannot say. But much effort is being expended toward that end. Much effort, and much money."

"I am but a businessman of modest means and cannot pay you more than I have already promised," Anil informed him flatly.

His gaunt face looking even more pinched than usual, the Rat was offended. "Have I asked for more? I tell you this only by way of providing information."

Anil was soothed. "So his company is looking for him, too. I'm not surprised." His expression darkened. "I don't care who's looking for him, they'd better not get in my way. I'll kill anybody who tries to kill my son. That is *my* obligation."

Bending, the Rat picked up a loose piece of gravel, checked to make sure no monitors or rangers were watching, and flung it into the artificial pool on the other side of the barrier. Startled by the splash, four antlered heads rose simultaneously to ascertain its source. Handsome animals, the Rat decided.

"Nothing is being said about killing. Only that if your son is found, a great reward awaits the finder." At Anil's look, the much smaller man hastened to add, "I am an honest man. You should know that from those who referred me to you. I am not a hare, to jump on a whim from one field to another. If I locate your son, I will inform only you of his whereabouts."

Anil nodded approvingly. "See that you do. I have prepared myself to kill two people. I can just as easily kill a third."

"Slaying your best source of information would be a poor way to obtain the information you seek," the Rat countered, unafraid.

The businessman had to grin. "You're as tough as my friend claimed. Tell me: what caste are you?"

The Rat smirked. Those of his teeth that were not broken were blackened, but it was a winning smile nonetheless. "Ask the priests of Deshnok. There is no caste among rats, which is one reason why they are so successful. They stick together."

Suddenly Anil found that he was uncomfortable in this man's presence. He was a respectable entrepreneur, and it shamed him to have to engage the services of such a person. But not half so much as Taneer had shamed him. "Find my son and my son's slut. Find them before his company does."

The Rat stepped back and inclined his head slightly, still displaying his wreck of a smile. "Someone surely will. When that happens, I hope it will be myself, or someone that I know."

He left the honorable merchant to contemplation of the swamp deer, and his private visions of righteous murder.

chapter viii

Originally founded by a rich merchant family from Jaipur, Shrinahji Market mixed both the bazaar and the bizarre with disingenuous equanimity. Having shopped there before, seeking unusual stock for his store, Sanjay knew his way around the enormous, multi-acrylic-domed complex. You could buy anything in Shrinahji: fruits and vegetables; consumer electronics; illegal electronics; sex in any size, shape, color, or preferred fetish; furniture; real estate; bootleg implants; the occasional human organ; spices and condiments; automobiles—even ancient locally manufactured Ambassador sedans that had been converted to standard fuel-cell power and were as revered as they were clunky.

One entire rambling building that had, in the American vernacular, just growed, resembled a misshapen collection of giant child's blocks. The multiplicity of huge acrylic domes that protected the market quarter sheltered the architectural amalgam from the elements, enabling its dealers and customers to set up and do business outside. The entire complex was devoted to books. Real books, printed on paper made from pulped tree mass. Like the wheezy, aerodynamically challenged Ambassador, such relics possessed much in the way of nostalgia value.

Far more upscale, and never set out on the hundreds of tables that backed up to storefronts, were ancient handwritten manuscripts boasting richly hued artwork and elaborate calligraphy. Some had been decorated with liquid gold and silver. There were maps for sale, and jewels of the Nizams that had escaped the attention of museums and collectors, and robotic astrologers that claimed to be more accurate than any human forecaster, not least because they were completely unbiased.

A city within a city, Shrinahji seethed with activity. Shrines and other religious facilities catered to the needs of Hindus, Buddhists, Christians, Jews, Muslims, Sikhs, Animists, and Zoroastrians. Political parties and groups had their own meeting places, the market accommodating the vocal needs of everyone from the BJP to the Dalit Army, from Shiv Sena to the Militant Vegans. In their ubiquity busy personal communicators approached plague level. Their ringing and calling had been banned, lest their conjoined cacophony make the conducting of normal business impossible. Other means of announcing incoming calls had to be adopted. The reigning joke was that there were more vibrating units in Shrinahji than in all the brothels in Southeast Asia.

Sanjay's unit remained in his pocket, quiescent and unmoving. Not wishing to be distracted by casual conversation, he had turned it off prior to entering the market. Now he strolled purposefully down Bagwan Street. A late-afternoon monsoon rain was washing the air outside. Half a dozen stories above his head he could just see the drops splattering on the curving, smoky acrylic that formed the roof over this part of the market.

A tax on all sales concluded inside a covered market paid for the aircon that made Shrinahji and its less famous, less well-established siblings so popular with merchants and customers alike. Entrance was restricted to those who could prove they had legitimate business to conduct inside. Without such controls the market would be overrun with tens of thousands of street dwellers desperately seeking shelter and surcease from the city's relentless heat. Unrestrained by the special laws that protected pedestrians pounding the pavements outside, drifting bouquets of fanciful advertisements assailed him like flurries of electronic snow, badgering him to visit this shop, eat at this restaurant, patronize this clothing store, seek out this sly seller of secrets. Such unrestrained, unsupervised capitalism was restricted to enclosed places like the market, where it would not upset the delicate sensibilities of those who were easily offended by rampant commercialism.

Sanjay reveled in it all—the noise, the pushing crowds, the vocal hawking, even the inescapable adverts. He was not so many years removed from the simple life of the village to have become jaded to such things. As he walked, it seemed to him that his left shoe, the one with the hidden compartment containing the tiny mollysphere, was slightly heavier than his right. It was all in his mind, he told himself. If anything, the unhollowed-out right shoe should be heavier.

Despite the best efforts of the most powerful atmospheric scrubbers the market ownership could install, the enormous complex was still fragrant with the stink of the thousands of merchants and customers who plied its multiple levels and hundreds of narrow accessways. At least there were no vehicles to contend with, Sanjay thought gratefully as he turned a corner. All deliveries and services entered the market via specially designated underground corridors. The only way to get around Shrinahji was to walk, or utilize an approved personal transport mechanism. Being small and silent, the latter were no impediment to the foot traffic they complemented. Like everything else that came into the market, you needed a permit to use one.

Sanjay preferred to walk. A personal transport would only have hindered his progress, since pedestrians always had the right of way. The noiseless electric transports were more useful for the aged, the crippled, and the lazy. He was none of these.

Halting at an intersection, people flowing around him, he frowned at suddenly having three choices, three directions from which to choose. At a touch of his communications bracelet a glowing, three-dimensional map of the market materialized in front of his face. Responding to voice commands directed at the bracelet, the map zoomed in response to the GPS built into the instrument until it fixed on his current position. Verbally, he entered an address. Shifting to an angled view, a green line appeared in the air, connecting the red dot that marked his position at the intersection with a building two blocks away. Satisfied, he deactivated the map, turned up the street that led off to his right, and resumed walking.

The building was old, but Sanjay was not put off by its appearance. Many historic structures near the center of the old city had been saved as part of Sagramanda's diverse and energetic preservation projects. As long as the building was of no special historical value, modern construction techniques allowed the interiors of buildings that sat on valuable property to be gutted and updated while preserving their original appearance from the street. Many sleek modern enterprises boasted compelling nineteenth- and twentieth-century facades.

The four-story structure that rose before him was a mixture of both. Announcing himself to Security at the main entrance, he waited while his ident was checked and his appointment confirmed. Granted entry, he saw at once that the building originally had been a haveli, or house of a wealthy merchant. It had been taken apart somewhere in Mandawa, transported across India, and reassembled inside Shrinahji. In purpose it was perfectly appropriate to its present address and location within the market, as well as his reason for coming here.

A central rectangular courtyard opened to the sky—or rather, to one of the multiple acrylic domes that roofed the market complex.

Unlike those that still stood in distant Rajasthan, subject to the whims and weather of the harsh Thar Desert, the interior of this magnificent old residence had been well preserved. The upper portion of one exposed courtyard wall, where it met the overhang of the second-floor walkway, was covered with decorative old paintings; triptychs of Indian life from a century and a half ago. Elephants with howdahs, camel caravans, Europeans in black hats, dancing girls; all followed one another around the wall in a procession of bright hues and lost innocence. Similar depictions graced the upper portions of the other three walls, with two exceptions. The decorations there were of recent vintage, and they moved.

A virtual of the highly endangered Indian lion preyed upon and brought down electronically terrified sambar deer. Elegant water birds, from egrets to spoonbills, frolicked in shallow lakes. Apsaras gave lessons to their descendants the nautch dancers while merchants in rich robes presented their wares to turbaned and bejeweled warlords who flaunted bejeweled knives and ferocious black beards. It was moving history, devoid only of noise. Adding accompanying sound might have been distracting to business. It was all very well and good, Sanjay mused as he moved through the courtyard, to honor one's past, but not at the expense of commerce.

The lift was located within a four-story-tall precast statue of Lakshmi, the goddess of wealth. The voluptuous sculpture was mildly sexist, without a doubt, but undeniably beckoning. Any businesswoman who objected could take her trade elsewhere. Such thoughts did not trouble Sanjay as he stepped into the lift. He came from a small village, and was a traditionalist. Supplying aesthetic balance, an abundance of virile, scantily dressed warriors pranced and fought mock battles as part of the wall décor. Fair was fair.

The office he sought was on the top, fourth floor, at the rear of the complex. Standing out front was the owner's symbol: a richly garbed camel. Not a real camel, of course. It was an excellent simulacrum, complete to the methodical, metronomic chewing of its cud. Sanjay studied it purposefully, striving to identify the breed on which the effigy had been based. Bikaneri, Jaisalmeri, or Gujarati? The superbly rendered hairy ears were a giveaway. Bikaneri, he decided. He had never been to Bikaner, but he had heard of its perfectly preserved palace and other wonders from the Rat. Bikaner was the nearest large city to the temple of the rats in Deshnok.

As for being able to recognize the differences between kinds of camels, Sanjay could because it was one of many things every poor Indian child learned. One never knew when the opportunity to own one of the wonderful beasts might present itself. Back in the days when most vehicles had been powered by ever more highly priced gasoline, camel cart drivers had looked down on frustrated vehicle owners and smirked, secure in the knowledge that their venerable means of transportation required neither petrol, nor lubrication, nor insurance, was unlikely to incur speeding tickets, used no imported parts, and in the absence of onboard computers or auto AIs was quite capable of parking itself.

All that had changed considerably with the advent of the hydrogen-driven, fuel-cell-powered car. But a camel was still cheaper to run.

Not this one, though. It was too sophisticated. As if to prove the point, the android dromedary looked down at him and said, in a no-nonsense preprogrammed voice, "State your business."

"I am Sanjay Ghosh." He checked his chronometer. "I have a ten o'clock appointment with Mr. Chhote Pandit."

The camel looked him up and down, the gleaming lens of one eye recording his outward appearance, the lens of the other probing deeper to check him for weapons. It detected, among other things, the mollysphere packed carefully in the secret compartment of his left shoe, but did not remark on it.

"Go on in," the camel directed him. Its business concluded, it resumed chewing its nonexistent cud. As he walked past, Sanjay couldn't keep from examining the robot's flanks. No doubt there were other, far more lethal devices buried within that faux furred body.

Pandit was not what Sanjay expected. Anticipating someone youngish, bright, and with an advanced degree from Bangalore or somewhere else in the southern Silicon Triangle, he instead found himself in a room more like an audience chamber or den than a modern office, facing a man considerably older but otherwise not unlike himself. As they shook hands and exchanged steepled fingers and head bows, it was all he could do to forebear from asking his host the name of the village he hailed from.

Taking a seat on a couch opposite another, Pandit gestured for his guest to sit. There was no table between them; only a fine rug predominantly woven of blue and red thread whose pattern Sanjay did not recognize. On the walls were delicate paintings of incredibly fine detail that hailed from the school of Rajasthan miniatures. Some of them looked old, though Sanjay was hardly an expert in such things.

"Persian," his host told him. "The rug," he added when his guest did not respond. "Royal Sarouk. Two hundred years old."

Suitably impressed, Sanjay made sure his feet rested lightly on the dense fibers. "It looks almost new."

Pandit smiled and nodded. "The hallmark of a good rug." He was a small old man, shorter even than Sanjay, with a wispy white beard and prominent sideburns like steel wool. His prominent ears stuck out from the sides of his head like those of a baby elephant, he was missing several teeth that could easily have been regenerated or replaced with synthetics, and he wore a plainly embroidered sherwani coat of ivory-hued cotton over an equally basic, pajama-like chundar. The only sign of modernity on his body—indeed, in the entire room—was the gold-tinged control bracelet encircling his left wrist and the chronometer on his right. Absently, Sanjay wondered what the former could summon. He suspected he might have the opportunity to find out. He did not have to wait long.

"Tea?" asked his host. When Sanjay nodded affirmatively, Pandit whispered to his bracelet.

Through some mechanism Sanjay could not discern, the priceless rug rolled itself up and off to one side. A portion of the wooden floor slid silently aside to reveal an exquisite low table cut from a single block of white marble. In full pietra dura style, the marble was inlaid with flowers, leaves, and birds fashioned from shards of precious and semiprecious stone: lapis lazuli from Afghanistan, carnelian, turquoise from Iran, jasper, agate, malachite from Africa, tiger eye, mother-of-pearl, and more. Built into the center of the table was a heating unit atop which sat a silver pot damascened in gold. Steam issued from the pot's curved spigot. Cups rested nearby, together with containers of milk, cream, and several kinds of sugar.

"Please." Pandit gestured for his guest to help himself. Sanjay fixed a cup, sat back on the comfortable couch, and sipped. He eyed the cup as he gestured with it. "Not marble?"

Pandit smiled back as he poured for himself. "Too easily stained by tea, as I'm sure you know." Adding sugar and milk, he sat back on the other couch and stirred slowly, regarding his visitor out of narrowed eyes. "You are a walking contradiction, Mr. Ghosh."

Sanjay maintained his poker face; his business face. "How is that to be, Mr. Pandit, sir?"

"You do not look in the least like the sort of person to be demanding the kind of money that is being asked. You look, and please do not feel slighted when I say this, like a dirt farmer."

Somehow Sanjay managed not to flush. He certainly would not have thought of responding with something like, "That's funny—so do you." Instead, he replied, "I am only a poor servant of another, who wishes to remain anonymous."

Pandit coughed slightly into his tea, availed himself of a longer swallow. "As am I, as am I. Both of us being middlemen, then, it should be easy for us to reach an understanding. I am sure you are being paid a commensurate fee. As I will be." Sanjay, properly, said nothing.

Abruptly, Pandit looked bored. "Well, let's get it over with. This should not take long. It cannot, because despite what you may think from appearances, I am a busy man. You have only been allotted this brief bit of my time on the personal recommendation of another whose information I value highly. Otherwise you would not have gotten past the entrance to this complex, much less into my ante office."

"I know that, Mr. Pandit, and I am grateful." Sanjay's response rang of honesty because it was just that. "I have only one thing to show you. It represents what my client has to offer for sale. I don't pretend to understand it. The details are unfamiliar to me personally. But I was assured by my client that when it was presented to you, you would know how to read between the lines it will make available to you to such an extent that you will be able to bring my client in contact with an appropriate buyer for what he is offering to sell."

"Yes, yes." Pandit checked his own chronometer impatiently. "Well, drink your tea and get on with it. Let's see this wonderful thing—whatever it is."

Without further comment Sanjay lifted his left leg and crossed it over his right, the better to access the hidden safety compartment in the sole of his shoe. Pandit paid hardly any attention to the process, as if such low-tech subterfuges were old news to him. Extracting the packet holding the small molly, the shopkeeper slid it across the inlaid tabletop to his host.

Pandit opened it and removed the contents. "Standard information storage device." Sharp eyes focused on his guest. "Is there anything special I should know before I try to access it?"

Sanjay looked appropriately innocent. "All I was told was that removing it from my shoe would allow it to be activated. I am not sophisticated in such things."

His host studied both mollysphere and merchant for a moment

before addressing his command bracelet once more. Mimicking the ascension of the beautiful coffee table, a small pedestal console rose out of the floor in front of the couch. Pandit popped the molly into one of its available receptacles and waited for the precision internal alignment of magnetic field and variable focal length lasers to lock in. He was mildly disappointed when the box unit generated only two-dimensional information.

His eyes widened, however, as he studied the readouts that were generated in the air before him. Eyeing their backside, Sanjay could make out words and diagrams, charts and numbers. It was doubtful that he would have been able to make sense of the highly technical terminology even if he had been sitting alongside Pandit on the other couch and viewing the display from the front. Though intensely curious, he did not say anything. For one thing, he did not want to break his host's sudden concentration. For another, if he were to view the display he might be asked to comment on its meaning, thus revealing the extent of his ignorance about the contents of the molly.

"By Mohini's girdle!" Pandit breathed softly as page after page of heads-up information automatically winked in and out of existence in front of him. He took a moment to peer around the display at his patient guest. "Have another cup of tea. Do you know what you have here?"

Sanjay might not be highly educated, but he was mentally agile. "Something of great value."

"Be obscure, then, if it pleases you." There was no rancor in Pandit's voice as he returned to studying the floating fount of information. Either his guest was truly ignorant of the molly's contents, or else he was playing dumb for commercial reasons. While Pandit might prefer to believe the former, from a business standpoint it was much safer to believe the latter. The older man's reaction rendered Sanjay even more curious about the molly's contents. Just what was it that the furtive Taneer had given him to sell?

Whatever it was, the mollysphere's sales pitch was having the intended effect. Chhote Pandit was not merely interested: he was entranced.

Fine tea or no fine tea, Sanjay was beginning to squirm when his host finally shifted to the other end of his couch, leaving the molly activated and the last page of information hanging in the air. As Sanjay waited, the display winked out. Frowning, Pandit spoke again into his command bracelet. Nothing happened.

"That's odd. The storage sphere you gave me now reads empty." He studied something out of Sanjay's line of sight. "Not just empty, but as if it had never been written to."

His guest was apologetic. "I was told by the person who wishes to sell this information that you would be able to view it one time only. It was quantum secured."

"Ah." Pandit leaned back in his couch and nodded understandingly. "Viewing the information simultaneously destroys it. A sensible precaution. It means that one option open to me, that of holding you against your will and stealing this information, is no longer applicable. Nothing personal, you understand. In business of this nature, one must always consider every available option."

"Naturally." Sanjay maintained his composure. "Then you find my client's merchandise worthy of consideration?" Given the price Taneer was asking, Sanjay would not have been in the least surprised if his host had sneered or even laughed at the query.

Instead, Chhote Pandit fell to stroking his wispy beard with the thumb and forefinger of his left hand. "I admit I was initially more than skeptical. But the presentation provided ample proof that your client can deliver what is promised."

Sanjay tried not to hold his breath. "And the proposed fee arrangements?" The reply stunned him.

"I would only be passing along the indicated materials to the final purchaser, as per your request, but from what little I know of such things, I would count it a bargain."

Despite his promise to himself to conceal anything like an emotional reaction for the duration of the meeting, Sanjay found himself startled. He recovered as rapidly as possible.

"My client will be pleased to hear that."

"There is only one problem." Pandit removed his hand from his beard and gestured absently in the direction of the gleaming console, as if its presence in the room could explain everything. "I am not sure I am equipped to negotiate a transaction of this magnitude."

Sanjay frowned. "I was reliably informed that—"

His host cut him off with a wave of his right hand. "Oh, I did not say I could not do it. It is just that business of this nature comes along once in a man's lifetime, and I want to be sure of the schematics before I can proceed. But I am certainly willing to try! Oh yes, I am certainly willing to try." The look in his eyes was one Sanjay had come to know well. It was the same whether one saw it in the face of a fellow Indian, or a Chinese, or a European, or an African.

Greed knows no ethnicity.

A fresh thought came to his host. Instinctively he looked around, back toward the entrance Sanjay had used. "Did anyone see you come in here? Not just to my office, but to the complex? Do you think there was any possibility you may have been followed?"

The shopkeeper's muscles tightened. By accepting the proposition of the customer Taneer, Sanjay had known he was going to be operating in territory hitherto unfamiliar to him, but to see the venerable businessman sitting on the couch suddenly tense and look toward his own doorway left him feeling more uneasy than he had anticipated.

"I do not think so. There was no reason for anyone to follow me." He offered what he hoped was a reassuring smile. "My client has been very circumspect in every aspect of his dealings with me, and I with him."

Pandit relaxed slightly. "See to it that it remains so. Where something of this importance is involved, civility tends to be the first casualty." His somberness gave way to a winning smile, missing teeth notwithstanding. "To say our relationship in this matter is to be mutually possible is to speak the mother of all understatements. Provided neither of us ends up dead, of course."

"Of course," Sanjay agreed with a calmness he did not feel.

"We should conduct future dealings in person as much as we can. These days, it is easier to trace and read an electronic communication than a live person. Provided you do not mind coming back here." Pandit's eyes were fixed on his guest. The intensity of their gaze and the intelligence behind them both belied the age of their owner.

"I will do whatever my client thinks best."

"Spoken like an honest broker. I promise that I will be no less." Pandit paused a moment, thoughtful, then asked, "You really do not have any idea what you have gotten yourself into, do you?"

"I am focused on making a profit, so that I can bring my family out of the village where I was born," Sanjay replied, a little stiffly. "Besides, I gave my client my word."

Rather than being put off by the response, Pandit appeared greatly pleased. "A child of the soil, come to this. Who says there is no opportunity in Mother India for upward mobility?" He rose from his couch, prompting Sanjay to do likewise. The two men shook hands.

"I will go to work on this immediately. Given what is at stake for both sides, I am sure your client will understand it will take a little time to put the necessary arrangements and precautions in place."

Sanjay thought back to what Taneer had told him. "Speed is of the essence for my client."

"I can imagine." Pandit chuckled. "I know that *I* wouldn't want to be in his position, given the nature of the information that storage unit contained." He shook a cautionary finger at the younger man. "Watch your step, and your back, Mr. Ghosh. This is not a game for children. But then, you are clearly aware of that, or you would not be involved to the extent that you are."

Pandit's words hung in Sanjay's memory as he exited the office, departed the complex, and made his way out of the great market. It was too late to back out now. Anyway, he didn't want to back out. He wanted his three percent. Presumably, Pandit's cut was among the information disseminated by the mollysphere he had brought to the office. Sanjay was understandably curious to know what it was. He did not expect "Mr. Mohan" to tell him. That would be bad business. Whatever else he was, Sanjay suspected that his unusual client was anything but a bad businessman.

Especially when the business at hand was exceptional enough to involve such very real tangibles as life and death.

It was late evening when Taneer left the little gift shop in a state of measured euphoria. The storekeeper, Sanjay Ghosh, had struggled to contain his own excitement as he related the details of his meeting with the counterpart he had chosen. Taneer was not surprised that this person, whom Ghosh quite properly left unnamed, had been overwhelmed by the offer: the researcher knew perfectly well the value of what he had to sell. But to have already struck a deal to move forward to the next stage, that of having the second merchant agree to put the merchandise on the open market and handle the resultant bids, was more than Taneer could have hoped for.

He had never doubted for a moment that from the instant of his abdication from his former employer, the hounds would be set loose on his trail. Thankfully, he had been able to make Depahli understand this. Therefore and obviously (as his uncle Dilip liked to say), the sooner a deal could be consummated, the better it would be for all concerned. He was under no illusions as to what would happen to him if the minions deployed (during the Raj one might have said "sepoyed," he reflected with a small smile) by his company found him first. In that event, his beloved Depahli would find herself attending not to the details of a marriage but to those of a funeral.

As he turned down a side street whose brand-new sidewalk fronted an empty lot littered with garbage and slabs of upturned concrete from which twisted rebars protruded like tormented brown snakes, he reflected on how right he had been in his selection of an intermediary. The shopkeeper Sanjay Ghosh was clever enough to follow instructions but not clever enough to think of a way to outsmart his client. Recognition of his own shortcomings would help to keep him honest. It also did not hurt that the two men had established something of a personal rapport. Though he would not trust the shopkeeper any more than he would anyone else except the final buyer with the full particulars of what he had to sell, Taneer found himself liking the immigrant from the countryside more and more each time they met. He could only hope it was not all a polite, businesslike sham, and that his feelings, as well as his instincts, were reciprocated.

If all went well, the entire risky business could be concluded in a few days. Sanjay had assured him that the contact he had made had sufficient status to engage interested buyers on the appropriate scale. That contact had promised to get back to the shopkeeper with firm offers and a high bid before the end of the week. Sanjay could not keep a touch of awe from his voice as he reported this.

"We're both going to be rich, my friend," Taneer had assured him.

Sanjay had nodded. "You are going to be much richer—but I have no problem with that. I am only taking a commission."

"Some 'commission,'" the scientist had responded, whereupon both men shared a laugh.

Was that a shadow behind him?

Without thinking, he looked back sharply. He was not the only one using the sidewalk on this side of the busy street. There was no such thing as an empty sidewalk in Sagramanda. If not thick with pedestrians, it was occupied by the homeless. Any open space greater than a meter square was considered fair game for squatters.

A particularly tall man had halted by a makeshift lunch counter and was buying what at a distance appeared to be patra ni machhi—fish in banana leaf. That was a Parsi dish, not a specialty of the state where Sagramanda lay. Food from Mumbai—and originally from Persia. Could the man be Iranian? Certainly his height caused him to stand out among the average city dweller. You are being paranoid, Taneer accused himself.

Paranoia is healthy, his brain reminded him. He resumed walking. But instead of following his usual path toward the nearest subway station, he turned left at the next corner instead of right. Using the excuse of crossing the street, he managed a surreptitious glance back the way he had come.

Munching on his fish, the tall man was still behind him. The distance separating them had not changed.

Don't panic, he told himself. It is not impossible that you are both heading in a similar direction. It may be nothing more than coincidence. He kept walking long after he would normally have been aboard the first subway car heading for the next station in his carefully worked-out roundabout route home. And it was getting dark.

Was the tall man closing the distance between them? Without constantly looking back over his shoulder it was impossible to tell. And if he gave in to that impulse to repeatedly check on the other man's location, it would signal to the other that his purpose had been discovered. What would happen then? Taneer lengthened his stride and increased his speed. When he finally decided to risk another glance backward, he found that he had opened up some distance between himself and his shadow. Deliberately, he maintained the new, faster pace.

Another half an hour passed before he felt reasonably confident he had either lost his pursuer or else had sloughed off someone who had not been tracking him in the first place. Ten minutes' additional walking at a much slower pace served to confirm his hopes. He was not upset. Far better to burn a little time and be sure than to rush and commit a fatal mistake. There was only one problem.

It was dark, and he was lost.

So focused had he been on trying to lose a possible tail without giving himself away that he had neglected to properly keep track of his surroundings. Always a fast walker anyway, he had covered a respectable number of kilometers in less than an hour. A glance up at a street sign's softly glowing luminescent letters indicated that he had arrived at the intersection of Saranad and Aberdeen. The intersection was notable for several things: an alarming lack of light, either from passing vehicles or storefronts; an absence of purposeful pedestrian traffic; and the feeling of complete disorientation that had come over him.

No matter. Better to be momentarily lost and unnoticed than in familiar surroundings and hunted. He would seek directions from a shopkeeper.

But of the few shops that were not gutted and abandoned, all were shut tight. None were boarded up, of course, because the homeless would steal the boards to fashion makeshift homes of their own. From the vicinity of their wretched residences of clapboard, scavenged metal, and plastic, the hollow eyes of the enduringly destitute eyed him with curiosity. The dominant scent in the night air was one of urine and human waste thickened to a lugubrious miasma by the unrelenting humidity. It struck him that he must be by far the most well-dressed and most prosperous-looking individual on the street, perhaps in the entire neighborhood. That was not necessarily a good thing. Not on a moonless night in a zone devoid of busy shops and cafes.

Then, quite without warning, the attention that had been increasingly focused on him shifted. Figures standing or sitting in alleys melted back into the narrow slot canyons of concrete and stone from whence they had initially emerged. Synthetic sheeting was unrolled to drape disheveled families in plastic shrouds. Those who were healthy enough began to walk faster, then to run. They all seemed to be looking in the same direction, back up the street down which Taneer had come. Could it be the tall man? If so, what had he done, what rep-

utation preceded him, to inspire such fright in so many with nothing
to lose?

Turning to gaze in the same direction, he saw not one but several
figures coming toward him. Bunched tightly together, they advanced
slowly, in several lines. He did not know whether to be relieved or
afraid. On the one hand there was no sign of a tall man among them.
In fact, as they drew nearer he saw that there was no sign of a man of
any height among them. The methodically advancing group was composed entirely of women.

He seemed frozen to the spot. Not knowing where he was, entirely
ignorant of his immediate surroundings, he had no idea which way to
run. Could he stare these women down? Or would they simply ignore
him and walk on by? Surely they couldn't be robbers. Not because
there was no such thing as female bandits. From Phoolan Devi on
down, the country had a rich tradition of notorious dacoits of both
sexes. It was just that from what he had already seen there was nothing
in this neighborhood worth stealing. A chill ran down his back. Body
parts, perhaps. There was a nasty underground market in body parts
harvested largely, though not exclusively, for export.

He was almost right.

One thing was made clear immediately. As they drew near enough
for him to meet their eyes, it was evident that their attention was
focused on him and him alone. None were looking elsewhere. With a
start, he realized that they might have been following him for some
time. Intent on monitoring the whereabouts of the tall man, who an
uneasy Taneer now realized had probably been nothing more than
another wandering citizen engaged in perfectly ordinary everyday
business, he had neglected to note if he was being trailed by anyone
else. He had allowed himself to become preoccupied with one person
to the exclusion of all others. The wrong person.

Were the members of this group among the many who had been
engaged by his furious former employer to find him? He kicked him-

self mentally. He should have known better than to be watchful only of men. But if that was the case, why were there so many? He counted a dozen of them. An excessive number of professional trackers to run down one lone scientist, surely. And if that was not the case, if they were not bounty hunters or company security personnel or independent investigators, then what did they want with him? Thoughts of organlegging returned. But as a well-read, well-informed citizen, he had never encountered a report or heard tell of an all-female gang of organ thieves.

Was he misinterpreting the hunger in their eyes, and they were not after him at all? A case of mistaken identity, perhaps. Bands of women, especially poor women, often organized themselves to mete out vigilante justice in vast swathes of the immense city where law enforcement was lax and the sight of a policeman infrequent. The hunger in their eyes . . . The hunger.

Oh God, he thought abruptly as he started to back up. Oh Vishnu. Depahli, I love you. He knew what they were now, these relentlessly advancing poor women with their burning, intent eyes. The knives were coming out now, emerging from the depths of cheap, ragged saris and puffy blouses. Cheap but razor-sharp, the blades glittered as brightly as the eyes of those who gripped them. They *were* after his body, but not just his transplantable organs, and not to sell. They wanted *all* of him.

Admikhana. Man-eaters. Cannibals.

As the lowest of the low, the poorest of the poor, society expected them to eke out a pitiful existence until disease and especially starvation overtook them. Except that some years ago, no one could say exactly when, three such women had impertinently refused to remain complicit in their own quiet, courteous demise. All had children. No matter what their mothers consumed and no matter how it affected them in this life or the next, these women had determined that their children would thrive and survive on a diet of normal mother's milk.

The foundation of that milk was immaterial. It was the survival of the children that mattered. It justified everything. Anything.

Though never boasting many formal adherents, the cult the triumvirate of poor women had founded had grown large enough to alarm the authorities. Despite repeated efforts, they had never been able to completely stamp it out. There were too many poor women, too many starving children. The moral rationalizations offered by the cult were sufficient to sustain its always fluctuating membership. Besides, it was only one of hundreds of cults old and new that boasted believers scattered throughout the city's vastness.

They weren't going to sell him, a terrified Taneer realized as he backed up. They were going to gut and eat him. Horrific servants of a noble purpose, they began to spread out, to cut off any possible retreat. Before that could happen, he turned and bolted into the night.

Upraised dirks and dirty kitchen knives flashing, hems of silk and cotton rising and flapping about their legs like the wings of ascending bats, the Admikhana broke into a run behind him. The piercing ululation that rose from their throats as if from a chorus of stoned banshees was bloodthirsty in every sense of the word, and not merely a metaphor.

chapter ix

Getting around the hotel was no more difficult than entering it. All one had to do, Jena reflected, was dress appropriately and act as if you owned the place. Here, her sun-darkened skin was assumed to be the product of long hours spent whiling away the afternoons at luxurious beach resorts, instead of simply surviving from day to day beneath the burning tropical heat like everyone else in Sagramanda.

She had discarded her modified sari in favor of an outfit that would not have drawn a frown in Montmarte or Lyon, or for that matter New York or Zurich. Handsome photophobic skirt and blouse, credible shoes, long narrow shoulder bag, passable fake pearl necklace and earrings comprised the kind of elegant yet casual travel gear any sensible European woman would choose to wear during a visit to India. The tall, traditionally uniformed, magnificently mustachioed Bengali doorman was quick to offer the usual salute and open the heavy glass door for her without asking to see any kind of identification.

Striding through the open, multistory lobby, she kept her gaze forward and purposeful. She was not attractive enough to draw lengthy stares. Not in this five star hotel, a favorite of visiting film stars and other notables. The indifference suited her purposes perfectly. Though she acted as if she owned the place, she had never been here before. It was important, when she was in a hotel mood, never to visit any hotel more than once. In a city the size of Sagramanda, that was not a problem.

High overhead, virtuals of scenes from the Ramayana and Mahabharata played out silently on the slightly concave ceiling. Glancing up, she caught a glimpse of Hanuman the Monkey God triumphing over the demon-king Ravana, as he did every hour on the hour. It was an impressive display, made all the more so by the fact that she couldn't spot the projectors.

The mongoose that confronted her stood up on its hind legs and inquired politely if there was anything she needed. It was a deft mechanical, and a clever change from the usual miniature elephant. Hotels of this class were always looking for any edge over the competition. Indicating that she was fine, she thanked the device and found her way out back.

The poolside bar was comfortably cool thanks to the invisible air curtain that kept the outdoor facility at half the chill of the main lobby. Choosing a chair by one of the small, elevated, mushroom-shaped tables, she ordered a drink and settled down to study the pool itself. It was a trilevel job, the two upper levels connected to the lower by transparent waterslides and waterfalls. Both of the upper pools were fashioned of transparent acrylic, so that swimmers could look out at the world beyond while those seated nearby or swimming in the main pool below could watch the upper-level swimmers cavort. Rainforest vegetation abounded, giving the setting the appearance of some movie-set jungle paradise. Miniature versions of the air screen that sealed off the bar area ensured that the vegetation was not doused with lethally chlorinated pool water.

That portion of the pool area not facing the hotel was enclosed by a two-story-high fence topped with electrified wire and a silent laser alarm beam. On the other side of the fence was a service alley that was the sometime home of perhaps a thousand people. Clapboard lean-tos and empty shipping boxes served as shelters for those who had taken up residence in the narrow lane; at least, they did so until a particularly wide delivery truck or utilities vehicle needed to make use of the passage. Then people would scatter frantically in all directions as their transitory residences were smashed to pieces or crushed flat, whereupon they would wordlessly set themselves to the laborious task of rebuilding them anew. Occasionally a ripe coconut, or mango, or papaya would fall into the alley from one of the branches of the decorative landscaping that overhung the security wall, whereupon a small war over its possession would ensue.

The residents of the hotel, of course, never had any contact with the residents of the alley, and the hotel's indomitable security staff ensured it stayed that way.

None of the alley's citizens would have dreamed, or had the means, to bluff their way inside the hotel. For Jena it was easy. Any decently dressed European, especially a single woman, who entered the hotel was assumed either to be staying there, or visiting a guest, or meeting someone on business. It could be said that the latter was the case for her. It was just that she had not yet chosen someone to meet.

She sat for an hour; nursing her drink, then another. Watching, waiting, appraising, calculating. A middle-aged Italian couple sat down at the table next to her and exchanged polite greetings in broken English. She chatted with them while they ordered, waited until a plate of satay arrived at their mushroom table, watched as the individual thermotropic skewers cooked the chunks of pork and chicken from within, did not bother them as they ate, and decided against asking to see their room so she could compare it with her own. Despite his age, the man was a bit too big, a shade too physically competent-looking. Jena did not buy trouble. The couple departed smiling, utterly unaware how near they had come to participating in an afternoon of sudden death and dismemberment.

Eyes narrowing only slightly, she picked up her drink and walked over to another table.

"Hi. Mind if I join you? I hate drinking alone, and it doesn't look like the person I was supposed to meet here is going to show up."

She guessed the other woman to be about her own age, perhaps a year or two younger. With the Chinese it was sometimes difficult to tell. The woman wore an expensive sun-repellent wrap around a form-fitting swimsuit. Her black hair was cut short and fashionable. The only jewelry she wore was a single earring, so long that its tip brushed her clavicle. A waterfall of color played through it, controlled by the internal chip.

After studying Jena's face, the woman gestured courteously at an empty seat, "Why not?" Her English was excellent, and no surprise.

"I am Marie-Louise." Jean extended a hand, shook the other woman's. The grip was firm but not overbearing. "From French Guiana."

That piqued the other's curiosity. "Xinzhou Mai-ling. Everybody calls me May. French Guiana?" She eyed her visitor with obvious interest. "I have never met a person from that place. What do you do there?" She laughed lightly as she set the drink down. The steadily fizzing contents were blue, Jena noted. "What *is* there to do there?"

"Not very much, it is true. I work for Arianaspace."

"*Shih?*" This time interest mixed with surprise. "Are you an astronaut? Or as we say, a taikonaut?"

Jena laughed. Rapport had been established. "Nothing so exciting. I'm a technician. I am here for a conference." She did not say what kind of conference. Nor would she, unless she was pressed to elucidate, in which case she would have to elaborate further on things she had read on the Net while constructing her current cover.

Fortunately, May Xinzhou was not particularly interested in the details of her new European friend's profession. She was much more interested in the Frenchwoman herself. She was an executive for a major white goods manufacturer in Guangdong and was in Sagramanda exploring wholesaling possibilities. Jena could not help her there, but she could help relieve the ennui the other woman anticipated having to deal with until her next appointment, which was not until tomorrow morning.

"These Indians," she confided well into her fourth drink, "the men they are always so very surprised when they find out there is such a thing as female Chinese executive. Some of them cannot deal with it. Those who only want to talk figures and look at fiscal projections are no problem." She giggled. "You are staying here too?"

"Of course," Jena lied effortlessly as she sipped. "I'm trying to find a way to relax myself." She raised a hand and pointed to the far side of the pool where a dark stairway could be seen leading downward. "I understand this hotel has an excellent Ayurvedic facility. If you want, we could continue this conversation while really taking it easy."

The executive half turned on her stool. "I have heard about Ayurvedic massage, but I have never tried. Because I know nothing about it and would not know where to start."

"I know all about it," Jena assured her. She hopped off her stool, still holding her current drink. "Come on. I guarantee the experience will relax you completely."

"Hokay. It will be something to tell my friends back home."

As they walked toward the stairway, Jena frowned suddenly. "*Merde*—I must have left my access in my room, and I can't remember the code."

"No problem, no problem," her new acquaintance assured her. "I have mine with me." She smiled graciously. "I am on full expense account. Time to make use of some of it."

"Thanks," Jena said simply. "That's good of you."

The big male was hungry, but he was also confused, and uncertain. Days ago, he had made an easy kill south of the area he was now prowling. Liking the taste of the strange meat and hoping for more of the same, he had intended to return as soon as his stomach demanded refilling. But on his initial approach to the place he had sensed and heard unusual noises. Advancing with great caution through the cloud-heavy night, he had espied something unnatural moving through the brush not far from where he had made the kill.

The creature patrolling the edge of the jungle marched on eight legs. It had only a single eye, curiously dead, that scanned its surroundings from the end of a thin neck. There was no visible mouth to worry about, certainly no teeth, but the tiger was wary nonetheless. The cylindrical, armored body emitted a steady hum so subtle that many animals would have been hard-pressed to detect it. Not the tiger. It sounded more like a buzzing, flying thing than anything else, but there was no evidence of wings. Most peculiar of all, the smell that emanated from it was a faint, thick stink the likes of which the tiger had not encountered before. Then there was the matter of the internal light that was visible for just an instant when one of the creature's rear legs flexed.

Anything never encountered before was to be regarded with great suspicion. Given the creature's much smaller size, younger, bolder males and females might have decided to attack first, taste second, and evaluate later. Not the big male. He had not reached his present mature age and size from acting impetuously. From his hiding place in the thick underbrush, he pierced the night with vision six times sharper than that of a human as he watched the strange being trundle down its chosen path. It made no move either to enter the jungle proper or drift toward the well-kept dwellings beyond. The single-mindedness of purpose it exhibited was impressive.

Silently, the tiger tracked it for a while longer. Once, he shifted his place of concealment to follow the thing, maintaining the distance between them. To see a quarter ton of tiger moving in absolute silence through the jungle on footpads big enough to completely blot out a man's face is something to remember—or to terrify, depending on the thrust of the cat's movements and one's proximity to it. The eight-legged creature did not react to being stalked. Nor did it pause to drink, or to browse, or to try and catch something to eat.

Suspicious, the big male retreated, backing up until he was well out of sight of the odd being and then turning to retreat into deeper, darker jungle. He did not trust what he did not know, especially the eerie smell. Hungry as he was, the big cat would look elsewhere for tonight's twenty kilos of meat. He would have been even more wary had he been able to read and understand the markings on the creature's side, one of which said in both subdued English and Sanskrit script:

DEPARTMENT OF WILDLIFE AND GAME
SUNDARBANS NATIONAL PRESERVE
Mobile Tranquilization and Capture Unit A-23

Only one attendant was on duty in the facility. Jena studiously examined the three-dimensional artwork on the wall while her new executive friend checked them in. In response to the attendant's query as to whether they required a live masseuse, the Frenchwoman replied in the negative, without turning her head to face the attendant. When she and May entered their assigned cubicle, Jena was confident that the bored employee had not managed so much as a glimpse of her face.

As befitted a hotel of this class, the subterranean room was intimate and welcoming. Responding to her room flasher, a soothing male voice husked as they passed through an open portal into the sanctum, "Welcome, Mai-ling Xinzhou and guest." Jena tensed slightly. But as hoped, since she was clearly with the Chinese executive and already inside the hotel grounds, the facility's subsidiary security system did not feel compelled to ask her for additional identification.

There were four private grottos and no human attendants. That was the nice thing about exclusive places like the hotel, Jena reflected. Management respected the privacy of its guests above all else. Even better, none of the other cubicles were presently occupied.

"Preferences?" inquired Mai-ling. "Please remember that I am new to this." Jena noted that not everything the executive said rang true. But then, she had already figured as much. The mix of anticipation and mild excitement in the other woman's voice was unmistakable.

"It doesn't matter." Jena touched the "Open" button on the nearest cubicle. "I'm sure they're all identical. Private and soundproofed."

With a soft whoosh of air, a door decorated with Ayurvedic symbols drew aside to reveal a small room. Virtuals of forest scenery—lush trees and rippling springs, blossoming flowers, lullabying songbirds—immediately added depth and dimension to the surroundings. Overhead, a curved ceiling was filled with fluffy white clouds backlit by gentle sunshine. The musical equivalent of falling water, the trembling tones of a sitar filled the chamber in concert with the dulcet crooning of the oboe-like shehnai. Standing between two raised, padded platforms, the delighted Mai-ling smiled like a schoolgirl who had just unexpectedly been presented with a new dress.

"I am relaxed already, and I believe we have not even started, yes?"

Nodding, Jena reached for the tab under her left arm that would disengage her outfit. "Get undressed and lie down on one of the tables. I'll take the other one."

As the visiting businesswoman complied, Jena carefully folded and set her own attire aside. By the time both women were completely naked, their cubicle had pumped enough perfume into the room for it to smell like an ancient harem. The carefully compiled blend of fragrances scented their nude bodies with droplets of warm mist.

A bit awkwardly, Mai-ling climbed onto one platform and lay down on her stomach. "Like this?"

Reclining supplely on the other platform, Jena gestured approvingly. "Stretch your arms out in front of you. Like this." While demonstrating, she began to search impatiently for an activation control. It was not necessary. The room was simply taking its time, allowing them to get comfortable before treatment commenced.

Now a different male voice greeted them. "Welcome, guests, to the ashtahvaidyan Ayurvedic experience. Please lie back and relax while your specific composition and body types are scanned in preparation for the receiving of treatment. Be so kind as to keep your eyes closed until the brief period of preparation is complete."

Both women shut their eyes as a laser spent half a minute scanning each of them from head to toe. When that process was complete, the inner portions of both platforms sank less than a centimeter into their receptacles, except for the dense foam pillowlike portions that supported their heads.

"Please relax while your beds are filled with a light application of the appropriate massage oil," the voice told them. Jena felt the familiar warm glow of precisely blended liquid filling the basin in which she lay. Moments later they were instructed to turn over onto their backs, then back onto their stomachs once again.

Giggling drifted across to her from the other table. "I feel like duck in a wok," the delighted executive told her new friend. "I warn you—if I see vegetables being added, I am going to get out!"

Jena made herself smile. "Just relax. Let the oil penetrate your skin."

"The special blend that has been prepared for you," the room voice murmured, "contains a typical Ayurvedic mix of sesame oil, extract of sweet flag, round zedory, beech, nightshade, Uraria lagopoids, deodar pine, fennel, sandalwood oil, eaglewood, valerian, costus, cardamom, musk root, country mallow, and winter cherry. It is designed to relax and invigorate your specific body types."

"Definitely sounds like it would go good with duck," Mai-ling commented, but this time without laughing. She was beginning to loosen up as the lightly warmed oils penetrated and soothed her skin.

"Ayurveda is one of the oldest systems of medicine in the world," the comforting voice assured her. "It is designed to work on both the physical and mental levels."

"I do not know yet about the physical," the executive sighed, "but mentally I am definitely starting to unwind."

"Just let go," the voice urged her, "while I work on your marmas." A soft thrumming filled the room, not loud enough to drown out the soothing music.

"My what?" Through her rising torpor, the naked businesswoman managed to sound slightly alarmed.

"Marmas," Jena explained as the humming grew nearer and more personal, "are energy points within the body. They respond to physical manipulation. Massage." She allowed herself to relax, too. It would be foolish to waste the opportunity.

The humming sound originated with the motors that lowered long rectangular shapes from the ceiling. Only slightly smaller than the bed-platforms directly below, each was densely covered with hundreds of synthetic rubberoid fingers, each of which could be individually programmed. Mai-ling let out a small "Oh" of surprise as the prewarmed, rounded tips of the full-body massager above her made contact with her bare, oil-slick skin. With a precision no human masseuse could match, the fingers contracted until the upper platform was perfectly molded to her body from the back of her head to her upthrust heels, as if she were a priceless porcelain doll being measured for form-fitting shipping foam.

The synthetic fingers began to move; rubbing, pressing, manipulating, working the oil into her muscles and joints, relieving stress, gently but firmly pushing and stretching, relying on the intimate details that had been recorded by the scanning laser.

"Heavenly!" the executive sighed.

"Much more effective than its human counterparts," Jena agreed. "It's like having a dozen specialists work on you simultaneously instead of just one tired and maybe bored masseur. In addition to freeing you from stress and tension, Ayurvedic massage is supposed to be able to cure rheumatism, sciatica, bursitis, and many other ailments of the joints and muscles."

Arching her body, she pushed firmly upward with her back and buttocks. As she did so, the platform containing the massaging synthetic fingers automatically retreated, allowing her to swing her legs off the platform and sit up. Head turned the other way, by now completely at ease and half asleep, the drowsy visitor from Guangdong took no notice of the other woman's silent and deliberate movements.

Prowling restlessly northward, the big cat cut through the forest in a wide arc, not approaching the edge of the jungle again until it was several kilometers from the place where it had encountered the TC device. Once more it found itself confronting a professionally maintained greensward fronting a jumble of multistory dwellings. These expensive townhomes were only two and three stories high, with open space separating every cross-shaped quad of housing. Their inhabitants paid a premium for considerable interior space and a location on the border of the world-renowned reserve.

In this wealthier, more developed neighborhood, a barrier of charged cables the height of several men separated landscaping from jungle. Other special wires had been laid below the surface, carrying current underground to repel anything smart or active enough to try digging beneath the fence. A meter off the ground, the steady, subdued beam of a blue sensor laser was flanked by two of the softly buzzing cables. Anything living that made contact with them would receive a jolt powerful enough to discourage even a determined elephant or rhino, of which there were many living in the preserve. Anything that also broke the beam of the sensor would trigger an alert plus a swift response from the privately maintained ranger stations that were situated at intervals along the border with the reserve. A sloping, dry moat designed to keep children away from the fence paralleled the barrier on its north-south run. Evenly spaced warning signs provided the same function for adults.

Neither Ritu, in her stone-washed green jeans and sun-repellent matching blouse, or Vinod in his trendy one-piece pseudo-chamois relaxer, gave any thought to their surroundings as they ran, hand in hand, toward the fence line. Both from comparatively well-off families, each with a year left at university, she attractive and he handsome, they cavorted with the air of those in their early twenties who were convinced they were immortal and destined for Great Things.

"We shouldn't be doing this," she giggled nervously but expectantly as she looked back toward the receding shape of her parent's quad.

"I know." Vinod squeezed her hand a little tighter as he led her on. "Isn't that why we are doing it?"

They shared the delicious, knowing smile of those tempting the forbidden as he guided her toward the place he had found. Here and there, large natural conglomerations of gray granite had been left standing among the lawns, flowers, and decorative bushes by the quad's builders. The natural rock piles provided places for children to play, older juveniles to scramble and fight, and adults to sit quietly. The two university students intended to use the outcropping Vinod had chosen to sit, but not quietly. And truth be told, to do something other than sit.

They were alone, which was the idea. Vinod's flashlight illuminated the way. They were hurrying across grass, well away from the
nearest winding, paved walking path.

A little out of breath, he slowed as they neared the stone outcrop.
The beam of his flashlight played across the rocks. Though the waxing
slim sliver of moon was hidden behind clouds and not visible tonight,
the whitened, ghostly aspect of the raw granite was suitably lunar.

"Come on," he urged her. In the dim light, his teeth were whiter
than the rocks.

"What?" Uncertain, she gestured with a nod of her head. "Up *there?*"

"Why not?" He grinned challengingly. "Afraid of heights?"

"Hardly," she shot back. "It just does not look very . . . comforting."

"You can lay your head on my lap," he told her.

"Yes, you would like that, wouldn't you?" After a moment to let
the tease sink in, she matched his grin with one of her own. "All right.
But mind your hands on the way up."

He started toward the nearest slope. "On the way up, I promise.
After that . . ." A multitude of possible interpretations were left dangling in the air. Significantly, she did not bother to swat them away.

It was an easy climb. Children made it. But at this hour of the
night there were no children about, nor any others their own age. It
was midweek, after all, and people had to get up in the morning to go
to work, or to class. Not even the warning lights of a nocturnal jogger
utilizing the nearest paved path materialized to interrupt the solitude
they sought. Somewhere deep in the woods on the other side of the
security fence, a brilliantly blued lilac-breasted roller warbled in confusion. A diurnal bird, it was not normally active this late at night.

"I can't thank you enough for this suggestion." Gently cupped
between upper and lower platforms, body massaged by hundreds of

tenderly, precisely programmed synthetic fingertips, the visiting businesswoman's voice had dropped to a completely contented whisper.
"How long should we stay like this? Is the treatment timed, or can we
stay as long as we wish?"

"I believe such automated systems charge by the half hour. It should
be charged automatically to your room." Slipping, literally, off the platform, Jena made her way to the open closet where she had placed her
clothes. The room's subdued light glistened off the oil on her skin.

"Have to stay for an hour, then," Mai-ling murmured. "Remember,
it's all on expense account."

Jena did not reply. Instead, she took out and unsealed the long carrying bag she had brought with her and reached inside. The steel of the
sword that she extracted had been polished to a mirror-bright shine.
Its presence did not alarm the room's programming. Nor would a hotel
of this class think of installing security cameras in so exclusive a venue,
lest a single outraged guest sue for invasion of privacy.

The tip of the sword hanging from her clenched right fist nearly
scraped the floor as the naked Jena quietly approached the occupied
bed-platform. Through the perfumed mist that filled the massage
chamber, the gleaming, oiled, nude body of the visiting female executive was visible as a pale streak between the upper massage platform
and the lower basin. Chinese egg roll, the expatriate Frenchwoman
thought, without a flicker of a smile.

"You have a beautiful body," she murmured, barely audible above
the tinkling, seductive strains of sitar and shehnai.

"Umm." Mai-ling started to turn her head to face her newfound
friend. "How do I get this to let me turn over?"

"Just turn," Jena told her softly. "The unit's sensors will detect
your movement and respond accordingly."

"Okay." The other woman started to roll onto her back. "You
know, this setup is wonderful, but sometimes there's no substitute for
the *human* touch."

"Believe me, I know," a somber-voiced Jena admitted without hesitation.

The look of expectation and anticipation on the businesswoman's face hardly had time to turn to horror as the sword descended.

Vinod helped Ritu to the crest. The rock outcropping fell off more sharply on the other side. From this vantage point they were able to look directly over the reserve's underbrush and into its trees. He amused himself by switching the flashlight off and then suddenly shining it into the branches. Once, the beam picked out a family of macaques moving through the canopy. Other than that, the forest was asleep.

"When we get married . . . ," he began as they sat down and in one single, smooth motion slipped his right arm around her waist.

"Just a moment, Vinod." Her voice slowed him, but she made no move to push his arm away. "We are not even engaged yet. I want a modern marriage, yes. Nothing arranged. But I am not sure I am ready for it yet. There is the matter of finishing my degree, and—"

Leaning close, he tenderly kissed her shoulder. She resolutely continued not to pull away. "There are such things as married students, Ritu. We would not be the first such couple in history." Continuing to touch her lightly, his lips slowly ascended, climbing toward her neck. Sitting atop the outcropping enveloped in tropical night, she shivered slightly.

"Vinod, this isn't right."

"Odd," he murmured as his lips reached her cheek. "It feels so very right."

She had no more words for when he began to kiss her. Besides, it was difficult to speak with two tongues in your mouth. A sound, however, made her draw back sharply.

"What?" Vinod was simultaneously alarmed and surprised. "What did I do?"

She was not looking at him. She was staring intently over the fence, into the forest. Her words were whispered. "I heard something."

He relaxed. Whatever it was that had startled her, the important thing was that he was not responsible. He moved to resume where they had left off. "Macaques. Monkeys. The wind."

"Maybe—no, there it is again." Leaning away from him, she squinted as she tried to see deeper into the trees. "Let me have your flashlight."

Grumbling to himself, he removed the thumb-sized device from his breast pocket. "Monkeys," he repeated, but without much enthusiasm. Usually it was his younger brother who ruined such moments. Frustrated, he followed the beam of light as she moved it around. He tried to sound understanding. "I don't see what—"

He never did see. In a demonstration of incredible power and unrivaled agility, the tiger exploded out of the tree it had climbed opposite the outcropping. It cleared the top of the fence and landed, roaring, as much on top of the wide-eyed Vinod as it did on bare rock. Ritu screamed and fell to one side. Her boyfriend had time to do neither. As she rolled and scrambled down the rocks, she heard above the blood-chilling snarling a momentary quick, sharp sound like the snapping of a broomstick. Far behind her, the first lights were coming on in the nearest townhouse quad.

Lying on the grass at the bottom of the outcropping, she found herself staring upward, openmouthed. Even in the dim light she was able to make out the massive shape of the tiger. It held something limp in its jaws. If she had not known it was Vinod, she would not have been able to tell, because the face was completely obscured by blood. His head hung downward at a perfect right angle from his neck. The sound she had heard had been the tiger's jaws snapping his spine. She was too terrified to scream. Only once, when she thought the tiger looked down at her, did she come close.

Then it turned and, with the dead student clamped tightly in its mouth, leaped almost disdainfully back over the fence, landing this time not in a treetop but on the ground. As she stared half paralyzed and dead silent, it trotted off into the bush calmly carrying its kill in its jaws. She sat like that, unmoving, wide-open eyes locked on the silent jungle, until the residential complex's first concerned residents reached her and one put a tentative hand on her shoulder. The same shoulder that Vinod had so recently kissed. The human touch helped greatly.

It allowed her to start screaming again.

chapter 5

"**R**iot in progress." Her tone apologetic, Keshu's driver glanced over at the chief inspector. "It may take some time to get to the address you specified, sir."

He nodded absently. His mind was not on the traffic, or on the river of humanity off to his right that flowed east to west, paralleling the direction the unmarked patrol vehicle was trying to take. In another attempt to assist traffic flow in a city the likes of which humankind had never known, decades earlier the city authorities had somehow managed to get together long enough to agree to make all the main streets not only one way to vehicular traffic, but to pedestrian as well. To walk west to east through Beypore District, pedestrians had to go one block north to Pudumandapa, or one block south to Kerala Place. Such radical changes had not been written into law to make walking easy. They had been done to make it possible. Vehicular gridlock was frustrating. Pedestrian gridlock was often fatal.

Attesting to the efficiency with which the Department of Pedestrian Affairs enforced the laws, Keshu could see a pair of foot patrol
officers administering punishment to someone who had committed the
crime of attempting to walk against the one-way flow of traffic. It had
been before the inspector's time when vociferous argument had greeted
the radical proposal to reinstate physical chastisement as punishment
for such minor crimes. Considering himself a modern, enlightened citizen, he could not understand the reason behind the objections. Laws
were only respected when they were perceived to be effective.

What, after all, were the alternatives to beating such lawbreakers?
It had been shown that lectures on civic responsibility did nothing to
dissuade habitual offenders. Fining them was useless, since most had
no money. With its promise of a roof over one's head and two meals a
day, to a substantial portion of Sagramanda's swollen population the
promise of jail time was an inducement rather than a deterrent. What
remained to deter the repeat reprobate except the threat of physical
punishment?

From what he could see from inside the cocoon that was the patrol
car, the two officers appeared to be administering a level four thrashing:
use of open palms only with not less than two and not more than four
swift kicks. A minor infraction, then. Perhaps the man had come out of
an alley or a shop and had inadvertently turned the wrong way, only to
be unlucky enough to have been spotted by the pair of police. That
would likely have been his claim, anyway: the illegal walker's equivalent of a driver's insistence that he had not been drunk. Among the river
of pedestrians, all intent on their own business, hardly a one bothered
to turn to observe the swift meting out of justice.

One of the officers was male, the other female. The pairing was
necessary in a city with a Muslim population in the millions, since by
law no male officer could manhandle a female of that religious persua-
sion. Justice was not impaired, however, since the city's female officers
were just as well trained and equally as adept at meting out punish-

ment as their male counterparts. Besides ensuring that foot traffic flowed on the city's sidewalks and rampways, such officers were responsible for keeping people and animals off those main thoroughfares that had been designated for vehicular traffic only, as well as the sad, sorry task of keeping them clear of the kind of makeshift housing and temporary shelters that so sorely afflicted the older, more traditional parts of the metropolis.

As the car moved forward in fits and starts, he lost sight of the small drama. Occasionally, a pedestrian attempting to pass part of the flow would step off onto the street. This happened less often than might be expected since most vehicles, both public and private, were equipped with dispersers. Via conduits embedded in the carbon-metal car frames, an electric charge flowed from the vehicle's motor through the vehicle's exterior. Anyone coming in contact with this would receive a low-voltage jolt that was strong enough to make them want to avoid such contact, much less lean on a vehicle so equipped.

City vehicles were allowed to generate much more powerful charges. Unlike private cars and taxis whose repelling nuisance voltage was limited by law, those of fire engines and police cars responding to emergency calls could be cranked up to truly uncomfortable levels. Nobody in their right mind would attempt to get in the way of or hitch a ride on an ambulance with siren wailing. Touch a bumper or a door and the current flowing through it could knock a man off his feet and leave him quivering helplessly on the street for several minutes or more.

Trying to contain his irritation, he checked his wrist chronometer instead of asking the car's AI for the time. "How much longer until we can get through this?"

The driver pursed her lips. "Hard to say from here, sir." She indicated the heads-up schematic that hovered in the air between them and above the dash. "You can see the problem for yourself. There is not one riot, but two."

Keshu nodded and sighed. "What is it this morning? People still protesting the proposed infill for the new stadium up on the bend of the Hooghly?"

"No sir." The driver was a sergeant, middle-aged and experienced. Henna-tinged curls bunched up over the back of her collar; a current fashion that did not violate departmental dress code. "One involves about a thousand chanters protesting conditions in a couple of outlying northern region jails where mistreatment of alleged political prisoners is claimed to be rife." Leaning forward slightly, she checked a readout. "Latest information indicates four dead so far, a dozen protesters and two police seriously injured, with the situation being brought under control."

Keshu nodded. Nothing out of the ordinary. "And the other?"

"Something to do with Raj Tanur Khan's latest picture not being granted a license for general exhibition because of social censorship concerns. His fans are fighting with objectors from two religious groups who are trying to have the film banned outright." Again she eyed the relevant readout. "Twelve dead, forty-two seriously wounded. No breakdown on which side is dominating, but there are half a dozen mobile tactical squads now on the scene, with crowd dispersal and arrests in progress."

That was about right, the chief inspector mused. Far greater outrage and injury was being inflicted over the content of a film than over the behavior of human beings. There were times when the actions of the citizens of Sagramanda made the prospect of taking early retirement loom large in his thinking. Such thoughts eventually passed, however, most commonly for two reasons.

He loved the challenge of his job, and he loved the city that was his home.

Which made his exasperation at not being able to capture one particular suspected serial killer, or even latch onto a stronger lead as to that individual's identity, all the more frustrating.

He shifted in his seat. "If one disturbance is breaking up and Tactical is down on the other, it shouldn't take us too much longer to get to the Chatham." The driver said nothing, concentrating on making her way through the jam.

He could have taken a chopper. But five-star hotels were understandably uneasy about having police copters set down in their parking lots. It tended to provoke awkward questions from the guests. This need to respect the wishes of the influential and well-connected had already cost him an hour this morning. An hour that could have been spent more usefully than fuming helplessly in traffic. To be fair, while riots were a daily occurrence, they were usually avoidable. Encountering two of them at the same time was just bad luck. Then, just as he was ready to give vent to his frustration once more, they were safely around the corner, and the Chatham International hove into view.

Sheathed in fake sandstone and decorated with carvings of animals, plants, and temple dancers (but no gods) that had been brought forth not by artisans' hands but by a computer-controlled industrial lathe, the hotel combined Mughal architecture in the style of the Taj Mahal with the shikhara spires of a traditional Hindu temple. It was all very Disney. Keshu supposed the hotel's guests loved it. If only, he ruminated, the real India were so simple.

While unobtrusive, the gate barring the entrance to the main hotel lot was solid enough to stop a war elephant—or a runaway eighteen-wheeler being driven by a wild-eyed terrorist or extortionist. Picking up the special low-frequency broadcast from the police vehicle, it opened automatically to admit them. His driver parked near a pair of cruisers and a van housing a mobile forensics lab. Seeing him step out of the car, a junior officer introduced himself while Keshu stared at the architectural jumble that was the hotel. If not for his purpose in being there, he would have found the sight amusing.

"The fatality is still on site?" he asked the junior officer as the latter led him toward the nearest service entrance. It was flanked by two armed men; an officer from the department and a senior member of the hotel's security staff. Both nodded in recognition as the senior inspector and his escort passed between them.

"Yes, Inspector," the younger man assured him. "Forensics have been taking their time with it. When the crime fits an ongoing modus, nothing is to be disturbed until the chief investigating officer in charge of the pertinent file has been allowed to make his own observations." He stepped to one side and gestured. "I'll take you there, sir."

Straight from the manual, Keshu reflected, but he didn't upbraid the junior officer for reciting the blatantly obvious. One did not encourage improvement by slapping down those engaged in its pursuit.

Their route took them through service areas camouflaged with expensive landscaping, around the back of the hotel grounds, out of sight of the laughing, yelling guests frolicking unknowingly in the pool. Happening to glance through the vegetation, Keshu noted the fashionable slenderness of many of the swimmers and sunbathers. While they eschewed food and lay in the heat of the tropical sun out of choice, a few hundred meters down the road and a world away local people were starving unwillingly and dreaming impossibly distant dreams of shade and air-conditioning. *What a species*, he reflected.

The appalling handiwork of one of its more disagreeable extant representatives was to be found nearby, in the hotel's designer underground facility dedicated to the ancient healing arts of Ayurvedic massage and the extraction of millions more rupees in supplementary fees from paying guests. Discreet signage at the top of the stairs leading down to the entrance indicated that the hotel regretted that the facility in question was closed for temporary repairs. At the bottom of the stairway, Keshu found inconspicuous plainclothes officers ready to assist hotel security staff in gently but firmly turning away any curious wandering guest who might happen to stumble across the crime scene. Or Krishna forbid, hotel management's worst nightmare, a representative of the media.

So far, a sergeant on duty assured him, they had been able to keep this one off the Net and the vit. It was only a matter of time, of course, before the incident became common knowledge. In an age of near-universal access to and hunger for information, secrets were impossible to keep for very long. Where the police were concerned, this unstoppable flow of information cut both ways.

Acknowledging the duty sergeant's assistance, Keshu adjusted his turban slightly and looked past the officer toward the shadowy interior of the closed facility. An idiosyncratic mingling of aromas he could not recall having previously encountered emanated from somewhere within: sandalwood, rose, and human blood.

"Where is it?"

The sergeant jerked his head slightly in the direction of the facility's interior before starting in. His expression grim, Keshu followed.

Ignoring the forensics team that was still actively scouring the interior of the private massage chamber for evidence, the chief inspector studied the body without approaching or touching it. The poor victim was very definitely beyond the help of the Ayurvedic arts or anything else. Quite a lot of blood had been cleaned up. The woman's skin was pale and waxen. Kneeling, he had a look at the face on the front of the head that had rolled some distance away from the corpse after it had struck the floor and bounced, a consequence of having been neatly severed at the neck from the rest of the body.

The duty sergeant hovered nearby. "Mai-ling Xinzhou. Vice president Hiang Manufacturing Consortium, home office Guangdong Province, China." Unnecessarily, he added, "Had meetings scheduled with two local companies for this morning. Did not make either of them." He nodded at the headless cadaver. "Competitors playing rough?"

"What do you think?" To his surprise, Keshu found that he was angry. It was rare that he allowed what he felt inside to seep out, but this time he could not keep his feelings from communicating themselves to the sergeant.

The other man was clearly taken aback. "It was just a thought, Chief Inspector. I did not mean to appear disrespectful, either to you or to the victim."

"Forget it." Putting his hands on his knees, Keshu straightened and walked over to Bachchan. Having completed necessary chemical analysis of the body and its surroundings, the elderly forensics specialist was now imaging the corpse from every angle.

"*Whaeguru ji ka khalsa, waheguru ji ki Fateh,*" Keshu murmured to his fellow Sikh. "The Khalsa belong to God, Victory belongs to God," following which he added immediately, "Haven't you retired *yet?*"

It was a running joke in the department. Bachchan was one of those unfortunate men born with a long face and premature wrinkles, who had looked old when he was twenty and who was short to boot.

"How can I retire, when there are so many incompetents in the department?" His grin flashed through a perfectly trimmed beard that was gray fading to white. With a nod, he indicated the cadaver. "Poor woman. I know what you are going to ask, Chief Inspector, and here is your answer." Holding up his scanner, he let Keshu have a look at the readout. As the technician had implied, the inspector did not need to ask for an explanation.

"The pattern of the cut matches others already on file for similar cases."

"Enough of them, anyway." The tech nodded. "You had better catch this evil person or persons, Chief Inspector. They are not going to stop killing until they are caught."

"I know that." Mindful of the effect his tone had had on the sergeant, Keshu kept his response carefully neutral. "Don't you think I and my people are trying?"

Bending over, Bachchan ran the tips of the sensor-implanted glove on his left hand over the stump of the dead woman's neck. "You need to try harder, Chief Inspector, or you will never achieve mukti."

"This job isn't conducive to becoming a gurmukh," the inspector responded. "Candidate for residence in an asylum, maybe." He added something in Punjabi so that it would remain private between himself and the technician.

Straightening, Bachchan looked up at his nominal superior. "You must not let your frustration lead you to make this personal. One murderer is no different from another, because a victim is always just a victim."

"I know that's how I should look at it, my friend, but this is different." He gestured at the corpse. "A visiting Chinese businesswoman. Two Australian tourists. Local citizens respected and otherwise. Serial killings tend to follow patterns. They're sexual in nature, or the killer has a grudge against some business, or the government, or relatives. Nothing matches up here." Despite his determination to maintain control, his voice rose slightly. "There's no *pattern* to these slayings."

"Does not that suggest a kind of pattern in itself? Could not this seeming randomness be suggestive of something in the murderer's state of mind?"

"Yes, yes." Keshu agreed tiredly. "I've thought of that. But it makes it damn difficult to try and predict where she will strike next."

"'She'?" Bachchan's reaction showed that he had not been brought up to date on the latest suppositions.

"There are indications that the killer may be a woman, or perhaps a transvestite," Keshu informed him moodily.

His gaze returning to the corpse, Bachchan nodded solemnly. "Not a virtuous date. But if true, one with a strong arm, who has had much practice at their vocation."

"Practice?" Keshu frowned slightly.

Leaning forward again, the technician did not hesitate as he ran his gloved palm across the dead woman's open neck. "This decapitation was accomplished with a single blow. The sharpness of a blade aside, one does not make a cut like this without being well versed in the use of the chosen weapon."

Too well versed, Keshu mused. "I can understand that. If, as we are coming to believe, it is the same individual who is responsible for all these murders, then she has had plenty of practice indeed." Nodding farewell to the technician, he walked back to rejoin the duty sergeant.

"Witnesses?" he inquired tersely.

"Nothing yet." The sergeant indicated the electronic pad he held. "We have to be circumspect about it. The hotel management is naturally frantic to keep this as quiet as possible."

"I know." Keshu let his gaze take in the entire crime scene: the white walls presently devoid of full-depth virtuals, the curved ceiling stripped of its projected sky and clouds, the pair of massage beds; one with its marble-like victim. The blood stains on the floor. The disembodied head near the feet of another forensics tech. Unbidden, a line from the Sidhha Goshth came to him.

"'The perverse are gone astray and are under the sway of death.'"

A sudden and atypical wash of claustrophobia overtook him. He needed to get out, back into the sunshine and the heat, the city air that was far from fresh but was at least alive with familiar smells and not the stink of waning death. He needed a break from dreadfulness.

"Let me know the moment you have anything." He headed out before the sergeant could reply.

To help clear his mind, he and his wife spent the evening in their local Gurdwara, helping out in the langar, the community kitchen that was open to people of all faiths. On the way out he made sure to swipe his credcard through the reader at the entrance so that it would deduct his regular, voluntarily pledged sum to help with the running of the place of worship and the community service in which it was engaged.

The evening's prayers helped to settle his emotions, but not his thoughts. Every crime assigned to him that he could not solve caused him to lose sleep, but it had been a long time since he had taken the activities of any lawbreaker as a personal affront, as he was doing with this still-unidentified serial killer. The sheer randomness of the attacks, the indifference to the innocence of the slain, rankled him both personally and as a Sikh. The ineffectualness of the ongoing investigation was beginning to trouble him night and day. He could not put it out of his mind even as he recited the sohila, the prayer before retiring for the night.

"The Khalsa is of the Wondrous Destroyer of darkness." So the prayer went. It was incumbent on him to find and stop the person or persons responsible for these killings, not only professionally but because of who he was—and he was failing in that responsibility.

What was it Bachchan had said? "Could not the seeming randomness of the killings be suggestive of something in the murderer's state of mind?" Something like that. Randomness, randomness. The reason the killer was killing seemed to be nothing more than that he or she enjoyed killing. Reveling in murder. In death.

It gave him an idea, but he could only put it into practice tomorrow.

There were a number of cults that venerated death. Put the word out on the street and perhaps something useful would come back.

As it turned out, the following morning brought to light information more useful and specific than he could have hoped for. Nor could it have come at a better time, what with the pressure from his superiors to produce results threatening to become onerous. Not that he blamed them. As was inevitable, word had finally reached the media about the death of the visiting businesswoman and the gruesome manner of her passing. The Chinese embassy was now involved. Coming so close on the heels of the deaths of the two Australian tourists, the travails of his section were threatening to go global. It was the kind of international publicity his department, the municipality of Sagramanda, and the country at large could do without.

Efficacy arrived in the person of a familiar diminutive operative from downstairs. Mustering a smile and waving to one side the projections that were hovering above his desk, the chief inspector greeted his visitor.

"Ah, Mr. Subrata—the man who likes to search for patterns. I hope you've found a useful one."

The researcher permitted himself a half smile; about as effusive an expression as he allowed himself while on duty. "Better even than that, it may be hoped. A match. May I?" He extended the police spinner he was carrying.

In response to a positive gesture from his superior, Subrata switched on the compact device he was holding in his right hand. Exchanging codes with Keshu's desk, it inserted therein a number of items of information together with several three-dimensional images. As the images rotated, the chief inspector's excitement rose. One image was the computer-generated re-creation of the woman seen by the elderly museum guard in the company of the two Australian tourists just before they had turned up dead in the Hooghly. The second was brand-new, but similar enough to excite immediate comparisons. He asked his visitor for clarification.

Subrata halted the rotation of the second projection. "This composite is based on a description provided by the young man who was tending the poolside bar the afternoon of the Chinese businesswoman's murder. It depicts, as best he could recall, a woman seen sharing drinks with the deceased that same afternoon. Notice, sir, the similarities between the two separate descriptions."

"Unavoidable." Keshu had to restrain himself from thrusting a fist skyward. "Can you do a fusion?"

"Already programmed, sir." Murmuring into his spinner's pickup, Subrata complied. As both men watched, the two three-dimensional images merged into one. Unseen software smoothed and blended. Where two composites had hovered, a single woman now hung in the air between them.

"Doesn't look Indian," Keshu observed tautly. "That was apparent from the description provided by the guard at the museum. This confirms it."

"Not a Latin type, certainly not Oriental." The technician had resumed rotating the combined image. "Preliminary maxillary-cerebral structural analysis suggests a European or North American origin. She could still be a resident, or an expat working here."

"Those possibilities are already being considered," Keshu informed him. "But this finally gives us something solid to work with. See that suitable reproductions are distributed to all media as well as being put out on the street. Unless she is Muslim or a pretend Muslim and goes about veiled, sooner or later someone is bound to recognize and report her. Given that she's been seen unveiled by at least two witnesses, that may not even be a concern."

"Yes sir." The tech turned to go.

"Oh, and Mr. Subrata? My compliments to you and your associates downstairs. Very good work. With luck and continued persistence, hopefully we can take this person and her associates, should she have any, into custody before she can kill again."

"That is the hope of myself and my colleagues as well, sir." Subrata let himself out.

For the first time in weeks, a tiny bit of the gloom that had hovered over the chief inspector's every working day lifted. They had, at last, a plausible description of the possible killer—or at least someone who could be a link to the actual killer. It seemed too far-fetched for coincidence to expect that a museum guard and a hotel bartender had seen the same woman in the company of three unrelated people just prior to their untimely deaths.

Maintained by his desk, the representation continued to hang in the air before him. The impassive face was that of a still young woman, attractive without being striking. It could not show what lay within, what drove someone like this to commit or conspire to commit multiple murders. Though it was difficult to tell just from a computer-generated image, the visage hovering before him did not have the aspect of the criminally insane. All the more dangerous, then, for not being *non compos mentis.*

Privately, he was ashamed to admit he was relieved that the first solid lead they had obtained on the serial killer strongly suggested that she was not Indian. It distressed him to think that he could be so provincial.

chapter xi

There was no question about it. The man he had been trailing had picked up on the tail, broken into a near run, and taken an unexpected detour, seemingly all at the same time. In the gathering darkness and following from behind, Chal could not be positive it was the person he had been charged with finding: Taneer Buthlahee, missing scientist and absent employee of the very anxious and very nervous multinational concern to which his immediate employer Nayari-sahib kowtowed on a daily basis.

Though not familiar with the surroundings through which he now ran, Chal Schneemann recognized that both he and his quarry had entered and were moving steadily deeper into a part of the city for which the description "unsavory" would have been a marked understatement. The absence of nighttime pedestrian traffic, of open shops and stores, of virtually anything in the way of vehicular traffic either private or munic-

ipal, active or furtive, was sufficient to verify his initial hasty impres-
sions. He was not afraid to enter such an area. In the course of his singular career he had found himself forced to operate in far more threatening surroundings. But it did not make his task any easier.

How far should he go in his pursuit of the well-dressed younger
man he had been stalking? The information he had received that had
led him to track the individual in question had been suggestive rather
than positive. Wait at such and such a corner and you might see the
man you're looking for, he had been told. He had waited, in the heat
and crush, ignoring nattering tourists in their garish, unsuitable
clothes, watching and hoping.

Only one person all day seemed to fit the physical profile of the
absent researcher. Making a choice, he had abandoned the corner to
follow that individual. Just because the man had broken and fled still
did not mean it was Buthlahee. Anyone persuaded that they were being
followed by a stranger might respond in such a manner. Chal knew he
could not be certain until he confronted the man directly and made a
positive identification, either by shaking it out of his quarry or passing
the hand scanner resting in his inside shirt pocket over the man's face.

Of more concern right now was just finding him again. Did he
know his way around this bleak, blasted neighborhood? If so, he
might be hard to track down. The challenge invigorated Chal. An
active hunt was always more stimulating than pumping contacts for
information or sweating through a stakeout. There would be no
killing at the end of this one, of course, but though muted, the thrill
of the chase was still there.

His quarry had bolted down a certain street. Chal would go
another way. In the darkness and unfamiliar surroundings, his choice
amounted to little more than an educated guess. But it was a guess
based on the same decades of experience that kept him alive. Breaking
into a run, he lengthened his stride. He could run like this all night.
He expected to run like this for not more than a few minutes.

His heart pounding so hard it threatened to punch its way out of his chest, Taneer skidded around a corner, nearly stumbling over a pack of dogs that was sleeping on the sidewalk. Several of the mangy, four-legged ratbags stirred despondently as he leaped over them, but none had the energy to spare to give chase, or even to bark. But when the howling throng of hungry women appeared, the dogs rose and scattered as if a live grenade had landed in their midst. Undernourished as they were, the women would have fallen upon the unfortunate mongrels and butchered any they could have caught.

Scientist and dogs fled in different directions, the latter making much better time even though they were not nearly as well fed as the man. As he ran, dodging debris, clumps of feces, and piles of uncollected street trash, Taneer regretted having devoted so much of his youth to intellectual pursuits and so little to cricket or soccer. Without having measurably increased the distance between himself and his rabid pursuers, he was already panting heavily. He had the calories to burn, but the Admikhana had staying power—and inspiration in the form of starving children. They would catch him, and he would be chopped up and turned piecemeal into mother's milk. Like any good resident of the city he had always been in favor of recycling—but not where it involved him quite so intimately.

What part would they start with first? he found himself wondering as terror gave a boost to his legs. Or would they be as indiscriminate in their butchery as in their taste? It was not a heartening line of thought.

As desperate as they were for protein, they couldn't have much in the way of energy reserves. Nonathlete though he was, if he just kept his head—and his balance—he might yet outrun them. Or encounter a lonely police cruiser, or a city bus, or even a couple of sanitation workers. Cornering, killing, and quartering a lone pedestrian was one thing, but the presence of witnesses might be enough to dissuade them.

Despite his fervent prayers, the way ahead remained empty. Word the Admikhana were on the hunt had, through some unfathomable street gossip osmosis, managed to precede him. Dark, tapering alleys beckoned on both sides of the increasingly narrow street, but they reminded him too much of gaping serpentine gullets for him to chance seeking sanctuary in any of them. And if he elected to dart into one, and chose wrong, he might quickly find himself cornered in a place where no one would even be able to hear him scream.

Lights. He needed lights, and people, and activity. He needed to cast himself into the protective maelstrom of energy that was city nightlife.

Instead, he rounded one more corner only to run into another man.

The impact shook him twice: physically, from the unexpected bodily contact, and mentally, because as he staggered backward from the collision he recognized the shape he had run into as the man who had been pursuing him and who had caused him to stumble wildly into this insane part of the city in the first place.

What was worse, much worse, was that the man recognized *him*.

"Taneer Buthlahee." Though the voice was oddly calm, as if reciting one name lifted from a long invisible list, there was no mistaking the satisfaction that underlay the tone. "I've been looking for you for quite a while. It's been an expensive and often frustrating search. But now it's over." A long, lean arm reached for the scientist.

Without thought or hesitation, Taneer slapped it away. Always a mild sort, for him such a reaction bordered on the extreme. The explanation was that the response had been entirely instinctive.

A slim specter velcroed to the night, the taller man frowned. "Don't be difficult, now. I'm supposed to return you intact—or at least, coherent. I don't want to hurt you."

When he advanced a second time, his movements were a blur, and not just because they were masked by darkness. The man's other hand grabbed Taneer by the collar of his shirt before he could duck and spun him around. Though slender, the arm that slipped up to lock in place under his chin and across his neck was immovable. Reaching up with both hands, a struggling Taneer was unable to dislodge it. His fingers dragged futilely across flesh that was rippled with veins that bulged like tree roots. He might as well have been trying to untangle himself from one of the steel cables that held up the bridges over the Hooghly.

New voices filled the night. Shapes that were female but not especially feminine came barreling around the same corner he had just turned. Taneer's eyes widened at the sight of the homicidal mothers. With extreme terror shooting a burst of adrenaline through his system as forcefully as any pusher, he broke free of his captor's grasp, staggered a few steps, and took off running. Cursing in an especially crude jumble of English, Hindi, and German, Chal turned to corral his quarry, but found his attention diverted.

Never ones to discriminate in their choice of meat, the Admikhana were on him before he had taken another step.

Driven by a combination of frustration and anger at having had his objective snatched away from him, Chal Schneemann fought back. That he did not run like the other man, like most of the men they had pursued, slowed the reactions of the Admikhana somewhat. That he was well armed and clearly schooled in the use of the weapons he carried caused several of them to hesitate further. The brief delay was all a professional like himself needed.

Eyes wild with hunger and bloodlust, one woman brought her long knife around in a wide arc parallel to the street. Gauging the distance with knowledge born of long practice and too much experience, Chal simply leaned back just far enough for the blade to miss him by centimeters. In response, one hand withdrew from an inside breast pocket a small gun not much bigger than his open hand. The shot from it was as silent as it was deadly. The tiny syringet, no bigger than a small nail, struck his attacker in the neck. She looked surprised, brought the knife around for a backhand swing, swallowed hard once or twice, and collapsed as the potent neurotoxin contained in the hypod paralyzed the muscles in her upper body. Unable to breathe, much less to scream, she went down as if axed.

The gun that appeared in the tall man's other hand was larger, less subtle, and almost as fast-acting. The second-closest woman to him was knocked backward by the concussive force of the compact explosive shell that blew apart her sternum and shredded the vital organs within her chest. Unlike the silent syringet, the noise of the explosive shell shattering bone and flesh stunned most of the remaining attackers into momentary immobility. Clearly, the last thing they had expected when they had commenced their hunt of the other man was to encounter resistance in the person of a trained professional.

Only the two most desperate women continued with the assault. Unable to bring a weapon to bear properly, Chal leaped into the air, extended his right leg, spun completely around, and brought the heel of his right foot into contact with a small but ferocious woman's chin. Jawbone cracked, flesh fluttered, and eyes closed as she collapsed. The fourth attacker caught another of the explosive shells just above her left armpit. It blew off her arm.

That was enough for the surviving Admikhana. A potential death from hunger was bad, but at least it was not instantaneous, and might more easily be avoided. They retreated, leaving their broken, bleeding, and unconscious comrades behind. They could return for the meat later, when their unexpectedly adept adversary had moved on.

Hardly pausing to ensure that the fight was over, Chal crossed his hands over his chest and pocketed his weapons. A quick search of the street behind him showed no sign of the man he had almost caught. Expressionless, not even breathing hard, he broke into a steady, space-eating run that was more wolf-lope than runner's stride.

Bevaquf mahila, he groused under his breath as he efficiently scanned both sides of the street as well as the filthy pavement ahead. Stupid

women. Why did people always have to interfere in his business? He was
fully aware that he had killed three, possibly four of them. Self-defense,
though he needed no excuse. The deaths of rabble like that would raise
no eyebrows in the media, draw no attention from the local police. Like
the rest of the refuse that called the street its home, the carcasses would
probably be swept up and unceremoniously dumped in the nearest
municipal incinerator. If someone chose to claim a body or two, that was
none of his concern. Personally, he felt better knowing that such human
trash would not now be able to mate and produce more offspring.

Clearly, the homicidal women had been pursuing the scientist
when he had run smack into Chal. The other man's frantic terror and
unexpected resistance now had an explanation. Circumstances had
resulted in the professional sent to track him down ending up not only
extending Buthlahee's freedom but saving his life. Even as he ran on
while methodically searching every possible and potential hiding
place, the irony of the encounter did not escape Chal.

Where had the elusive little shit gotten himself off to? Hitherto
calm and in complete control, Schneemann began to lose his temper
when he noticed that his unadorned but finely crafted shirt had suf-
fered cuts and tears in several places. The four Admikhana had not
gone down without making contact.

Now he would have to visit a tailor: how annoying.

Lights began to appear up ahead. He was emerging from the edge
of the squalid zone into one occupied by lower-middle-class families
and their businesses. Street vendors hawked fast snack food like pap-
padams with meat toppings and deep-fried pakoras. Small storefronts
sold everything from cheap Chinese toys to portable electronics, while
pay-as-you-go terminals offered communications access, information,
and multiple entertainment downloads. While a few small utes and
private cars were in evidence, vehicular traffic was dominated by the
more affordable, electrically powered tri-wheeled rickshaws.

What was his quarry likely to do now? Not keep running. Their brief physical contact had been enough to tell Chal that the scientist was no athlete. He was much more likely to seek transportation than to stay on foot.

Feeling he was about due for a break, the tall tracker got one when he spotted the well-dressed shape of his target hailing an automated taxi. Breaking into a sprint, he bent low and tried to hide himself among the crowd. But the street was too well lit and he was too tall.

Spotting his pursuer approaching rapidly, a frantic Taneer had to wait for the door to open before he could throw himself inside the cab. While the automated vehicle's voice inquired politely as to where its passenger wished to go, Taneer yelped wildly, "Security, security!"

"I have already locked the doors," the cab assured him in calm, unthreatening, preprogrammed tones. "Destination, please?"

Panicky, looking out the back window for signs of his pursuer, Taneer almost gave the address of the apartment complex where he lived with Depahli. Just before he spoke it, he reminded himself that he knew nothing whatsoever of any sophisticated electronics his tracker might be carrying. So instead of home he called out the first innocuous address that came to him: that of a bank in the city's commercial center. From there he would be able to take public transportation in any direction, eventually working himself by a carefully circuitous route back to the apartment. But first he had to shake the company man who had somehow tracked him down.

The taxi started off, but his relief was short-lived. Traffic control in this lower-class, largely residential district was a fraction of that maintained on the main thoroughfares. Cattle lay uncollected and unshifted along the central median, cargo rickshaws illegally piled four and five times their height and twice their width with enormous bundles blocked lanes theoretically reserved for cars and real trucks, while electric-powered Tata trolleys fought for driving space with fuel-cell-driven Ashok-Leyland trucks.

As there was no driver, he did not need to lean forward as he urgently addressed the vehicle's AI. "Can't we go any faster? I'm already running late."

Since the taxi utilized sophisticated electronic sensors to perceive its surroundings, the traditional forward windshield existed only to allow fares to see where they were going. The vehicle was as aware of this as its passenger.

"As you can see, sir, this is a very busy street, and I am forbidden by law and by my coding from forcing a path. I assure you that I am doing my best."

There was nothing Taneer could do except fight down his anxiety and feed his patience. Switching to another taxi would gain him nothing. All were equipped with the same city-regulated programming. With its smaller profile, a rickshaw might make better time through the throng, but all powered rickshaws had open sides. He felt safer in the sealed, air-conditioned confines of the cab.

His choice to stay put was validated when a lean, determined figure drew up alongside the vehicle and bent low to squint inside. Taneer found the lack of any expression whatsoever on the lean, drawn visage that peered inward far more frightening than any scowl or grimace.

"*Out*," the man ordered him, his voice muffled but not completely muted by the intervening window. Terrified, Taneer could only gape back at his pursuer and shake his head forcefully.

A reaching hand grabbed the exterior handle and tugged experimentally. Chal was not surprised to find the door locked. He started to reach inside his shirt pocket for the little pistol that fired the tiny shells that made very large holes in things, but hesitated. Already, some people were stopping what they were doing to stare at the odd sight of a man running alongside a moving cab. Krishna damn all interfering witnesses, he thought as he dug into a pants' pocket and withdrew his scanner. Keeping pace with the slowly moving taxi, he spoke sharply into the device.

As soon as he saw his pursuer take out the pocket scanner, Taneer activated several programs built into his command bracelet. So he was ready when the scanner found the taxi's code for its door locks and a soft buzz indicated that they were being deactivated. Before the tall man could grab the door handle, the scientist hit a control that instantly reprogrammed the coding. An electronic click sounded, indicating that the doors had relocked themselves.

Frowning, Chal worked the scanner again. For a second time, it insisted that it had solved the small matter of the taxi's internal security and had deactivated the relevant segment of the vehicle's programming. Yet when he tried the door again, he found it still locked tight. Peering in, he could see that his frightened quarry had retreated to the far side of the single bench seat and was working with a bracelet communicator. The tracker addressed his scanner a third time.

In this fashion they advanced up the street, one man seated inside the cab with the other running alongside, the two of them dueling with wireless electronics and embedded, adaptive programs much as their predecessors in another age might have sparred on horseback with swords or pistols. Responsive and insufficiently intelligent to be confused, the taxi's doors unlocked and relocked, opened and resecured themselves. Each time, Taneer's electronic riposte was just a step enough ahead of his pursuer's reprogramming to relock the doors before Chal could wrench one open.

"Ah," announced the taxi's voice, unconcerned with and uninvolved in the intense struggle that was taking place between passenger and pedestrian, "we have a break in traffic. Please relax, sir, and I will have you at your destination as soon as is legally possible."

When the cab accelerated beyond his ability to keep pace with it, a winded Chal put away his unexpectedly ineffective scanner and pulled his gun. Witnesses or no witnesses, he was not about to let his quarry escape a third time. He would fire to disable the taxi and invent some excuse to satisfy the anticipated horde of curious onlookers the attack would draw. But he had waited too long. Fast as he was, by the time he had the weapon out and aimed, a dozen pedestrians, a trio of rickshaws, and one cow had filled in the space between him and the rapidly retreating cab. The pedestrians he could avoid, the rickshaws he could pay compensation for, but if he killed the cow, the mass of devoted Hindus who comprised the majority of the crowd were likely to set on him and beat him to a bloody pulp. It was with great reluctance that he put the gun away.

Furious and frustrated, it was all he could do to keep from screaming his disappointment as the taxi carrying his long-sought-after quarry disappeared into the night, swallowed up by the swarming multitude of men, women, children, cattle, dogs, and assorted exotics.

Taneer kept looking out the side windows and twisting around to stare out the back until he was absolutely certain there was no sign of his pursuer. Even so, he did not relax until the taxi spoke to him in a concerned, if wholly synthetic, voice.

"Pardon me, sir, but in compliance with metropolitan taxi code regulations two hundred seventy through two hundred eighty-four, I am required as part of service and safety rules to monitor the health of my passengers at all times. In respect of that, I note that your respiration is significantly elevated above the initial readings taken when you first entered and engaged my services, and that your heart rate has repeatedly surged above levels deemed safe by the Municipal Health Authority of the city of Sagramanda for one of your approximate age and build. Do you wish me to detour to the nearest hospital?"

Reminding himself that he was dealing with programming and not with a human driver, Taneer composed an appropriate response while making an effort to slow both his heart and his breathing. "I'll be fine. Proceed to the designated destination, please. You may continue to monitor my vital signs." At a thought, he added, "Should I at any time fail to respond adequately to your inquiries, feel free to abort the requested destination and take me to a hospital."

There, he thought. If his relentless pursuer somehow managed to get in front of the taxi and shoot or otherwise injure him while he was still in the cab, the vehicle was now programmed to take him to a hospital and into the presence of witnesses, regardless of what the tracker did. It was a sensible and hopefully unnecessary precaution.

Pulling the bottom of his shirt out of his waistband, he used the hem to mop up the sweat that was still pouring off his face despite the taxi's efforts to cool the interior of the cab. His hairbreadth escape into the taxi meant he had managed two near-misses tonight. That was two too many, he knew. Having lost his quarry twice, Taneer doubted his pursuer would allow him to get away a third time. Therefore, there must be no third time.

Some things would have to change. Though he had taken pains to repeatedly emphasize to Sanjay Ghosh the need to move forward in negotiations with all possible speed, he was going to have to insist on it now. Available time and space was contracting rapidly around him. Contrary to current physical theory, his universe was showing distinct signs of collapsing. Ghosh was going to have to make a deal with a buyer, and fast—even if it meant cutting the price Taneer was asking. Better to have half the money and be alive to enjoy it than hold out for the full amount and end up dead as well as broke.

Could the uncomplicated ex-farmer pull it off? Taneer had to admit the shopkeeper had done well so far. He was just going to have to do well a little faster. As the cab sped onward into the night and toward safety, it struck the scientist that despite their disparity in education and accomplishment, both men were about the same age and wanted the same things. Having from the first sought only straightforward, unemotional help in pursuing his dealings, Taneer recognized with a start how much he had come to depend on the shopkeeper. Everything was now riding on the other man's skills as a negotiator and a businessman. The money, his future, that of him and Depahli together; everything. And not only that.

Perhaps also his life, Taneer felt as he recalled the last intense glare of the grim tracker as the man had begun to fall behind the accelerating taxi.

chapter xii

Sanjay was wrapping the rug when the call on his secure number came through. He was reluctant to take it. An early rule he had learned in this business was that when a customer agreed to a purchase it was prudent to conclude it as quickly as possible lest at the last minute they change their mind and ask for their money back. Even when a price had been agreed upon and a credcard debited, ever-fickle tourists had been known to insist on canceling the purchase. Someone decided they didn't like the color, or the item was too big, or they had gone overbudget on their vacation. This had happened to Sanjay several times before he caught on.

So he rolled and wrapped the rug with its gold and silver thread, hand-applied beadwork, and sewn-in bits of mirror as expeditiously as possible lest the bored Taiwanese parents and their giggling teenagers decide to move on without taking it. They were very happy with the price they had bargained him down to. Fashioned from a patchwork of elaborate, elegant wedding blouses all sewn together on a heavy backing, the decorative rug was an expensive item to begin with. No doubt his customers felt the obsequious shopkeeper badly needed to make the sale or he would not have come down so far on the price. They were confident in this because they had compared their acquisition with the cost of similar rugs for sale all up and down the street.

They were right about the price of the item, on which they were indeed getting an excellent deal. What they did not realize was that Sanjay would make back the difference together with a little extra by bumping up the cost of shipping and insurance. He did not feel guilty for doing this. After all, if his customers went away happy, and he was happy, then what was there to argue about?

The communicator would not shut up, and he could see that it was distracting his customers. In a burst of activity and a blur of hands he managed to finish the wrapping, double-check the total charge, and shoo his contented clientele outside onto the street before the device ceased demanding his attention. So anxious was he to take the call that he almost forgot to darken his windows and activate the exterior sign that said "Band/Closed." That way, if his visitors from the far east did change their minds, they would not be able to contact him until it was too late and the rug had already "shipped"—even if only to his back storeroom, where it would await eventual transport.

His satisfaction in completing the sale was muted when he saw that the communication was not only marked "urgent" but was triple-encrypted. Only a handful of trusted suppliers and buyers had the ability to put something that significant through to his machine. They, and one other.

"You're sure nobody can intercept this?"

"Yes sir, Mr. Mohan, sir." Inwardly, Sanjay sighed. He had been compelled to repeatedly reassure his exceptional client as to the state-of-the-art status of his shop's communications system. But no matter how many times he did so the assurance never seemed to stick. Reminding himself silently that he existed only to serve his customer, he patiently repeated himself yet again.

"As I have told you previously, sir, once I have privatized my shop, no detection equipment can penetrate the electronic shielding and scrambling except those senders who possess the necessary key coding. And as everything is quantum encrypted before it is received by me, I am assured that the mere act of trying to intercept it would result in the secure communication being terminated. As before, you can speak with confidence that our conversation is completely private. Otherwise we would not be talking now." He frowned slightly. "You already know this. Is there some reason for you to perhaps be more concerned than before? Something you are not telling me, sir?"

"The last time I visited you, I was followed," Taneer told him. "Someone working on behalf of my ex-employers, I'm sure. I had more opportunities than was healthy to memorize his face. Tall guy, lean and muscular, part European or American. I just barely got away from him, and nearly got myself killed in the process."

"Oh my goodness gracious, sir! I hope you are all right." Sanjay was genuinely upset. Not so much because he particularly liked his sometimes overbearing, condescending client, but because the other man promised to make him rich; a task the gentleman who called himself Mr. Mohan would be unable to complete if he got himself dead.

"I'm okay, thanks," came the heartening reply. "But I can't come back to your place, and we can't see each other in person. At least not for a while, until I'm sure it's completely safe."

Sanjay found himself looking past his counter, through the shop, toward the darkened windows and the barely visible street beyond. "Tell me honestly, sir: do you think I am safe? Not that I care so much about myself," he lied facilely, "but I have a devoted wife and two fine children to think about."

"Nobody's interested in you." Sanjay took no offense at this cava-

lier and rather blunt appraisal of his evident nonimportance. It was
after all nothing more than a statement of reality. "It's me they want."
There was a pause on the other end before the client resumed. "If they
should connect us, and someone should confront you, don't try to hold
anything back. Don't let yourself get hurt. Tell them whatever they
want to know. I don't want anyone else getting in trouble because of
me and what I've done."

Suddenly Sanjay found that he did like the other man. "I will take
care," he assured his client. "I have been very careful so far. So then, you
do not think this person who came after you can connect you directly
to me and my shop?"

"I don't know. But I didn't notice him until I was well away from
your place. It may be that he was only told to look for me in the area,
and is still unaware of our relationship. For both our sakes we need to
make sure he remains ignorant in that respect."

Sanjay nodded, even though there was no one in the shop to
observe the gesture. "Then it truly is best if you do not come into my
establishment anymore."

"Agreed. We'll conduct the rest of our business via communicator
and box. I don't foresee any difficulty. The added distance shouldn't
impact our dealings." The scientist's tone softened slightly. "Though I
will miss your tea."

Sanjay smiled. "When our business is finished, you can buy all the
tea you want, I think. A whole plantation. Or two."

"I'm not interested in getting into the tea business," Taneer told
him, evidently not detecting the humor in the shopkeeper's response.
"What I *am* interested in is concluding ours as rapidly as possible.
How soon can you make the final arrangements?"

Leaning back in his chair, Sanjay tried to conjure a reply that would
satisfy his client. "My goodness, Mr. Mohan, sir: it is not as simple as
trying to auction off a truckload of chickens, you know. I am still
waiting for all the bids to come in. I do not know how familiar you are

with business dealings, but the longer one waits and the more disinterested he seems, the better the price that can eventually be obtained."

The shakiness of the voice on the other end of the secure communication was not the fault of a poor connection. "Sanjay, my friend, we don't have *time*. If this person finds me again, I doubt I'll be able to get away from him. I could see it in his face. I don't doubt that if he feels it necessary, he will do whatever it takes to secure my cooperation. Or yours, you should know. You have to strike a deal now, while we still have the freedom to do so."

Sanjay nodded reflexively. "Very well, Mr. Mohan, sir. You are the instigator here, whereas I am only a humble facilitator working on a commission. Of three percent."

Exasperation replaced anxiety on the communicator. "Please, my friend. No last-minute renegotiations. I don't have time for that, either. If you're finding our agreement unsatisfactory, I can always—"

"No, no, sir!" Sanjay cut the other man off quickly. "Please excuse me. I meant no offense. You must understand, it is the way I was brought up. Surely you cannot blame a fellow for trying?"

"All right," the voice conceded. "But no more foolishness. This is a deadly serious business, as you should know from the stakes involved. How soon can you close the deal?"

Sanjay considered. "I will go today, if I can get an appointment, to speak with the intermediary who is working to arrange the sale on our behalf. I will explain to him what you have said. But in order to push the business forward, I need your permission to threaten to break off all talkings if the kind of speed you are requesting is not forthcoming."

"Tell him whatever you like," Taneer told the shopkeeper. "Do whatever you have to do. But we must have a deal and make the exchange this week."

"I understand from where you are coming, sir. I will do my very best."

"Oh, and Mr. Ghosh?"

"Sir?"

"Be careful, and don't accept any help from those of whose relia-
bility you are not personally certain."

Sanjay found himself smiling again. "In my business, Mr. Mohan,
sir, one learns very quickly about such things, or one morning he wakes
up to find he no longer is the operator of a going concern."

A few brief closing pleasantries, and the communication was terminated. As soon as his client was off the line, Sanjay began making
encrypted calls of his own. As expected, his contact was as reluctant as
he had been to rush a transaction of such magnitude. And just as he
had been, his contact did not dare risk losing his share of the deal. It
might be done, Sanjay was told. It *had* to be done, he riposted. Otherwise, the entire complex transaction risked falling to pieces.

The intermediary wanted confirmation of final details in person.
Sanjay agreed to a meeting that very afternoon. Concluding the conversation, he made hurried preparations to close up shop for the rest of
the day. Urgent family business was the explanation he gave to the
merchants who operated the stores on either side of his. They nodded
knowingly and sympathetically, not believing him for a minute,
having themselves utilized the same generic excuse to cover the doing
of secret business. But they would watch over his shop just as carefully,
had the situation been reversed, as he would have watched over theirs.

Almost, he determined to go straight to Shrinahji. Since time had
become so important to his client, the last thing he wanted was to be
late for the important appointment he had managed to secure. At the
last minute he recalled Mr. Mohan's admonition to always employ a
roundabout route when traveling on behalf of their mutual business.

It was well that he did. He was only halfway to the great market
when it occurred to him that the same three people were on the back
of the city bus that he had seen riding in the same subway car with him
when he had left the central district. Two men and a woman. Trying
to size them up without staring in their direction, he grew decidedly
uneasy not at the sight of the men, but of the woman. Her expression

was furtive and uncertain, as if she did not know where to aim her eyes. A woman in the company of two men should not look so uneasy. Also, he did not like the way she kept fiddling with the pallav, or end piece, of her sari. She kept pulling and pushing it up higher on her left shoulder, as if she was using the silken folds to hide something there.

It could be coincidence, of course. The three might really be traveling the same route that he was. Furthermore, neither of the two men fit the description of his client's tracker. They were of average height, and neither looked in the least bit European. Nor had Mr. Mohan said anything about a woman.

Sanjay knew he could not take any chances.

Exiting the bus at the next stop, well in advance of his intended destination, he found himself in an upper-middle-class commercial district. Drifting adverts assailed him, clamoring for him to try, buy, and not be shy about sampling the latest range of domestic products, imports, and joint-venture goods. Pushing through a loosely regulated street-storm of light and noise entreating him to acquire a new car, new furniture, new entertainment options, new hair, new body odor, and old vits recalibrated for contemporary playback devices, he worked his way through the comparatively well-dressed, well-groomed crowd of upwardly mobile service personnel, students, and technocrats who jammed the eastern sidewalk.

A single backward glance was enough to confirm his escalating fears. The somber ménage à trois was still behind him, following at a discreet distance, striving assiduously to look everywhere but in his direction while not losing track of him.

He began wildly searching his immediate vicinity. Would they just continue to follow him? Or if they could catch him out alone somewhere, in a store or while waiting for transportation, would they decide their presence had been detected and choose to confront him instead? With questions, and the means to persuade him to provide the answers they sought?

He determined not to give them the opportunity. Though he found himself in a strange neighborhood, there was nothing alien about his surroundings. It mimicked its cultural and social counterparts throughout the city. Storefronts emblazoned with "Sale!" signs offered Bata shoes, Nike sneakers, and cheap socks from China. The broad windows of kapri ki dukan—clothing stores—featured remarkably lifelike holoquins whose flashed-on garb changed every couple of minutes. Larger shops flogged every imaginable size and variety of consumer electronics from Japan, China, Europe, and Southeast Asia as well as the familiar homegrown brands. This not being a tourist area, there were few shops akin to his own.

There was the usual line outside the local Starbeans. Ignoring the frowns of those waiting he forced his way inside, claiming that he was meeting friends already arrived. Pushing through the milling, chattering crowd, he worked his way up to the counter. One of a dozen automated serving stations politely inquired if it could take his order.

He had to make it look real. After a moment's thought he replied, "I'll have a couple of chocolate-chip vadas, please, with a chota masala chaicchino." While he waited for the lentil doughnuts and the spicy frozen drink, he kept glancing surreptitiously in the direction of the entrance.

His heart sank when he saw the single-minded trio enter. Trying to remain inconspicuous, they approached the end of the counter nearest the door and placed orders of their own. That, at least, was a good sign. Sanjay doubted they would have bothered to do so had they believed their anonymity had been compromised.

His order arrived. So nervous was he that he had to flash his credcard three times under the reader before it would accept the charge. Moving away from the counter, he did his best to appear nonchalant as he slowly wended his way toward the rear of the establishment. It did not concern him that every seat and stool was taken by office workers on break or students from the nearby university. He had no intention of sitting down.

The small doughnuts went down fast, the cardamom and ginger in the chaicchino tickling his palate. Beyond that, he barely noticed the food or drink. As expected, there were bathrooms in the back and lines for both. That didn't bother him, either. He no more had time to piss than he did to sit.

There was no alarm on the rear doorway. Besides complying with municipal regulations requiring a second exit, it offered another way into the coffeehouse. The fact that no one was using it told him all he needed to know about the nature of what he was likely to find out back. Shoving hard against the door, he stepped out of the upscale enterprise and into another world.

The air in the alley stank of illegally flushed washwater, uncollected trash, decomposing food, the presence of undocumented night-dwellers, rotting appliances, and the presence of monkeys, rats, mice, and snakes, all compounded by the furnace-like heat of midday. But this was an upper-class neighborhood, and so the service alley was cleaner than many all-too-public streets he had walked in poorer neighborhoods.

An automatic closer had pulled the door shut behind him. Had his pursuers noted his escape, and were they even now moving to follow him? And if they confronted him in the alley, out of sight of witnesses, would their impatience lead them to put their questions to him directly, rather than continuing to follow to see where he might lead?

Should he run left, or right? Leftwards led to a narrowing and darkening of the passage, where the upper floors of commercial buildings nearly touched and where a man could be beaten to within a heartbeat of his life without awareness of his battering impinging on the consciousness of any of the thousands of busy pedestrians swarming through the shops and on the main street beyond. Not the best option.

To his right—to his right sat two figures, indifferent to the world but not unaware of their surroundings. One was old, while his companion was older. The first had a neatly trimmed short beard that was

peppered with gray and hair bound up to one side in long black semi-
dreads. The senior of the pair wore his hair in long braids and boasted a
gray-black beard as dense and untouched as the rusting wire fence on the
Ghosh family farm back home. Ash had been used to mark their cheeks
and the sun-seared arms that emerged from folds of bright carrot-colored
clothing, while their foreheads bore decorative marks in gold and orange.

The men were sadhus, wandering holy ascetics, who for the most
part eschewed the trappings of Earthly existence in their search for the
True Path, Enlightenment, Nirvana, Realization, Kavayla, Nirguna
Brahman, or however one chose to define the ultimate seeking after
knowledge. Pithy aphorisms drawn from venerated Sanskrit texts
floated across the three-centimeter-wide transparent flexible headband
that ran across the forehead of the less ancient of the pair, a moving (in
both senses of the word) testament to a lifelong commitment to the
dispelling of ignorance. The ancient sayings glowed brightly for all to
see, no less ethically efficacious for being solar powered.

The elder sat with his back propped up against the rear wall of the
building that housed the Starbeans Sanjay had just fled. One hand
helped to support the chillum, or straight pipe, that protruded from
his mouth. The aromatic smoke that rose from its bowl reflected the
traditional packing of tobacco and hashish, though this particular
modern chillum added both chip-driven filter and concentrator to the
otherwise old-fashioned pipe.

Glancing in Sanjay's direction, the younger man greeted him
politely while extending a hand, palm upward, in the shopkeeper's direction. Sadhus survived on the generosity of others, exchanging good
wishes and prayers for alms. Sanjay had no time to waste on the giving
of either. He started past them, heading for the far end of the alley where
people could be seen rushing busily back and forth on the intersecting
main street. His luck was holding: the back door behind him remained
closed. He could not rely on that for very long. If those following had
not missed him by now, they surely would very soon.

Gnarly fingers reached out to clutch at his pants. "Namaste, sir. Kripaya, please, can you not spare a few rupees for wise men on pilgrimage?"

Both sadhus looked too well established and too comfortable to be on a pilgrimage to anywhere but their local hash dealer, Sanjay decided quickly. But this modest indirection did not obviate their holiness. Whether in motion, standing, or seated, a holy man was ever on pilgrimage. Unable to dislodge the surprisingly strong fingers, glancing frantically back toward the door that he expected to see burst open at any minute to reveal his three restless pursuers, Sanjay fumbled in his pocket for loose paper. At fifty rupees to the U.S. dollar, only beggars and the truly poor bothered with coins, while the well-to-do hardly ever carried cash anymore.

Finally finding a ten-rupee note, he handed it to the grateful ascetic, who promptly loosened his fingers. As Sanjay moved to go, the man looked up at him and smiled broadly. "No special blessing for you, good sir? And if not for you, is there no one in your circle in need of prayer?"

Sanjay was about to snap that there was not, when a better response occurred to him. "Yes, as a matter of fact, there is." He indicated the coffeehouse's still shut back door. "Three people, two men and a woman, are very likely to be soon coming quickly out of that doorway. Wise men such as yourselves will immediately see from their countenances that they are much troubled in mind." Fumbling again in his pocket, this time he extracted a hundred rupee note and passed it to the sadhu. As he did so, the older man sucked harder on his pungent pipe and nodded appreciatively.

"Do what you can to help them," Sanjay urged both men. "Try to ease their stress. I promise you they need your prayers and intervention more than I."

"You are a generous and caring man." Carefully pocketing the second banknote, the younger sadhu pressed his palms together in front of him, steeple-fashion, and nodded. "One who has concerns for

the welfare of others is thrice blessed. Though we have already performed the morning puja, we will try our best to help these others who
are in need of spiritual salving."

Sanjay hurriedly put his own palms together in front of him, closed
his eyes, bowed his head quickly, and rushed off up the alley. As he did
so there came the sound of a door opening violently behind him, followed by a feminine shout of "There he is!" Though short by Western
standards, Sanjay still had the strong legs a farmer developed chasing
down stray chickens and vagrant goats. Now as he sprinted madly for
the main street ahead, he thought not of chickens and goats but of the
leopard that had eaten his dog, and tried to imagine not one but three
hungry carnivores behind him.

The first of the hungry carnivores found his way intercepted by a
bearded scarecrow clad in bright orange. "Stop!" With upraised hand
and ash-decorated palm, the senior of the two sadhus had risen to block
the bounty hunter's path. "Are you wise in the ways of Lord Krishna? Do
you recite the proper evening prayers? I sense that you are full of discon-
nection and discontent and that your dharma is weak. We would help
you." He extended his other hand, that still held the smoking chillum.

"Get out of my way, old father!" Irritated, the much younger man
moved to step around the senior ascetic.

As he did so, he was brought up short by a sudden projection from
the headband of the younger sadhu. A tall, well-formed blue man clad
in tiger and elephant skin smiled back at him. The figure's long,
matted hair was tied into an elegant yet functional knot. Two of his
four arms held a trident and a damaru, a small drum. The remaining
two were held in the postures known as abhaya and varada mudras,
confronting the three trackers. With one hand upraised, Shiva greeted
them. The tracker swallowed, hesitated.

The woman pushed forward. "It's only a virtual, you idiot! Step
through it. Or if it offends you to do so, then go around." She gestured
anxiously. "He's getting away!" She started forward.

"Bad karma flows from you as waste from the mouths of the Ganges," declared the elder holy man. "You should work to cleanse yourselves." So saying, he blew a puff of smoke directly into the face of the irate woman.

It made her cough. Angrily, she turned toward him, reaching for something carried in a pocket. Then she wavered, swaying slightly. Contradicting Sanjay's original supposition, the chillum contained a considerably more powerful mix of blended substances than just hash and tobacco.

"Get . . ." The woman broke off and swallowed, unable to complete the sentence. Alarmed, both of her companions rushed to support her.

As they did so the third eye of Shiva, the one set between his brows, opened. It was the eye of wisdom, the opening of which serves to destroy unworthy selves and false illusions. As both of the male trackers turned toward it, the projection slammed into their wide-open retinas and stunned their brains. All in good cause, of course. The sadhus would never dream of harming anyone. Especially these three, who were so clearly suffering.

"Relax, please," murmured the senior sadhu soothingly. "Let Lord Shiva work on your imperfections. Let him destroy your illusions, desires, and ignorance, your evil and negative nature, the effects of bad karma, your passions and emotions and all the many things that stand between you and God as impediments to your progress and inner transformation." Approaching each of the three mesmerized trackers in turn, he gently blew smoke from his chillum into their faces.

"Be at your ease, for those who rush about aimlessly in this world will reap their fretfulness tenfold in their next incarnation."

Responding to the sadhu's suggestion the three dazed trackers sat down there in the alley and, one by one, fell into a contented and sudden sleep. At the far end of the passageway, Sanjay was stepping up into the powered rickshaw he had hailed.

By the time his three groggy pursuers awoke from their photonar-

cotic sleep, rested in body if not necessarily in mind, both their quarry
and the two elderly sadhus had long since moved on.

The glassy eye of the suspicious robot camel studied him with the same
scrutiny as before, but it finished the inspection more swiftly. Basic
biometric information obtained during his previous visit, Sanjay suspected, was already stored in the elaborate automaton's memory.

Somewhat to his surprise he was directed not to the same meeting
room as before but to a much smaller room high up in one of the
building's two towers. Noticing them on his prior visit, he had
thought them merely decorative.

The room was tiny and cramped, with hardly space enough to
accommodate him and Chhote Pandit. The view out the single small
window was spectacular, encompassing as it did a good portion of
frantic, frenetic Shrinahji Market. As on his previous visit, there was
tea. This time it was dispensed not from a tea service rising from the
floor, but from the right breast of a three-foot-tall automated silver
apsara that removed itself from a niche in the wall and executed a perfect, sensuous odissi as it danced over to them. If the intention was to
take a visitor's mind off the business at hand and leave him slightly
unsettled, it more than succeeded.

Grinning, Pandit whispered to the gold control bracelet he wore. The
gleaming apsara dipped its other breast toward Sanjay's cup. "Cream?"

Trying hard not to appear more dumbfounded than he was, Sanjay
nodded slowly, entranced by the sophisticated automaton. Chai service
completed, it executed several additional dance steps as it backed off.
Returning to the storage niche and plugging its reflective derrière into
its charger, it settled back into Wait mode.

Enjoying his guest's startled reaction, Pandit sipped daintily from his
own cup. "As you may know, humanoid robots are far more costly than

the purely functional kind." He cackled with amusement while gazing possessively in the direction of the mechanical. "Ones that can dance as well as serve tea like this are absurdly expensive. This one is taken from the template of an apsara found on the second level of the temple to the Sun God at Konark. An expensive toy. I will not tell you what she cost, except to say that the silver shell was the cheapest component."

Betraying his lack of sophistication, Sanjay could not take his eyes from the now-motionless figure. "I do not care what it cost. I want to see it in action again."

Lowering his head to hide his laughter, Pandit tolerated his guest's artlessness because he had encountered it before. "Then drink your tea and state your business, and it's possible you might be served again." Looking up, his expression as pleasant as ever, he added while stroking his frizzle of a beard, "Or I might call for servants larger and less metallic to throw you out that window, if I feel that you're pissing on my valuable time. You insisted that we arrange this meeting or that any and all dealings would be called off." Clasping his hands together in front of him, he leaned forward slightly, cutting in half the distance between their respective chairs.

"I do not like to be pushed, Mr. Ghosh. Or crudely cajoled, much less threatened. If not for what the mollysphere you brought me contained, you would not only not be seeing me now, you might not be seeing anything at all."

A lifetime spent dealing with scorching summers and frigid winters, with predatory beasts and corrupt officials, had toughened Sanjay. To take just one example, he knew that starvation was a greater threat to survival than a gun. His host's blatant warning left him attentive but not shaken.

"I must remind you, Mr. Pandit, sir, that what has been done and what is being done is being carried out specifically according to the wishes of my client, and that while I personally might have approached today's get-together differently, as a conscientious agent in this matter

I had no choice but to follow the wishes of the one who is employing me in this capacity."

His host grunted grudgingly. "All right—I understand. But since he isn't here, I can only threaten you."

Sanjay nodded as if he had found himself in similar situations many times before, when in fact this was the very first. "I appreciate your position as well, Mr. Pandit, sir."

"Well then," his host muttered, "to business, and the need for this unseemly urgency." He brightened. "And then, more tea."

Sanjay took a deep breath and began. "Recently, I am most sorry to have to say, my client was trailed and nearly killed by a professional tracker most probably working for his former employer. Only today, I myself was followed by three people." When Pandit looked startled the shopkeeper hastened to add, "There is no reason for concern. I was able to lose them long before I arrived at the market."

His host nodded slowly. "It is good that you understand the need to take proper precautions. We are dealing here with sums more common to exchanges among governments than between individuals and private concerns." He gestured amiably. "Of course, anyone who attempted to break into my place of business would immediately be electrocuted, incinerated, intercepted, or shot."

"I had assumed as much." Sanjay swallowed hard and tried not to look uneasy.

It was possible that he succeeded. Or perhaps old Pandit was too preoccupied, or too polite, to take notice. "Imminent death has a way of wonderfully focusing the mind. I understand now your client's need for speed. I have engaged with a number of different potential customers. There are one or two who I believe to be on the brink of coming to terms." Suddenly clapping a hand to each knee, he broke out in a wide grin that emphasized the gaps in his teeth.

"We will do this thing! *I* myself will do this thing. I will see it done as you ask. Not because I am a considerate person. Not because I am concerned for the safety of your client—or for yours, for that matter. I will do it because I would be loath to lose this commission!" Breaking out into gales of laughter, more witchlike than hearty, he managed to choke out a command to his semiautonomous apsara. Emerging from her niche, she resumed dancing, this time choosing to essay a complex bharat natyam from Tamil Nadu: less sensuous than the odissi but more involved. The serving of tea, as yet, did not come into play. Doubtless that required another verbal command from her proud owner.

"Within twenty-four hours I pledge that I will get back to you with a concrete offer that you can convey to your client," Pandit promised. "To ensure the speediest possible acceptance, he may have to come down somewhat on his asking price." Aged but wiry shoulders shrugged. "That is a decision for him to make. Me, I would be more than content with a tenth of what he is asking. But as a merchant yourself, you understand the need to begin bargaining with the most outrageous asking price."

Sanjay felt himself nodding absently by way of reply. His attention was focused on the silver dancer. Grinning like the wizened monkey-god Hanuman, whom he somewhat resembled, Pandit reached out to put a hand on his guest's knee. That finally drew the shopkeeper's concentration back to his host.

"Twenty-four hours. Chhote Pandit's word is his bond. Then it will all be up to your client."

Their business concluded, Sanjay had the delicious pleasure of being uniquely served one more time by the extraordinary automaton. Tea was sipped, dancing observed, music listened to. Ten minutes later Pandit rose, a signal that the meeting was at an end.

"Be careful, my friend." He wagged a warning finger at the departing Sanjay, who was not surprised to find two very large gentlemen of serious mien awaiting his exit. "Try not to get yourself killed; at least not until tomorrow evening after we have concluded this matter."

"Do not worry," Sanjay told him. "I am most assuredly not going back to my shop. I am not even going home, in case that is being watched. I will spend the night in a truck driver's hostel. Trackers would have to be very clever indeed to find me there, and braver still to try kidnapping someone from such a rough place. Tonight I will contact my client. Tomorrow, you and I will speak via secure communicator." He hesitated. "I will tell you one thing, sir, and then I ask that you tell me a thing."

Pandit nodded sharply, once. "Tell and ask, then."

"I believe that my client will accept any reasonable offer you can secure." There was no harm in saying this, Sanjay knew, because as agents for the sale both his commission and that of Pandit would rise or fall according to the final offer. "That is what I have to tell you. As to the asking . . ." He hesitated for a moment, not wishing to appear any more ignorant than he doubtless already had.

"I know the sum that is being stipulated. It seems impossible to me, the kind of figure that is met only in dreams, or in the stories of Mughals and maharajahs, sultans and nizams. Yet my client has not wavered in his asking price, and in the course of our previous meeting neither did you. What I want to ask is this, and you of course do not have to answer if you feel it is not in your interests." With the air of a man laboring under a cloud of disbelief, he took a step back into the lightly scented chamber.

"Is what my client has to sell *really* worth such an astonishing sum?"

It was silent in the little room for a moment, a state of affairs not entirely due to its sound-muting capabilities. Then Chhote Pandit looked over at the shopkeeper and replied easily, without a hint of a smile.

"Cheap at the price."

Chapter XIII

Despite his assurances it took longer than Pandit had promised to settle on a price, obtain an agreement, and lock down the relevant terms. About five hours longer. He conveyed the details to Sanjay Ghosh via the roundabout encrypted means the grand old merchant and modest younger merchant had previously agreed upon. Sanjay, in turn, communicated them to Taneer Buthlahee, whose relief as he readily agreed was palpable even over secured communications. Best of all, the buyer shared Taneer's desire to conclude the business as rapidly as possible. Tomorrow at the soonest, since the banking establishments in both India and Europe whose services would be required were already closed and the necessary instruments and transfers could not be put through until they reopened.

Though he would continue to work through the shopkeeper, Taneer insisted on making the final arrangements and conveying their details to the buyer himself, in real time. That meant either engaging in a simultaneous three-way communicator exchange—much more difficult to keep private—or being with Sanjay while the two of them utilized the facilities of a single open line to talk to the purchaser. The latter arrangement had the additional advantage of allowing them to communicate privately by signs or in writing or even just via eye contact while still remaining in constant contact with the buyer.

But where to conduct such business, and on such short notice, this very night? Via communicator, Sanjay suggested that they meet at the trucker's hostel where he was staying. The idea did not appeal to Taneer. Too much potential for secondary violence, too many possible eavesdropping ears. It had to be a more public place, with as many witnesses as possible in the event something went wrong. Preferably somewhere with a significant police presence. Both men racked their brains for a suitable venue.

In the end, it was Depahli who came up with the solution.

Ramapark was one of the most recent, and successful, additions to the city's sometimes bewildering abundance of entertainment venues. While the well-to-do could afford to have elaborate personal entertainment systems installed in their homes, thus saving them the trouble and danger of mingling with their millions of less fortunate fellow citizens, such expensive luxuries were not available to the vast majority of Sagramanda's inhabitants. Hence the creation of frequently small and simple, but occasionally vast and elaborate, carnivals of culture and pleasure. Ten-year-old Ramapark fell into the latter category, and had proved stimulating enough to intrigue even the wealthy into going slumming in search of its delights.

Based on the great epic of the Ramayana, a tale set three thousand years in the past had been adapted and updated for contemporary enjoyment. Located on the western side of the Hooghly, the thousands of lights that illuminated the park after dark drew packed crowds on weekends and was reasonably busy on weekdays, not least because most of its rides and attractions were air-conditioned. In the same way, movie houses during the mid-twentieth century had often filled their seats with people less interested in what was being shown on ancient screens than they were in escaping the summer heat.

Surrounded by an artificial moat that made use of Hooghly water, entrance to the park from the parking lot and public transport station was over a wide causeway built to resemble the stone bridge Hanuman had raised from south India to Ceylon so Rama could invade that country to recover his kidnapped wife, Sita. As he joined the throng of happy families and couples in moving toward the great arched, illuminated entrance, Sanjay vowed to one day bring his own family here for a visit. Chakra and the children would love it, from the automated servants of Hanuman the Monkey-God, who were shown working on the bridge, to the soaring virtuals of Ravan's demons, who strove futilely to harry them in their efforts.

Inside the walls, constructed to resemble Sugriva's fabled city of Kishkindha, sound competed with light for the attention of the park's visitors. People flocked to eat dinner at one of the park's many restaurants or the stalls that served specialties from all over India. Wide-eyed children clung with one hand to parents and with the other to souvenirs like the internally illuminated balloons in the shape of heroes from the Ramayana story. Shops sold everything from figures of the epic's many characters to replicas of Maricha's deer and Hanuman's asoka flowers. "Reproductions" of Sita's jewelry were especially popular among young girls, while boys favored miniatures of Rama's bow and arrows or the sandals he had given to Bharat.

Never having been to the park before, Sanjay found it difficult to concentrate on the work at hand. He was here on business, serious business, and not for relaxation. Still, it was hard not to be seduced by the glitter and glow of the many rides and attractions on offer. He was particularly drawn to the opportunity to participate in an enormous enclosed ride where for ten minutes at a time, fifty individuals could reenact the great battle in the sky between Rama in his chariot and the evil Ravan in his sky carriage. Rama's arrows and Ravan's darts were all virtual, of course, but that did nothing to mute the genuine excitement. A place like this, he reflected, could make one feel like a child again.

A check of his chronometer indicated that he was already running a little late. Too late, and his client Mr. Mohan might grow nervous and leave. That would not be good for their always-tenuous relationship. Sanjay tried to walk faster, but the press of bodies around him made it difficult. In such packed surroundings, he could not run. The consequences of running over some distracted child would slow him down even more.

Passing the opportunity to take Sumantra's chariot ride or win prizes by finding the jewel in the lock of Sita's hair, he worked his way through the multitude until he found himself walking past two opposing rows of park games that harkened back to a simpler, less technologically advanced era. In another time and place, they would have been called carny games. Step right up, folks, and try your skills here! Win cheap prizes! These consisted primarily of overlarge, inexpensively produced stuffed animals and Ramayana figures or wildly blinking low-priced electronics imported from the low-labor factories of China or the SADC.

He passed on the stentorian blandishments of a human hawker who urged him to try his luck at throwing the healing herbs of Hanuman at the foul poisons of Indrajit as he searched for the venue specified by his client. It was located at the end of the aisle, on the left. There, people paid to shoot at Varan's Raksha warriors with virtual arrows shot from real bows. Imbued with individual internal programming and the appropriate electronics, the bows responded to aim and strength of pull and "fired" accordingly at virtual targets that swooped and darted in three dimensions at the rear of the high-tech booth. When a Raksha was hit, it perished in an explosion of light and color garish enough to satisfy the most demanding twelve-year-old—or his excited father.

As Sanjay approached, there were only three people utilizing the booth's facilities: a frowning teenager of about fourteen who was rapidly exhausting the credit on his park card, and a young couple. The shopkeeper recognized his client immediately. When the figure with him turned slightly, Sanjay found himself taken aback by her attractiveness. Though the capacious sari she wore concealed any hint of curves (deliberately, perhaps?), he felt confident that the beauty he saw in her face must surely be duplicated all the way to the toes of her sandal-clad feet. There was something else about her he could not quite put a finger on, however. A suggestion of hardness, perhaps. This was a flower that would not surrender its petals easily.

Taneer finished firing his bow. He'd been at it for a while now, too preoccupied to pay much attention to what he was doing, more interested in conveying the appearance of an average park-goer. Even so, he was irritated at his lack of success. He had been brought up not to lose at anything, and even the meaningless diversion of the game threatened to distract him from his purpose in coming here. Recognizing the expression on his face, Depahli was amused at his inability to win a prize neither of them wanted. They were here to put the final touches on acquiring a real prize.

She had to touch him on the shoulder and turn him slightly to face the quiet gentleman who had come up behind them and stood waiting patiently for Taneer to finish with the game.

"Sanjay, my friend." Gesturing, Taneer led the shopkeeper away from the booth and deeper into the park.

"Mr. Mohan," Sanjay replied courteously.

Depahli looked at him in such a way that the scientist felt moved to take a step forward, in the direction of trust. "Events have pro-

gressed to the point where I think you might as well know my real
name, Sanjay. If things don't go as we hope, you might need to know
it to facilitate alternatives. My name is Taneer Buthlahee." As they
walked on, he introduced the exquisite woman at his side. "This is my
fiancée, Depahli De."

Steepling his palms together, Sanjay bowed slightly in her direction. "I am both honored and charmed, though if you will permit me,
I must confess that I am more charmed than honored."

Depahli laughed. It was a bold, forthright expression of delight
without a hint of fragility about it. "A pleasure to meet you, too,
Sanjay." Her tone turned playful and she squeezed her consort's arm.
"Has dear Taneer promised to make you rich also?"

The scientist just shook his head. One could only restrain Depahli
so far, and then stand back while she said whatever was on her mind.

"We have a most equitable business arrangement, yes," Sanjay told
her, smiling.

A trio of young girls rushed past. Dressed in colortropic pants that
shifted hues to match their emotions and Western-style blouses puffed
at the sleeves in the current style, they carried self-icing drink cups
that, thanks to their electrostatically charged rims, kept the contents
from sloshing out as the girls ran. They were giggling and smirking,
bubbling over with adolescent feminine secrets that were important
only to them. As a proper father, Sanjay wondered what they had been
up to. Black entwined ponytails swaying, the tallest girl wore one of
the new vest tops that was open vertically all the way to her waist.
Opposing magnetized hems were all that kept it from flopping open
with each step. Reflexive disapproval caused him to shake his head.
Who could fathom the fashions of today's teenagers?

"Something wrong, Sanjay?" No longer ever completely at ease
since his encounter with the lanky tracker, an edgy Taneer tried to scan
the crowd without making himself conspicuous.

"No, Mr. Moh . . . Mr. Buthlahee. Everything is fine. I was not followed on my way here, and I assume the same is true for you." He smiled and nodded reassuringly at Depahli, whose return smile of gratitude was by itself enough to make a man momentarily forget his wife. Removing his communicator from a pocket, he raised it to his mouth.

"Whenever you are ready I will open the necessary connection on my secure line, and you can give the final instructions to the person who has been designated as spokesperson for the purchasing company. I was informed by our mutual contact that this person will be acting as the sole representative for the remainder of the sale."

Taneer nodded, searched the crowd again. He was looking particularly for a tall, lean individual with European as well as Indian features. Though several visiting European families were present, he saw no one resembling the man who had nearly run him to ground. Content and happy, enjoying their night at the park, innocent people eddied around the trio.

The plaza they emerged onto was busy, bright, and noisy, crowded with families resting from their exertions. Designed to resemble the courtyard of the ancient palace of Ayodhya, the slightly raised platform was one of several such meeting places within the park complex. Automated snack vendors kicked out floating virtuals praising the attractions of their ice cream, samosas, sandesh, rosogulla, the almost impossibly sweet gulab jamun, and other treats. Larger stalls offered every kind of fast food, from vegetarian to hamburgers, shashlik to satay. Open space, and a family crowd that was talkative without being deafening: it was exactly what Taneer wanted for a setting in which to conduct the forthcoming critical conversation.

Turning a slow circle, he took a last, wary glance around before nodding at his middleman. "Go ahead, Sanjay."

Bringing out his communicator, the shopkeeper entered a number. It connected him with a special autodialer that then made the secondary connection. This ensured that even if the communication was somehow intercepted, it could not be traced back to its point of origin.

The Rat had turned him on to it, and Sanjay had found it very useful when dealing with suppliers of inventory of the nontrinket kind.

By mutual agreement, visual as well as audio links were activated. It was conceded that knowing what everyone looked like would be reassuring to all parties concerned. There was a pause, no doubt prompted by security concerns at the other end, and then the communicator's small screen cleared to show the face of a heavyset middle-aged man of European extraction. Innate dignity showed through the effects of his extensive and expensive cosmetic surgery.

"Mr. Ghosh?" The tone was mannered, the English polished, but with a distinctive accent Sanjay could not identify. He did not let it concern him. The man's origins were no more his business than was the identity of the people the respondent represented. Chhote Pandit had vouched for him, and that was all Sanjay needed.

"I am here. What shall I call you, sir?"

The man did not smile. As it developed, he was not to smile throughout the entire course of their conversation. Neither was he condescending or discourteous. Sanjay had dealt with virtuals that were more human.

"Mr. Karlovy will do. As your Mr. Pandit has told you, the members of the consortium I speak for have agreed to your terms. We are ready, indeed anxious, to conclude the transaction."

Responding to a nod from Taneer, Sanjay obediently passed him the communicator. At the sight of the scientist, Mr. Karlovy's expression changed. It was still not quite a smile, but he was clearly pleased.

"Mr. Buthlahee. It is both a great honor and a considerable relief to see that you continue to exist in the flesh, and not as mere rumor. Do you know that you have made yourself, in certain knowledgeable circles, the most wanted man on the planet who has not committed mass murder?"

"It's always nice to be popular," Taneer shot back, unwilling to be flattered. "I'm looking to change that status as soon as possible."

"A yearning in which my group fervently wishes to assist you. How, where, and when might we best expedite our mutual business?"

Though Sanjay did his part by continuing to scan the laid-back crowd while his client chatted on the communicator, he could not keep from eavesdropping. In this he was not ashamed. His future revolved around a successful conclusion to this business as much as did Taneer's.

"Do you know the Parganas District, in the southeastern part of the city, that borders on the Sundarbans?" Taneer was saying into the communicator's pickup.

Mr. Karlovy was noncommittal. "Being only a visitor here myself, I know very little of your gargantuan conurbation. Without wishing to appear rude, there is very little of it that I wish to know. Only where we are to meet. Rest assured I have access to people who know it intimately, and can find their way to any meeting place of your choosing."

"Good." Taneer proceeded to provide the other man with appropriate instructions.

When "Gosaba Inurb" was mentioned, Sanjay's eyes widened. He knew the place, too. Many people who followed the news knew of it. When Taneer became even more specific, Sanjay was hard-pressed to keep his apprehension from showing.

His concerns were confirmed when, after Taneer finished, the man who called himself Mr. Karlovy turned to his left to whisper to someone out of range of his audio pickup. Peeking past the scientist's arm, Sanjay gave the man at the other end of the communication link credit for not losing his composure. At least, not visibly. But it was possible his words, when he spoke again, reflected just the slightest diminishment of self-assurance.

"I am informed that, of all things in this day and age, there is in the area you specify a wild tiger that has come out of the jungle and on two separate occasions has attacked and quite possibly consumed a young child and a grown man."

Taneer clearly relished the effect his directive had produced. So did

Depahli, who squeezed his arm while remaining out of range of the communicator's pickup lens. "That's right. A tiger. In this day and age. The Department of Wildlife and Game has assured the populace that it has the situation under control, though the people who are resident in the area remain somewhat skeptical."

"I cannot say that I would blame them," Mr. Karlovy replied feelingly. "Is this your idea of a joke, Mr. Buthlahee? Some form of local humor to which I, as a foreign visitor, am not privy?"

Taneer took pains not to smile. "It's no joke, sir. With the stakes what they are, there can be no joking around. I want a secure place for our meeting. I am sure that you wish nothing less. What more private location at which to consummate our business than the one place in all Sagramanda where at the present time no one except a handful of animal specialists dares to set foot?"

"Perhaps," the European replied, "sound reason underlies their reticence."

"Sir . . . ," Sanjay started to say, trying to draw his client's attention. But Taneer had worked it all out beforehand, and would not be swayed.

"No one will bother us there. No one will interrupt us," the scientist assured his reluctant customer. "This isn't the sixteenth century, Mr. Karlovy. I've researched a place where we can meet that's just inside the border of the preserve. No one will intrude on us, no one will stumble across our business, and we will be in, out, and done with it all in a few minutes with the aid of cars, not elephants. The odds of us encountering anything more threatening than a deer are quite small. Surely you know how the media seizes on such a story and immediately blows it all out of proportion, sensationalizing and exaggerating every detail?"

"Well . . ." Karlovy hesitated, murmured again to someone off-pickup, then returned his attention to the waiting researcher. "You are correct in saying that our business will not take long to conclude, and I must admit I do like the idea of conducting it well away from any prying eyes, be they organic or electronic. Isolation has its good points. Very well: your choice of time and venue is accepted."

Next to Taneer, Depahli hugged him in a way that caused Sanjay to blush. Her elation proved premature.

"Now that I have let you choose the time and place of our meeting," the European was saying, "I am afraid that I must make a stipulation of my own." Both Sanjay and Taneer were immediately on guard.

"What is it?" the scientist asked warily.

Karlovy's tone turned even more serious than previously. "The down payment on the amount you have requested and that has been mutually agreed upon is considerable. I know that your preference is for a simple one-on-one, face-to-face exchange. While I was willing to agree to this, certain other members of the consortium I represent were not. You will please excuse their unseemly suspicion, but where a cash sum of this amount is involved, their demands were inflexible." His expression was somber. "They insist that for the duration of the exchange I be accompanied by an armed bodyguard."

Taneer's first reaction was to break off the communication and instruct Sanjay to go back to Chhote Pandit and begin the negotiations all over again. But of course he couldn't do that. Not with trackers closing in on both him and the shopkeeper. Keeping his face out of range of the communicator's pickup, he licked his lips and exchanged an anxious glance with Depahli.

Though he could not, for the moment, see the scientist, the European plainly sensed his unease. "I know this is counter to what you wished, Mr. Buthlahee. But I assure you that the point is not negotiable. I tried my best, but several important individuals were unshakable in their demand." He paused, then added with an almost-smile, "Think of it, despite your admirable assurance that all the odds are against such a thing happening, as real protection in the event the wandering animal should after all choose to put in an appearance at an inopportune moment."

Taneer wasn't worried about some nomadic cat. The only thing he feared during the forthcoming transaction was the possible interpolation of a predator of the two-legged kind. Caught off guard for the first time since the exchange had commenced, he wavered and worried over what to do.

Yet again, it was Depahli who provided a potential solution. She put her lips close to his left ear, whispering to him so her words would not be picked up.

"If this funny Mr. Karlovy insists on bringing along a bodyguard, then you should have the right to bring one, too."

"That's fine," he murmured tightly back to her as he pressed the audiovisual Mute button on the communicator, temporarily shutting them off from the expectant European, "except that I don't happen to know any professional killers, or bodyguards. I don't suppose that you happen to, either?"

"No," she told him. "Besides, it has to be someone you can trust completely. Even if you had the time and the necessary sources, you couldn't just go out and hire somebody. Not for this. Fortunately, you already have someone who has not only already proven his trustworthiness, but who is intimately familiar with this entire business." Stepping back, she turned and gestured.

"What . . . ?" It took a moment for the import of her words to coalesce in the scientist's mystified mind.

Seeing them both looking in his direction, Sanjay suddenly wished himself anywhere but there, on that warm, humid night in the Ramapark plaza by the left bank of the Hooghly.

"Not to be in any way insulting, but—are you both crazy?" He spread his hands out in front of him. "Look at me. I am a shopkeeper, not a strongman. Before that, I was a farmer. I can handle a computer, and box access, and a hoe and a shovel. I have a gun in my shop, yes, but I have never had to use it, and if Krishna wills it, I never will." His gaze flicked back and forth between the perceptibly calculating Taneer and his delectable but evidently crazy consort. "You cannot possibly consider asking me to do this!"

"Three percent." While mild as ever, Taneer's tone was implacable. "Three percent of a sum you could never have imagined accruing to you, Sanjay Ghosh."

"Three percent of all the jewels in Rajasthan mean nothing to a dead man," the shopkeeper reasonably pointed out.

Suddenly, fingers were running along his right arm, dancing up his shoulder, lightly stroking his cheek. He wanted to pull away, knew he should pull away, but could not. He might only be a shopkeeper and an ex-farmer, but he was human.

"Dear Sanjay. Sweet, perceptive, clever Sanjay," Depahli cooed into his ear. "We have no time. No time to haggle, no time to go shopping for some great dim-witted hulk who might double-cross us in the end no matter how much care we take in our hiring. We need someone *now*. Someone we can trust. Someone who will not betray us because he has too much at stake." Her lips touched his ear. "We need you."

Legs trembling slightly, and not entirely from fear, he heard a voice that must have been his saying, "All right, okay, very well. I will do it. At least, I will try to do it. But not for you, Mr. Taneer, sir." He finally managed to pull away from her. "And not for you, Ms. Depahli. I will do it for my family."

She smiled at him as she stepped back. "She may be poor, Sanjay, but your wife is a fortunate woman. And if all goes as it should, she will soon no longer be poor. I know you can do this."

He forced himself to still the shaking that threatened to overcome him. "Then you know more than I do, Depahli memsahib."

Nodding at them both, Taneer unblocked the communicator. On the small screen, the European was visibly concerned. He relaxed when Taneer's visage appeared once more at his end of the link.

"Ah, Mr. Buthlahee. For a moment there I was fearful that my small request might have caused you to act precipitously."

Taneer recovered quickly "On the contrary, Mr. Karlovy, upon reflection, not only do I not see a problem with your request, and understand the reasoning behind it, but I find it of sufficient merit to warrant imitation." He summoned up as ferocious a grin as he could manage. "In addition to a lady friend, who will be unarmed, I'll be bringing along a bodyguard of my own."

Rather than unsettling the European, the older man reacted as if Taneer's announcement was nothing less than what he expected. "Of course you will. That is only natural. I personally will be glad of the additional security." He raised a hand. "Until tomorrow, then, at the agreed-upon place and time."

"Tomorrow," Taneer concurred.

The communicator went dark and silent as the link was mutually cut. Children dashed past the trio while fretful parents warned them not to run lest they trip and ruin their clothing. Autovendors continued to hawk foods whose primary ingredient was cane sugar, fructose, and assorted other artificial sweeteners. Music filled the air. The fireworks and laser show that featured three-dimensional virtuals enacting the climactic battle in the sky between Rama and Varan was about to begin.

Events had been set in motion that could not be stopped.

Of the three, Sanjay was breathing the hardest while showing the least enthusiasm. When Depahli moved to reassure him, he almost jumped back from her.

"Please do not come any closer, Ms. Depahli! Out of my shop I have sold narcotics from Afghanistan and Nepal and Tibet that have less effect on men than you do."

She smiled amiably. "What a flattering thing to say, Mr. Ghosh. I would blush, if I remembered how."

"This cannot work," he muttered tersely. "How can this possibly work? I am no mercenary, no gunman." He looked back at them imploringly. "What do you expect me to do?"

"Fake it," Depahli told him bluntly. Even Taneer looked at her doubtfully. Seeing both their uncertainty, she elaborated. "Sanjay, are you a fan of the cinema?"

He was taken aback. "Every Indian is a fan of the cinema. It is in our blood, I believe."

"Good. Think back to some of your favorite films. Which ones had the worst villains? The most vile, wicked bad guys? Bandits and robbers, murderers and revolutionaries? Every child plays at such things. When they grow up, those who are good at it become actors. We are all of us who go to the cinema actors, in our heads if not in our lives."

"I see what you are proposing," he replied thoughtfully, "but if I go through with this I will not be acting in my head. What of this businessman's bodyguard? He will be a professional. He will see through this puppet-play in an instant."

She laughed lightly. "Don't be so certain, Sanjay. And don't be in such a rush to sell yourself short. Every good shopkeeper knows how to act: poor, desperate, overworked, in desperate need of just one sale to keep food on the table and creditors from his door. I'm sure you do it every day, with your customers. Remember: we will be in a strange, dark place that will be unfamiliar to both these persons. In such circumstances everyone will be a little nervous, a little on edge. And both sides will be in a hurry to complete the business. If all goes as planned, the exchange will be over and done with before anyone has time to ponder individual suspicions about anyone else."

Encouraged, Taneer stepped forward. "Depahli's right, Sanjay. You only have to be convincing for a couple of minutes. I bet you can do that."

"A couple of minutes." Sanjay considered. Years ago, he and Chakra had splurged, had taken what few spare rupees they had managed to accumulate and gone into the nearest sizable town to have dinner out and to see a film. Its title—he didn't remember the title. But the villain of the piece, a serpentine monster with a vast mustache and glittering eyes, had lied and cheated and slaughtered women and children with scene-chewing relish. He would never forget that face, that devil's expression, those unblinking eyes.

He could do nothing about the mustache, but standing there, he widened his own much smaller one deliberately, flared his nostrils, swelled his chest, brought his arms slightly forward at the shoulders, and glared at each of his business partners in turn. Depahli almost broke out laughing, but fortunately managed to restrain herself.

"That's very good, Sanjay. Very good! But remember that you are not on screen or in a vit, and that your audience will be both smaller and nearer. Don't breathe so hard—you're pretending to be a body-guard, not a dragon."

"You might consider keeping one hand close to your heart, as if it's ready to slide at any moment into your vest toward the gun you have hol-stered there," Taneer suggested thoughtfully, studying his new escort.

Sanjay slumped slightly. "But I do not have a gun holstered there. Oh," he added quickly, a smile of understanding spreading across his face. "I understand. They will not know that." He frowned. "But I do not have a vest, either. At least, not one that would be suitable for such a deception."

"Get one," Depahli suggested. "Black. With shirt, pants, and shoes to match—not sandals. You don't have time to train for the part, but you can at least look it."

Around them, the shouts and yells of bouncing, delighted children and smiling adults convinced their money had been well spent turned their heads and craned their necks as noble Rama's chariot soared through lights and explosions to confront the evil Ravan's monstrous sky-carriage. Among those watching the display were two men and one woman who could only hope that their own looming, critical confronta-tion proceeded with considerably less in the way of actual fireworks.

chapter xiv

Chal Schneemann leaned back in his chair and, for the first time in many days, relaxed. At least, he relaxed as much as he ever could while still on the job. Though the high-rise hotel he had chosen for his base of operations had excellent security of its own, he would not have felt completely safe without taking his own safety measures even if he had located in a suite next to one occupied by the president of the United States.

He had taken all his normal precautions. To the consternation of the staff at the front desk and in contrast to the sweeping views offered by other rooms, he had insisted on a suite as high up as possible but with the smallest windows available, a seeming contradiction in desires. In addition, the excellent blackout curtains that covered those windows were kept permanently drawn. He slept on the side of the bed as far from the bedroom window as possible. Working in the suite's other room, he positioned his chair so that it was not directly in line with either the covered window or the second door that opened onto the hallway. And still he never felt completely secure.

Such feelings had kept him alive in a profession where retirement was frequently prevented by means most violent.

Two portable miniunits sat on the desk. One held nothing but information. The other was utilized for nothing but box access. The only link between the two devices was wireless and highly proprietary. In the event some exceedingly clever outside entity managed to pierce box security and tried to access the storage unit, number two would die. Should it fail to respond properly and the unauthorized link be made, number one would die. The loss of equipment would not bother him. Both units could be replaced, and the information they contained was backed up elsewhere and not linked to anything except an old-fashioned lock and key.

While from the outside both units appeared relatively normal, their highly customized electronic viscera would have amazed any tech lucky enough to be granted a look at them. At considerable personal expense to their owner, they had been customized and put together with illegal and to a large extent military components. These enabled the pair, especially when operating in tandem, to perform operations no similar units outside a government entity ought to be able to do. Intercept and decode quantum-encrypted transmissioins, for example.

The success of such a procedure, which might best be likened to electronic surgery, was what was presently enabling Chal to ease back against the body-conforming hotel chair. Hands clasped behind his head, he murmured a soft verbal command that instructed the box unit to replay what it had just observed and recorded.

The processing was not perfect. Constantly variable security recoding during the process of transmission made it difficult for his interception software to keep up. There were skips and breaks. But enough had been snatched out of the ether to tell him what he needed to know.

He had been monitoring the communications of Sanjay Ghosh ever since he had just missed catching the shopkeeper himself outside his establishment. The tip-off that had allowed him to locate the shop had given him all he needed to penetrate the enterprise's relevant utility and track down Ghosh's communications signatures. He planned to use these to try and locate the shopkeeper for questioning, even though Ghosh had been smart enough not to return to his place of business or to his residence ever since Schneemann's all-too-brief personal encounter with Taneer Buthlahee.

But this was better. Much better.

To his delight, Ghosh had not only met again with the tracker's real quarry, the truant scientist, but had used the same personal communicator to make contact with the representative of a consortium that planned to furtively purchase the discovery that rightly belonged to Mr. Nayari's company. It was hard to run down the location of a mobile communicator that was active only for short periods at a time and whose owner kept moving around, but with luck and persistence it could be done.

How thoughtful, then, how kind of the simple shopkeeper to lend his compromised communicator to the real object of Chal's interest. And how considerate of the obstinate Mr. Buthlahee to provide specific instructions to his would-be buyer as to where and when the two of them should meet. Chal eyed his tandem electronics with satisfaction. Their cost had been astronomical—and worth every dollar. For the unique equipment, it was just as easy to intercept, capture, and download video as audio.

Already familiar with Buthlahee and Ghosh's appearance, he now also knew what the buyer Mr. Karlovy looked like, and had acquired a glimpse of Buthlahee's girlfriend as well. Another time, another assignment, he might have looked forward to a diversion, a bit of enforced dalliance with such an alluring creature, made all the spicier by having her paramour restrained nearby and forced to watch. Not this time. The stakes were too high. Sex, of whatever variety and fetish he preferred, could be indulged in later, with no risk and at far less expense.

In addition to himself, Buthlahee had spoken of being accompanied to tomorrow night's meeting place by hired protection to match what the buyer insisted on bringing along with him. If both sides adhered to their guarantees, that made four potential adversaries to deal with, two of them professionals. Possibly five, if the scientist's consort chose to join him, though she did not really figure into his calculations. For that matter, neither did the scientist or the buyer. Of those who planned to be in attendance, Chal knew he need only be concerned with the two pros.

Provided he got the drop on them, to employ an ancient cliché that was no less valid for its age, it should not be a problem. He could hire and bring along temporary help of his own, of course. There was enough time between now and tomorrow night to make the necessary arrangements. But with only two real antagonists to worry about, he did not think it necessary. He had dealt with and on at least one occasion dispatched twice that number. Surprise was the key to success in such situations. That should not be a problem. No one would be expecting a third party to put in an appearance, least of all the two bodyguards on hand for the occasion. He anticipated no difficulty.

While anticipating none, he would prepare for every possible eventuality. Obsession over detail was another character trait that had contributed mightily to his success and continued survival. Though always ready to extemporize, he never entered into a dangerous situation unprepared.

Unquestionably, a great deal of money was involved. Nayari had implied as much on more than one occasion. The buyer, Mr. Karlovy, had spoken circumspectly of a "down payment" he was to hand over. As a matter of professional interest, Chal found himself speculating on the amount. After neutralizing the two bodyguards, he could easily steal it, of course. It never occurred to him to do so.

Once, early in his career, he had been hired to deliver a sum of cash to ransom the son of an important Malaysian businessman. With time on his hands until he was due to turn the money over, he had peeked inside the carbon-fiber container that had been handed to him. It had contained, as near as he could hurriedly calculate, between five and seven million U.S. dollars. Concluding his examination, he had closed and resealed the case, and had not so much as looked inside again.

Word swiftly made the relevant rounds about those in his line of work who reneged on their responsibilities. Five or seven million dollars would buy many things, but in a world linked by several modes of virtually instantaneous communication, it would not buy permanent anonymity. Recidivists in his profession inevitably tended to be found and terminated, often messily. Renege on his assignment, take the money and run, and he would be doing no more than switching places with the scientist Buthlahee. Ultimately, he would be found, and sooner or later his career as well as his life would be brought to an abrupt and brutal end by others of his own kind.

Besides, he always had and still continued to take pride in being the best at his work. While it would not win him the Nobel Prize, or land him on the front of *The Economist*'s box page, in certain important circles it did lend him a distinctive aura that was both feared and respected. He prized that. And it was not as if he didn't live well. Following the successful conclusion of this assignment, he would be able to live even better.

Unclasping his hands, he leaned forward and murmured instructions to the box unit. It took hardly a moment for it to generate a map, in relief and with accompanying reports on access routes, predicted weather, and assorted other pertinent factors, showing the exact location specified by Buthlahee for the clandestine meeting that was to take place at ten o'clock the following evening. Chal transferred it to his mated pocket unit and ran off a hardcopy as backup. Then he put both units in secure sleep mode, rose, and walked into the bedroom.

The lockable privacy closet held three sets of clothing, each hung equidistant from the other. One was for the street. One was for dining out in nice restaurants or attending meetings with individuals like Nayari. The third, a one-piece construct woven from special synthetics, could best be described as work clothes.

Whistling softly to himself, he removed the latter, hung it on the back of the bathroom door, and set about checking its pockets and specially embedded systems for gear that was not designed to aid in the execution of such mundane vocations as, say, plumbing or home electrical repair.

Keshu was on his way home in the shuttle chopper when his pocket communicator buzzed for attention. The tone indicated it was his official channel. Irritated, he considered deactivating the call and ignoring it. Most likely it was nothing that couldn't wait until morning. It was already after six, and even traffic in the carefully structured air above Sagramanda was busy. He was hungry and tired, and his wife was a superb cook. He was anxious to get home, enjoy one of her marvelous dinners, settle into his favorite massage chair, and pick up the history of Southwest Africa he had been reading. He definitely did not want to have to deal with business.

Maddeningly boorish, the communicator continued to trill at him. The chopper's constrained cockpit offered nowhere to run. Intent on his work, the shuttle pilot studiously ignored his passenger's incoming private message. As it always did, Keshu's damnable sense of duty overrode his personal desires. Grumbling a suitable phrase, he proceeded to acknowledge the incoming call.

He recognized the voice. Subrata from downstairs. The tireless bridge to, among other sections, Forensics. The individual who was invisible—except when he had something to say. The kind of man on whose hard work and back great works were raised. With a sigh, he muttered the command that would allow two-way communication.

"Chief Inspector Singh?"

"Yes, what is it, Mr. Subrata?" Keshu's annoyance increased as the shuttle slowed to give more room to a pair of air ambulances speeding past on their way to some unknown medical crisis. "I'm on my way home, you know."

"Yes, Chief Inspector. I know. I would not bother you, sir, if I—"

"—did not think this a matter of some importance," a prickly Keshu finished for him. "Get on with it, man."

"Yes, Chief Inspector." Though the communication was devoid of video, Keshu almost thought he could see the little man shuffling papers in front of him: mentally if not physically. "I, and those I am working with, believe we have identified a woman matching the description of the composite created by the department's visual facilitator."

Ignoring the crowded air lanes now, Keshu sat up a little straighter in his seat, the mandatory safety harness digging into his chest. "What woman?"

"The projected multiple murderer, Chief Inspector. The match is accurate to—"

"Hang percentages! Who is she? *Where* is she?" Even as he spoke, he was alerting the pilot, indicating with gestures that the man needed to be ready to receive new instructions.

The urgency in the chief inspector's voice did not fluster Subrata. Keshu was beginning to think that very little did. At least, not where the little man's work was concerned.

"Her name is Jena Chalmette. She is a French national who has been resident in India, in Sagramanda, for many years. Apparently, she changes her place of residence on a regular basis. Officers have already been to her apartment. She was not there."

Keshu cursed fluently and at length, but to himself. "Leads?"

"Better than that, Chief Inspector." Was that an uncharacteristic hint of glee in the sober-minded researcher's voice? "As soon as her identity was ascertained from a box match, a grade one-cee priority override was injected into the municipal surveillance system."

Keshu knew what that meant. Tens of thousands of individual pickups, vit sensors, and spotpoints maintained by the police department and scattered strategically about the city would have been alerted to search for one particular facial match. In addition, a grade one-cee override would temporarily coopt the functions of thousands more private surveillance systems to join in the hunt.

"And?" Keshu asked tersely.

The reply was more than he could have hoped for. Even worth missing one of his wife's superb dinners for. "We have her located."

The sense of relief that washed through Keshu was expansive enough to prevail over any feeling of triumph. Besides, any indulgence in the latter was premature. Locating someone was not the same as having them in custody.

"Order those officers on-site to maintain surveillance and keep their distance," Keshu instructed Subrata. "I want to be in on this one myself. Where is the suspect, and what is she doing?"

"Just a moment, Chief Inspector, and I'll patch you through to a Lieutenant Johar, who is the officer in charge on location."

Though to an energized Keshu the resultant pause seemed like forever, it took the ever-efficient Subrata only a moment to link the chief inspector's communicator with the officer on site.

"Chief Inspector Singh?" The voice that issued from the communicator's tiny but powerful built-in speaker was unfamiliar to Keshu. Though distorted by mild interference, it sounded capable enough.

Wasting no time on pleasantries, Keshu barked back, "Current location and disposition of the female foreign national Chalmette: report, Lieutenant."

Johar's prompt and efficient response justified Keshu's initial assessment of the officer. "At present, suspect is traveling south on automated public transport. There is a possibility, as yet uncomfirmable, that suspect is following a small group of students. Transport has just left Canning Central on way to Basanti Main."

Keshu found himself cursing again. Though still within his district, the foreign woman was far south of his present location. That made for awkward, but not insurmountable, logistics. While conversing with the lieutenant, he instructed the shuttle pilot to turn and head south as soon as airspace became available.

"How many people do you have on her and can they tell if she is armed?" he asked sharply.

"Two undercover officers, rotating observation, Chief Inspector. No visible weapons, but of course that is hardly conclusive. Do you want us to pick her up?"

"No, no," Keshu responded quickly. "We have to move very carefully here, Lieutenant. We have to have something irrefutable to take into court." He thought furiously. "I was told that officers have been to her apartment. I don't suppose they found anything incriminating, or I would already have been informed."

"I have seen the reports of the search, Chief Inspector. No weapons were found, if that is what you mean."

Keshu considered. "Anything less incriminating but still suggestive, Lieutenant? Media recordings of recent killings? Anything that might indicate souvenirs taken from one of the murder sites?"

"No, Chief Inspector. Nothing at all." The voice on the other end of the communicator hesitated. "There was one item that caught my attention, though. I thought it rather a strange thing to find in the living quarters of a foreigner, even one who qualifies as a long-term resident."

"Don't keep it a secret, Lieutenant," Keshu chided him impatiently.

"No, Chief Inspector. It was a shrine."

Acknowledging his orders, the shuttle was slowing and descending toward a staging area that bulged out of the right side of the expressway like a blister on an artery. He was already pumping a command request into the chopper's transmitter. As the pilot set down smoothly on the empty platform, Keshu continued questioning the distant but responsive lieutenant.

"What kind of shrine?"

"Very strange," the officer repeated, "It was as well maintained as any shrine in a well-to-do Indian home. When I saw mention of its existence in the report, I expected it to be a shrine to Ganesh or Krishna, those being the gods Westerners seem to find the most comforting. But it was not. It was a shrine to Kali."

Keshu swallowed hard. Leaning to his right, he peered out the transparent bubble of the shuttle, scanning the pollution-stained sky. "I don't know about you, Lieutenant, but I, for one, do find that suggestive."

"Yes, Chief Inspector," the distant officer agreed. "Also creepy."

"But not grounds for arrest, and certainly not for prosecution. We need much more than that, Lieutenant Johar. We can't remand a person into custody on the basis of uncharacteristic theological preferences, a perceived visual match with a computer simulation, or even for carrying a weapon that might match the one used in certain attacks." A black spot in the sky was growing steadily larger as it approached the platform on which he had ordered the shuttle to land.

"Tell your people to keep their distance, to make sure they aren't detected by the suspect, and not to do anything. Understand? They are not to approach the suspect in any way unless it looks like the woman is going to be alone with the students she may be following. At that time, and only under those circumstances, are your people allowed to move to stage two."

"Understood, Chief Inspector."

"I want to be very clear on this, Lieutenant." Keshu spoke slowly and emphatically. "If this woman *is* by chance the person we are after, and we alert her that we are on to her, she may change her modus completely. Or worse, leave India altogether. As a noncitizen, we cannot hold her. We need to be *absolutely certain* we have our killer before we pick her up, and that we have sufficient evidence to bring cause and to convict. Otherwise, we may not get a second chance. This case is too important to risk on second chances."

"I understand fully, Chief Inspector. It would be useful, I suppose, if she were to attack the students she seems to be following. Without being allowed to harm them, of course."

"Yes, catching a suspect in the act is always the ideal situation. We can but hope." Growing larger, the black spot resolved itself into a police stealth chopper. Switching gears, he added, "Downline your present location, Lieutenant. I'll be airborne again in a minute or two and on my way in your direction. And for the love of Guru Nanak, *keep your people clear of the suspect*."

The specially equipped chopper barely had time to touch down on the service platform before Keshu leaped aboard. In the waning light he hurried forward to take a seat behind the copilot. It took only seconds for his communicator to wirelessly relay the information the lieutenant had supplied and enter it into the chopper's navigation system. Upon confirmation from the pilot, the craft rose and turned south toward the indicated coordinates as it rapidly gained altitude.

Through the open sides of the craft the sounds of the great city wafted up to him. Black and lean as a cobra, the stealth chopper itself generated virtually no noise. Or rather, the sounds it made were smothered by the special noise-canceling electronics that were built into its propulsion system. Descending on unwary suspects, it could touch down with less commotion than a startled cat.

Endless commercial and industrial complexes and towering apartment blocks swiftly gave way to more prosperous inurbs whose fenced and patrolled interiors were interspersed with neighborhoods that varied from the desperately poor to the unspeakably poverty-riven. As the first arms of the Delta passed beneath the chopper, they in turn were replaced by the inurbs inhabited by the wealthy and the merely well-off. When the chopper began to descend, Keshu found himself wondering if after weeks and months of endless frustration they really might have the right person. Computer simulation matches had been wrong before. And even if Lieutenant Johar's people had locked onto the right suspect, there was no guarantee she was doing anything more than traveling south. To arrest and prosecute, he needed more than that; much more. Ideally, he needed a smoking gun.

Or a swinging sword.

Jena thought about trying to strike up a conversation with the students she was following. She knew they were students because of the way they acted, the style of MPAs they played with, and the matching Bangalore University Zoology departmental shirts they wore. They had backpacks that were up-to-the-minute stylish as well as practical, and fancy roll-up communicators, and gave every indication of being rich, educated, and innocent the same way certain flowers emit a musky stink to attract certain insects. They were perfect candidates to save from the brutal corruption and overwhelming despair with which the world was soon to mortally infect them.

Unusually, and usefully, the transport car in which all three of them were speeding south was busy, but not crowded. Standing and hanging onto one of the commuter bars, you could actually see through a window: never mind actually seeing the length of one of the slightly curved acrylic windows itself. Conversely, freed from the usual need simply to find enough personal space in which to breathe, it also meant other passengers would be more likely to notice the neatly dressed foreign woman introducing herself to the college-age locals. The immediate environment was public, and occupied by too many of the public. Better to wait, keep to herself, and continue to follow quietly until privacy as well as opportunity presented itself. She continued to peruse the bright-backgrounded scriptures unscrolling on the compact reader resting in her left hand, and waited.

Frustratingly, the boy and girl rode the car all the way to the end of the line. By the time they chose to exit, it was already dark outside. The evening was cloudy and with only a hint of moon, a condition Jena had thoughtfully ascertained before deciding to go out that night in search of others in need of salvation. Nor was the terminus station crowded, at least by Indian standards, when the pair finally disembarked. As they made their way through the station confines, past shops whose owners were activating security screens and autovendors that were shutting down for the night, they never noticed her. From her continued clandestine observation of them, she felt it was doubtful they noticed anything except each other, so intent were they on the young and handsome miracle that was themselves. In love, no doubt. Puppy love, kitty love, first love. Certain old memories that forever refused entombment rose, like bitter gorge, within her. She slapped them down. There was work to be done this night.

Despite her resolve and her eagerness, she nearly changed her mind when the older woman showed up to meet the couple. Stout and efficient, the newcomer was dressed not in sari or salwar, but in freshly laundered Western-style field gear. Peering over the top of her reader, Jena saw the newcomer namaste and then formally shake hands with each of the students in turn. That was more encouraging. It meant the possibility existed that not only had greeter and arrivals not met before, it also suggested that the students were new to this area and to their eventual destination. Unfamiliarity was the mother of confusion, and ever a useful partner in Jena's work.

Students and greeter climbed into an open-topped, fuel-cell-powered 4×4 equipped with bull bars, oversized wheels, all-wheel steering, and a pair of swiveling elevator observation seats mounted in the rear. Pocketing her reader and making her way in the same direction without ever following immediately behind the trio, Jena was able to make out the bold inscription on the side of the vehicle: Jhila-Biopatenschaften Biological Station. This only further confirmed her supposition that the young couple were students. Come over from their dorm for a night's, or longer, fieldwork. Used to reacting quickly to the unforeseen, she employed one of several aliased credcards in her bag to rent an electric trike from one of the numerous autohires located next to the station. When the 4×4 headed out of the parking lot and away from the terminal, its occupants were unknowingly being tracked by an equally silent if much smaller shadow.

In defiance of traffic regulations and those regulating the use of the rental, she drove with all the lights turned off. Should the driver of the vehicle in front of her happen to glance in her curving rearview, on such a dark night she was unlikely to see the much smaller, three-wheeled transport following behind. Jena was also careful to keep out of range of the other vehicle's animal detection avoidance system with which a 4×4 in this area was likely to be equipped. While its arc of sensitivity would be much greater forward of the vehicle on which it was mounted than it would be to the rear, she was taking no chances.

After a short drive during which the station receded into the distance behind them, the 4×4 slowed as it approached a gate in a tall, high security fence. Sizing up the situation swiftly, Jena did not slow proportionately. Instead, she asked for and received a quick burst of speed from the trike that enabled her to pull up alongside the bigger vehicle. It positioned her on the right side of the 4×4, out of range of the gate's identification system that was mounted off to the left. So occupied with each other were the students that they did not even bother to glance in her direction. As for the car's driver, she was busy slipping an ident card into the gate sensor's reception slot. Meanwhile, Jena made a show of fumbling in her shoulder bag for a similar card, which she did not possess.

Accepting the driver's ID, the gate blocking the road ahead rolled back on its track to allow the 4×4 to drive through. Jena paralleled it until she was just inside the gate, then turned deliberately down a narrow road leading off to the right. Not until the bigger transport had driven on out of sight did she reverse course, accelerate quickly, and resume tracking the other vehicle.

Interesting, she mused as she bounced along in the wake of her quarry, immediately finding herself in deep, damp forest. This was a place she had never visited before. Night birds called querulously to one another from high in the trees while the occasional rattle of shadowy branches hinted at the presence of other, larger creatures. As she drove on, forced in the absence of the trike's lights to concentrate exclusively on the route ahead, she made note of her fascinating new surroundings, or as much of them as she could make out in the dark. Fervently committed but not single-minded, she was always interested in improving herself and adding to her store of knowledge about her adopted country.

Giving no sign that its occupants were in any way aware that they were being followed, the nearly silent 4×4 pushed deeper into forest and night. Before too long it turned onto a left-hand spur that was narrower than the main track. Nearly an hour of additional driving ensued, during which time Jena stoically ignored the increasing ache in her backside and legs. Pain and discomfort were mere intangibles that her ongoing studies had long ago taught her how to tolerate.

Eventually, the 4×4 slowed and turned right, heading toward a small but intense cluster of bright lights that resembled a constellation fallen to Earth. They were the only indication of a human presence in the vast darkness. From the vicinity of the lights, voices and a few slightly louder welcoming shouts could be heard. Clearly this was a substantial encampment, hardworking and well populated.

With no one around to see her sitting in the darkness on the idling trike, Jena dug her fingers tight into the handgrips and made no attempt to hide her disappointment. Her long journey down from the central part of the city, her singling out of the student pair as likely candidates

for redemption, her subsequent shadowing of them on the train and now
to this point: all had been for naught. She was fearless, but she was not
foolish. There were too many people around for her to proceed with her
intentions. Furthermore, a camp in a place like this would be actively
alert to any unauthorized intrusions, especially late at night. The odds
were bad, and she did not see how she could improve them. There was
nothing she could do. The scriptures taught one how to absorb disappointment. Working the trike's controls, she brought it around and
headed away from the camp, back the way she had come.

Still, having primed and prepared herself to do a night's work on
the Mother's behalf, she was reluctant to simply return home. Around
her the woods were alternately still and enticing. The huntress is never
quick to flee. If she was patient, and waited, and looked around for a
while, perhaps she might encounter others. A student or two camped
by themselves for the night while carrying out observations of the
forest's nocturnal life. A professor with a wide-eyed doctoral candidate
in tow. Even locals who serviced the camp. In her present state of
mind, she would settle for providing salvation even to one as simple as
an itinerant laundry-wallah.

So instead of turning down the road that had brought her to this
point and heading back toward the transport station, she urged the
trike forward and continued along the north-south road. Once past the
well-lit camp, it narrowed perceptibly. Cut barely wide enough
through the forest to accommodate the specially equipped 4×4, it provided plenty of driving room for the smaller trike.

She did not wonder at the need for such a thoroughfare in so isolated and unpopulated a place. Besides leading to a camp such as the
one she had left behind, it paralleled the lofty security fence, providing
service access. As she sped northward, she could hear periodic crackles
as the occasional insect or unlucky night bird flew into its multiple
strands and was instantly electrocuted.

Some time later, at the sight of motion up ahead, she slowed, wondering if these larger animals would meet the same fate or would simply be shocked into retreating. Then she saw that they were not animals.

She smiled.

Bringing the trike to an abrupt stop, she pushed the deactivated transport into a copse of thick, concealing bushes. Removing her long carry bag from the trike's luggage compartment, she slung it over her left shoulder and began to move silently forward, keeping low and under cover. There was plenty of time and she would take all that she needed.

As always, she was intensely curious about those whom she was about to redeem.

chapter xv

It was not difficult to decode the seal and open the access gate. The dozens of such gates strung out along the fence line were designed to hold back animals, not bank robbers or terrorists. The trick was to realize the entry while preventing the gate from sending notification back to its central monitor that it had been opened without authorization.

Sanjay watched admiringly as Taneer swiftly and efficiently compromised the gate's sensors. It was a trick he knew could be done, but he certainly could not have done it himself. As soon as the three of them had stepped through, the scientist reactivated the gate behind them to maintain the fiction of a continuous, uninterrupted connection. The two men they were supposed to meet should already be waiting for them, having accessed the location by another route. The utilization of two different entry points and two separate approaches to the meeting place had been agreed on as much to assuage the buyer's fears as to enhance security for the forthcoming exchange.

"I don't like it here, Taneer." A fount of bravado in the city, Depahli retained the same atavistic fear of the jungle that was common to the majority of country folk. "Why couldn't we have done this somewhere in the city center? The main transport terminus, maybe, or one of the airport lounges."

"You know why, Depa." Cold beam in hand, the scientist illuminated the narrow but well-maintained service trail that was leading them deeper into the woods. "Too many potential witnesses, too many curious onlookers. If only one person witnessed the exchange, that would be one person who could identify all of us later. The buyer's representative feels the same way. He doesn't want this done in public any more than I do." He glanced over at the third member of their little group. "Sanjay, are you all right? For someone who's supposed to be pretending to be a ruthless bodyguard, you're looking a little pale."

In truth, the farther they walked and the more distance they put between themselves and the fence line, the less comfortable the shopkeeper felt.

"Permit me to point out that you have no experience of places like this, Mr. Buthlahee, sir. I grew up in surroundings that were similar but still not half so impenetrable. There are things in the forest that go bump in the night that you do not want to bump into."

"Relax," Taneer chided him. "We're still close to the fence line and the cluster of inurb buildings just on the other side." He waggled his beam across the trail. "There are three of us, and each of us has a light." A hand gestured at the dark woods. "Anything out there is much more likely to run from us than we are from it. It's true I may not have your firsthand experiences, but I've read a great deal about our native animals and their habits. It's not as if we are walking to Bangladesh."

Sanjay was not reassured. "Tell that to the first cobra we see waiting in ambush on the side of the trail."

Depahli shuddered and tried to crowd a little closer to her lover.

But Taneer was right. As they continued to advance and the dense, undisturbed vegetation drew even closer around them, even the nocturnal birds seemed to shun their lights. As for snakes, the only one they saw was a king snake, not a king cobra, too small to frighten even Depahli.

Jena was enjoying herself. Though the heat of excitement burned steadily within, it was late enough so that her surroundings had cooled down. The appearance of the two men and one woman had gone a long way toward mitigating her disappointment at having to abandon her intention to set free the two students and their guide. Three take the place of three, she mused. Obviously, these were the innocents who had been intended for her all along.

Something was itching her ankle. Glancing down and pulling up her left pants' leg slightly, she saw that something thin, black, glistening, and about six centimeters long had attached itself to her flesh. It looked like a tiny, wet sausage. She eyed the lively leech for a long moment, then let the fabric fall back into place. It was an omen. Someone else would have declared it was just an opportunistic parasite, but Jena knew better. Give blood, take blood. It would be churlish of her to deny the small creature its due. Ignoring the itching, which was barely noticeable, she moved on.

She was careful to keep her distance, sometimes utilizing the trail behind the trio, at other times ducking back into the brush. Only very rarely did one of the three bright beams being carried by her quarry aim backward in her direction. Those she was trailing were clearly concerned with what lay ahead, not behind. What were they doing out here, in the forest preserve, in the middle of the night? They did not look like students. One of them was exceptionally well dressed in a manner suggesting that he was in possession of unpleasant knowledge. She would have to watch him carefully. The other two concerned her not at all.

She felt that she could make her move at any time. But that would terminate the delicious sense of anticipation she always felt, a kind of lubricious homicidal foreplay. Besides, the more distance they put between themselves and the fence line, the less likelihood there was of anyone in the apartment complex on the other side overhearing any sounds. It would be a pleasant change to be able to conduct her liberating activities at leisure, without having to worry about the noise that all too often attended her ministrations. She continued to follow, and to anticipate, and to watch.

Keshu studied the readout on his spinner. The video was being forwarded to him from sensors mounted on the silent police drone currently hovering above the forest floor. Though the highly sensitive infrared detectors were picking up multiple targets, the unit's scopes and sensors had been programmed to emphasize anything that fit the human profile. It was left to those viewing the information to distinguish between night-loving monkeys and humans, a task that size comparison alone made relatively easy.

Next to him, Lieutenant Johar looked up from his own spinner. Half a dozen special police wearing night camouflage clustered not far behind them, while a pair of noise-negating stealth choppers hovered off to the west, above the nearest public housing. Each carried an additional complement of cops patiently awaiting orders for deployment.

Keshu was tired. Having covered many kilometers via chopper, he and his hastily assembled team had been tracking Chalmette ever since she had stepped off the commuter train at the end of its line. Fairly quickly they ascertained that she, in turn, was indeed following a pair of students. From a distance, the chief inspector had watched with grudging admiration as the foreign woman had used her own quarry to enable her to slip inside the restricted area of the preserve.

From then on it had been a matter of staying patient: tracking, tailing the foreigner as she trailed the field station 4×4 that had picked up the unknowing students. Not daring to risk losing her but still loath to pick her up without irrefutable evidence of wrongdoing on her part, he had reluctantly issued the order to start moving in when their target paused and turned away from the field station. But when she had surprisingly chosen to continue onward, paralleling the fence line instead of returning to the station, he had hastily countermanded his own order. Maybe, just maybe, an opportunity might yet present itself to catch her engaging in something prosecutable.

The process of tiresomely tracking her through the forest continued. Despite their hopes, he and Johar were starting to believe they were going to have to give up and decide whether or not to let the woman return to her apartment or pick her up on some pretext. That was when the three newcomers had put in their unexpected appearance. Their illegal entry into the preserve provided sufficient grounds for their arrest, but the thought of issuing the necessary order never entered Keshu's head. Especially not when the real object of his interest abandoned her trike and began to stalk the newly arrived trio.

He was not surprised. Her rapid and effortless switch from one set of potential prey to another fit the modus that the department psychs had put together for her. To a random killer unconcerned with the background or personalities of her quarry, one set of victims was as good as another. How cold she must be inside, he thought. How ethically bankrupt. He had dealt with, had helped to bring to justice, and had seen numerous murderers slain, but none quite like this implacable, unfathomable foreign woman.

Cheese, he thought absently as he studied the moving readout on his spinner, was a far more amenable French export.

From the moment she had pushed her trike into the bushes, there was no doubt to anyone observing her subsequent actions that her intent was to follow the trio of unanticipated forest visitors. Focused on his likely serial killer, Keshu wasted no mental capital trying to divine the newcomers' motivation. They might be researchers, or illegal lepidopterist collectors, or rare plant thieves. They might be friends out for an evening's excitement, or in the process of settling a bet. He doubted they were poachers because the starlight sensor on the drone did not show them carrying anything that might be poaching equipment. They might constitute a bizarre ménage à trois searching for a suitably exotic location in which to consummate their particular sexual needs.

It mattered to him only in the most cursory manner. Of the four ambulatory heat images visible on his spinner's readout, he had eyes only for one.

"Want me to signal some of the boys to move in more closely, sir?" Johar whispered even though they were well out of hearing range of both the naïve trio and the deadly female shadow that was stalking them.

"No." Keshu knew that the lieutenant was worried that if and when the foreign woman attacked, his people might be too far away to get there in time to put a halt to her intended mayhem. There was a risk, certainly, in continuing to keep their distance, but he felt it worth it to acquire the conclusive proof of guilt a court would demand. Even if they were seconds too late to intervene physically, each officer had been instructed that when given orders to move in, they were to make as much noise as possible. From experience, Keshu knew that might well be enough to halt the woman in her tracks.

But there was still an element of threat to the intended victims. He was helped in making his decision from the knowledge that by reason of their illegal entry they had already broken the law.

"We have to wait until the last possible moment," he rumbled tersely. The look on the lieutenant's face was visible even in the darkness. "All right then—the moment *before* the last possible moment.

But we have to hold back until the foreign woman commits. At least until she draws a weapon. Otherwise, even if she is carrying, we cannot prove intent."

Johar nodded to show that he understood. What he did not show was how thankful he was that it was the chief inspector and not him who would have to decide how long to wait before giving the order to move in and save the three trespassers.

"How much longer, Taneer?" Depahli's feet were starting to hurt. It had been a long time since she had traded in bare feet for sandals, and then sandals for fancy shoes, and her feet were protesting the regression. At least, she thought, nothing had leaped out of the looming, dark jungle to confront them. Perhaps Taneer was right and it was perfectly safe after all. But no matter how much time passed without anything untoward happening, or how many times her beloved reassured her, she still could not entirely shake fears that had clung to her since childhood.

Sanjay was faring better. Trailing his employer and the beautiful girlfriend, he had almost convinced himself that he could pull off the requested impersonation. Taneer had assured him that the likelihood of any real trouble was very small because both sides wished for a speedy consummation of their agreement and terms had already been agreed upon. The shopkeeper had gone so far as to purchase not only an entirely new and alien outfit consisting of black pants, vest, and dark embroidered shirt, but shoes with built-in air lifts that made him appear five centimeters taller. His new, albeit artificial perspective on the world had further increased his confidence.

Some of it evaporated when they reached an open tank intended to supply water to roving animals. The facility had been built to resemble a natural watering hole. Both the well housing and supply pipe stood artfully concealed nearby. Waiting with obvious impatience by one side of the shimmering artificial pond was a large, neatly dressed European clad in walking shoes and expensive synthetic tropical silks. The ambient light from the beamer he held revealed him to be of exceptionally pale complexion, as if he was unused to being exposed to the sun.

His companion was Indian and much bigger. He was, in fact, the biggest Indian Sanjay had ever encountered in person, though many members of the national basketball team were taller. An impressive mustache, curving upward at the tips, shadowed bulging cheeks. Though fully clothed, it was clear that his arms were larger in diameter than the shopkeeper's legs.

Mindful of his responsibility, Sanjay tried to make himself appear even taller, adopted a grim, no-nonsense expression, and moved closer to the couple he was supposed to be "protecting."

Stepping forward, Taneer left Depahli behind with Sanjay and extended a hand. The European's palm was damp with sweat, as was his face. "Mr. Karlovy?"

"Rotten climate, this." It was a good thing the visitor was a respected businessman, because he was certainly no diplomat. "Don't know how you people stand it. Don't know how my ancestors stood it."

"It's easier to acclimate to a place when you are born there," Taneer replied without rancor. "As for the other thing, your ancestors stood it because there was money to be made here. Often, though not always, by stealing it." He smiled in the darkness as an owl hooted softly somewhere in the trees. "Which brings us to why we are both here now, tonight, suffering in the heat and humidity."

Karlovy nodded appreciatively. "A man of directness. As are most in your profession." Turning slightly, he gestured behind and to one side. "As agreed, I have brought one escort with me. This is Punjab."

The bodyguard crossed thick arms over his equally massive chest, assumed the pose of a mighty one, and grinned. "It is a nickname. My father was a connoisseur of old comic strips. I am actually from Nagpur. Not that either my name or my place of birth matter." The smile went away, to be replaced by something very different. Bravely, Sanjay did his best to match it. "I am here to make sure Mr. Karlovy is not robbed."

"Nobody's here to rob anybody." Taneer spoke soothingly to the big man, then turned his attention back to the European. "Let's do what we came to do."

Crouched low in the bushes nearby, Jena observed the byplay uncertainly. It mattered to her not in the least what the two new gentlemen were doing out in the middle of the forest, nor why they were meeting with the three she had been following. What was important was that there were now five where a few moments ago there had been three.

The opportunity was without equal in her experience. Five potential souls to set free. It would be a blessing above all others. But she hesitated. She had never before taken so many at one time. The wonderful isolation of the spot was more than she could have wished for. But still, five—and one of them looking to be a very chancy undertaking indeed. She could take the big man first, of course, but if she ran into difficulty there, even an unarmed foursome could give her trouble, if only with fists and feet and stones. They remained unaware of her presence, which gave her time to decide.

Should she risk it? She had trained herself to move fast, very fast, but she had already decided that success was incumbent on taking down the biggest of the five first, and swiftly. At least they seemed in no hurry to leave, with two of the men conversing softly while the others looked on.

If they all left together, that would tell her something. But if they split into two groups again, it would make her decision easier.

She decided to wait.

Keshu stared at the image the high-hovering, night-piercing drone was relaying to his readout. Who the devil were the two men who had just appeared on the screen, and what were they doing meeting the first three in the middle of the jungle, in the middle of the night? Sensitive though it was, because it was compelled to keep out of easy range of those it was tracking the drone could not pick up their conversation. So he had no idea what was being talked about. Poaching? Proposed illegal real estate incursions, that were always a problem on the borders of parks and preserves near and within the city? Trading in illegal drugs?

What mattered was that—it didn't matter. Legal, illegal, or purely recreational, any discussion taking place in the forest was not germane to his reason for being there. He and his officers were present for one reason and one only: to obtain convincing evidence on a possible serial killer and then reel her in. The suspect was still present, thank goodness, but her heat signature had stopped moving when the other pair had put in their unexpected appearance. Cursing silently to himself, he knew that it was entirely possible the arrival of the newcomers would intimidate her to a degree where she would simply withdraw, at which point he would have to make the difficult decision as to whether to order her arrest or not. The two recent arrivals, whoever they were and whatever their purpose, threatened to spoil everything.

He held his spinner up next to Johar's. The images were identical, which meant that the two apparent newcomers were just that and not electronic artifacts.

"Any idea who these new people might be, Lieutenant?"

"No, Chief Inspector. What can the five of them be doing here?" Johar stared off into the night, as though the answer might magically arise from the trees in the form of glowing, hovering words. "What do you want to do?"

It was, for once, a simple decision.

He decided to wait.

Their brief conversation concluded, Karlovy turned and walked back to the water tank, which was fashioned of cast resin to resemble natural stone. Moments passed. Taneer waited nonchalantly, though he was anything but indifferent. Depahli tried not to fidget. As for Sanjay and the one nicknamed Punjab, they exchanged steady, unwavering stares. It was the most difficult thing the shopkeeper had ever done in his life, including the time he had taken delivery of a packet of drugs from an unthinking courier while a traffic policeman was searching through his shop hoping to find a present for his wife.

When he rejoined them, the European was carrying what at first glance appeared to be an ordinary briefcase. Closer inspection under the light of Taneer's beam revealed it to be made of a material Sanjay did not recognize. Two strips of metal ran around it lengthwise, and it was thicker than most such he had seen. Karlovy proceeded to whisper to it, softly and at length. Then he manipulated something on the top of the case that Sanjay could not make out clearly in the wavering light. The case responded with an audible hum, as if releasing a cloud of electronic bees into the night, and the top softly clicked open. A single tiny LED illuminated the interior. The European held the open case out toward Taneer, as if presenting an offering. His voice was a monotone, neither enticing nor reproving.

"Ten million. As stipulated; one third in dollars, one third in euros, the rest in rupees. The down payment you requested in cash. As per our agreement the balance will be transferred later, by means and to the foreign account you specify. The bills have been tested for marks and stainchips. They are all clean. If you wish, I will wait while you perform a random testing."

Struggling to appear nonchalant, Taneer shrugged and took the case. Considerably less indifferent, Sanjay and Depahli eyed the contents in open disbelief. Even Punjab edged forward for a closer look. One did not see even that much fake currency in movies.

After a cursory inspection of the neatly bound bills, Taneer snapped the case shut. "Security transfer?" he queried the European.

Karlovy was clearly struggling to contain his impatience. "After I have received the commodity, please."

Taneer hesitated only briefly before reaching into a safety pocket. Squeezing the interior seal with thumb and forefinger allowed the sewn-in unit to read both prints, whereupon the armored lining parted, allowing him access to its contents. Taking out two glassine packets each no bigger than a playing card, he handed them to the European. Karlovy's continental savoir faire deserted him as he accepted the offering with fingers that trembled ever so slightly. One packet contained a single mollysphere. The other held concrete, irrefutable evidence that had sprung from the information contained on the storage device.

Unable to restrain himself, knowing he would never have the opportunity to see anything like this again, Sanjay leaned forward for a better look as the European played his hand beam over the two packets, examining their contents intently. On the one hand was the case containing more actual money than he would have believed existed in the world. On the other, the two small transparent packets.

Though he raised no objection and offered no comment, it did not seem to him in spite of everything he had been told to constitute a fair trade.

The European, however, was visibly thrilled. Without looking up from his inspection he instructed Taneer. "Security reset is on the top of the case. I have already primed it for you. Slide your thumb over it three times. The unit will beep three times to signify acceptance. Next to the pickup is a small integrated mike into which you may whisper whatever passwords you wish. Both must be utilized to reopen the case." He finally looked up from his examination. "A powdered explosive is integrated into the body of the case itself. Any unauthorized attempt to force the seal will result in an explosion that will destroy the contents as well as anyone in its immediate vicinity."

Taneer nodded knowingly, as if he dealt with this sort of thing every day. He indicated the packet containing the molly. "Anyone can access three-quarters of the information via a standard reader. Any attempt to access the remaining fourth will result in a permanent sphere wipe. You get the rest of the code when I receive the rest of the payment."

The European nodded understandingly. "All as we agreed. It will be a standard simultaneous quantum exchange. If either side holds back any element of the agreement, the transfer will not eventuate. My consortium receives the rest of the code; you get the information that allows you to access a certain safe deposit box in Zurich." Now he did smile, albeit austerely. "Where I presume you will be when the final transfer is made. All quite neat and clean, as such transactions are meant to be." Apparently feeling it was time to let his guard down a little bit, if only for reasons of diplomacy, he added, "You will like Zurich, I think. Everyone who goes there does." He drew the back of his left hand across his forehead. "A much more civilized climate."

Taneer nodded and smiled back. "We'll stop by there just long enough to conclude our business, I think, and then we'll be on our way elsewhere."

Jena had still not decided what to do: whether to remain where she was, retreat and ascribe the situation to bad karma, or wait and see if the group of five once again split into its original parts. She was still debating with herself, praying for guidance, when the big man who had accompanied the European suddenly twitched, started to turn where he stood, and fell over. He lay there on the ground; unmoving, a large hill-like silhouette in the darkness. His companion gaped down at him. She crouched lower in her hiding place as hand beams swung wildly, searching the night. One swept past just over her head. None of them happened to focus on the right spot—but she did.

Something else was coming out of the darkness.

Keshu stared at the readout on his spinner. The overhead view from the uncomplaining drone was still as responsive as it could be, but it was not nearly informative enough.

A sixth shape had suddenly appeared, to join the other five. It had not entered from one side of the screen or the other, as would normally be the case. The human heat signature had simply materialized as if out of nowhere. Adding to the confusion was that the largest of the original heat signatures had stopped moving and was beginning to fade slightly.

As an officer with long experience in interpreting such readouts, he did not need someone to explain to him what it meant when a human's infrared signature began to pale. It meant that the body in question was growing colder, and in this particular instance clearly not from exposure to the sultry night air of the jungle. As if the situation was not already complicated enough, the baffling appearance of a new figure was more problematical. Once again, experience supplied a realistic explanation.

"Inspector . . . ?" Johar prompted him. Looking baffled, the lieutenant was fixated on his own readout. "Pardon my English, but— what the hell?"

"The downed individual has been shot, or otherwise severely impacted," Keshu explained. "Probably, but we cannot be certain as yet, by this intruder. As for the newcomer, I would guess he arrived draped in a camo suit of some kind. Possibly illicit ex-military. It would mask not only his heat signature but his shape. A little light-bending goes a long way at night."

"Yes, sir," Johar agreed, visibly impressed that his superior was not impressed. "But what does it mean?"

"It means," Keshu told him, taking a long breath, "that our neat little plan of action and follow-up has taken on an unexpected dimension. One that I just as soon could have done without."

The lieutenant held his spinner up to his mouth, and waited. "Orders, Chief Inspector?"

Desire and knowledge wrestling within him, Keshu's lips tightened as he tried to fabricate the right response. Unable to conjure one, he stalled. No matter what sort of confrontation they had accidentally stumbled into, no matter its consequences, he had no choice but to remain focused on the reason for his presence here in the first place: the foreign woman Chalmette. As for the rest of it, whatever "it" turned out to be, like so much unexpected rubbish it could be cleaned up later.

For the second time that night, he decided to wait.

Ignoring the shocked starlit stares of the four individuals still standing, Chal Schneemann pushed back the hood of his camo suit as he walked up to the body of Punjab and deliberately kicked the prone man hard in the back of his head, above the spot where a tiny transparent dart now protruded from his neck. No sound emanated from the motionless figure. Always one to be sure, Chal moved around to the front of the body and kicked again, breaking the nose. Frozen to the spot next to Taneer, Depahli made a small whining noise as she looked on, wide-eyed.

Blood appeared, flowing freely from the bodyguard's face. Still no reaction. Satisfied, Chal shifted the muzzle of the small hand weapon he held in his right hand until it was aimed in the general direction of both the visiting businessman and the Indian scientist. Noting the direction of their stares, he gestured slightly with the gun.

"This uses highly compressed gas to fire syringets containing a powerful concentrated neurotoxin derived from the venom of the banded sea krait. It paralyzes muscles almost instantly. It freezes hearts." He indicated the large and rapidly chilling corpse off to his left. "I dislike having to kill a colleague, but there is simply too much at stake here to take chances." Shifting his gaze, he locked onto Taneer's face.

"I'm supposed to bring you back with me, alive." His eyes shifted imperceptibly to his left. "I assure you that's going to happen. Whether your lady friend comes with us or not is up to you."

Quaking in his air shoes, a frightened Sanjay wondered why, if this terrifying person wished to take no chances, he himself had not already also gone the way of the dead bodyguard. Then it occurred to him that the masquerade that had deceived the European businessman and his associate had not for an instant fooled this person. Whoever he was, he had straightaway seen the sham for what it was.

Whether he would still kill the poor shopkeeper or not was something that could not be predicted, nor inferred from the executioner's manner. Sanjay would not wait to find out. Silently, he began reciting his own final prayers. He would be sorry to die only because it meant he would not be able to see Chakra and the children again.

Somehow, he knew that trying to use them to appeal to this person would carry less weight with the tall, stolid-faced killer than a dead leaf falling from a tree.

Gun held in one level, perfectly steady hand, the other extended outward, palm up, Chal approached the wide-eyed Karlovy. "In addition to this gentleman, I am required to return with the two items you presently hold in your right hand. Please pass them over to me while you are still capable of doing so. I assure you I have no compunction about picking them up off the ground, should they happen to drop along with you."

Swallowing, Taneer took a step forward despite a terrified Depahli's best efforts to hold him back. He held out the security case.

"Take this. I'll open it for you. There's a lot of money inside. Millions more than you're being paid to do this, I'm sure." He raised his voice slightly. "Go on—take it!"

Barely glancing in the scientist's direction, Chal's gaze briefly flicked over the case. Its presence and contents were confirmation that the esteemed Mushtaq's sources had once again come through.

"You want to know the difference between an employee and a whore? An employee has one kind of reputation, a whore another. I value my reputation, Mr. Buthlahee. Besides, even if I were to take you up on your offer, others of my chosen profession would then be hired to look for me in turn. Not to mention that I would have to kill you—all of you—simply to buy a little time." He smiled pleasantly. "For a man of logic and reason, I don't think you've thought through your offer very thoroughly."

Taneer's lips tightened. "If they get me back, the company will forcibly extract the information they want from me. Then they may kill me anyway, or they may not."

The tracker pursed his lips slightly. "Not my concern."

Sanjay could not keep from blurting, "You will excuse me, please, but I must ask: what happens to the money?"

Smile widening, Chal studied the shopkeeper and whispered something under his breath. It might have been "peasant," or it might have been something even less flattering. Sanjay could not tell, nor did he really care.

"I suppose this gentleman"—and he indicated Karlovy—"will return it to his superiors. He'd better, or they're liable to hire someone like me to find him." Shifting his attention from Taneer and Sanjay, he inquired curiously of the frightened businessman, "I don't imagine they're going to be very pleased when you have to report the details of your failure here."

To his credit and despite his evident fear, Karlovy did not cower beneath the tracker's stare. "I shall plead extenuating circumstances."

To everyone's surprise, but not relief, Schneemann laughed. "I've been around long enough to hear myself described a great many ways, in a great many languages, but as 'extenuating circumstances'? That is a first." An auditory vapor, the laugh went away, fleeing into the night. Chal gestured anew with his upturned palm. "The items, please. Before I lose my sense of humor."

Keshu wanted to shake the spinner, to threaten it. He was going to have to make a decision, and soon, very soon, without the right kind of information he needed to make it.

"Chief Inspector, what's going on out there?" With a nod, Johar gestured in front of them, toward the trees that blocked contact and a proper view of what was transpiring deeper in the forest.

"I don't know." Keshu squinted at his readout. "None of them seem to be moving. Since they're not likely to be spending all this time in prayerful communion, I expect they must be talking to one another." As he had been doing all night, he kept switching rapidly back and forth between the overhead drone's infrared and magnified-starlight views. One was little more instructive than the other. "Without audio or daylight vision, I can't tell what's going on. Are they arguing? Are they old friends meeting up for a night's illegal campout?"

Johar looked over at his superior. There was sympathy in his voice. "We're going to have to do something soon, Chief Inspector." He indicated his own readout. "It looks like the suspect is on the move again."

Keshu's attention shot back to his own spinner. Damn! The foreign woman was showing signs of moving, all right—away from the others. Pick her up, or let it go. It was the same thorny choice he had been faced with all night.

He was tired. It wasn't fair. All the careful trailing and observation, the expensive surveillance, the number of personnel on site and holding as backup; everything added up to a considerable expenditure of time and money. If he called it off, he'd be asked in no uncertain terms to explain the decision. If he gave the order to pick up the woman Chalmette, he might have no case—and no chance to prosecute again in the future.

Why had all these other people decided to pick the same night and place to convene for their mysterious little gathering? Why couldn't they have done so a kilometer farther north, or south, or at a sensorium tea shop somewhere in the middle of the city, or at a damn meet-and-greet center at one of the city's five main airports? Why in Gurja's name did they have to end up doing this now, on his watch, here, tonight? Had he not been devout in his work, his home life, his prayers? What had he done to deserve this?"

"Chief Inspector?" In the darkness alongside him, Johar was staring a little harder than usual at the glowing screen of his spinner.

"What now, Lieutenant?" Somehow, Keshu managed to substitute resignation for exhaustion in his voice.

"It looks like we have another new heat signature, sir."

Oh great. Wonderful wondrous, an exasperated Keshu thought. Who could it be now? A wandering politician in search of nocturnal votes? Teenage forestry scouts desperate to earn commendations? Was there perhaps a small convention scheduled for this region he had not been informed about? He directed his attention to the far right-hand portion of his readout as the unseen distant drone slightly adjusted its position and magnification to accommodate the new arrival.

Recognition shot through him as if he had received a full jolt from one of his department's own advanced mob control stunners.

The telltale heat signature of the new arrival was far too big, and moving much too fast.

chapter xvi

Five people stood around the artificial water hole. A sixth had begun to retreat slowly through the dense undergrowth that concealed her. Given so many choices, all equally oblivious to its presence, the tiger logically settled on the one that had its back facing the jungle.

To his credit, Chal sensed the big cat's approach and whirled with almost superhuman speed. Expecting to find a human bearing down on him, he was sufficiently taken aback, for just an instant, to hold off pulling the trigger of his small but exceedingly deadly weapon. When instinct and reflex finally managed to overcome shock, it was too late.

Depahli screamed. Everyone screamed. In the darkness and shadows of the night, the tracker's blood spurted like black milk as the huge cat brought its jaws together across the man's neck. Paws big enough to completely cover a car hubcap slammed into the tracker; one digging deeply in his right shoulder, the other shredding his face like an angry child toying with a piece of burnt toast. Muscle was pulled away from bone, bone splintered. The tracker went down with the cat on top of him.

It was Sanjay who had enough surviving presence of mind to grab hold of his employer and his employer's girlfriend and pull them in the opposite direction.

"Run, Mr. Taneer, sir! And you too, lady! Run this way now, please, back to the fence! We need to get through the fence!"

"Y-yes." Stumbling backward in the clutch of the shopkeeper's determined fingers, a shocked Taneer had to rip his gaze away from the nightmarish scene in front of him. Once, the tiger looked up, glaring green eyes meeting his own. He had seen tigers before; in zoological parks, from elephant back in Bandhavgarh. But not like this. It stunned him, threatened to root him to the spot as effectively as an infinitesimal dose of the deadly fluid contained in the tracker's syringets. Only when the big cat looked down to check on its unmoving prey did the scientist find his feet again. It helped that Depahli, too, was now tugging at him.

Together the three of them turned and sprinted, stumbled, staggered back the way they had come. Only Sanjay dared to occasionally check back over his shoulder to see if the cat was in the mood to take multiple prey tonight. Mercifully, the jungle trail behind him remained empty in the pale starlight.

What was it with him and cats, anyway?

They were halfway back to the fence line before Taneer realized he was still clutching the security case tightly to his chest.

Mr. Vaclav, alias Karlovy Milesclova, was used to dealing with the dangers of large, civilized cities. He knew how to negotiate with muggers, with prostitutes plying their trade on public streets, with beggars and the desperately drug-addicted. He knew how to find his way rapidly and efficiently through airports and other congested public transportation termini. He understood traffic flow and corporate intrigue and social backbiting.

He had not wanted to be here, in Sagramanda, doing this thing. But the consortium's overboard had voted, and he had been designated. Or lost out, depending on one's perspective. More than willing to forgo the promised bonus, he had done his tactful best to beg off. His polite pleading had been turned down.

Now he found himself running for his life. Not from some addled street person with a knife, not from some bomb-throwing antiglobalization terrorist, not from some irate religious fanatic whose personal precepts the consortium he worked for had inadvertently offended, but from a tiger. A tiger, of all things! In this day and age! It was absurd, outrageous, unbelievable. That he, Vaclav Milesclova, executive vice president of an international family of companies whose name was known throughout the world, should be frantically huffing and puffing his way through the jungles of the subcontinent without a chauffeured Mercrysler or Rollsbach in sight, was too much to countenance.

Wild of eye, flushed of face, his heart pounding like a runaway bass drum despite all the hours he had spent on his office treadmill and electronic toner, he looked back. Nothing stirred in the dark behind him except the fronds of the plants he had brushed up against. The starlit path was devoid of devils and empty of pursuit. Though he knew nothing of the habits of wild creatures, it seemed to him quite possible that the beast might well be preoccupied with its fresh . . . meal. Shuddering, he turned to run on.

He tripped over an unkind tree root, and fell.

His face smacked into the dirt. Raising his head almost immediately, he wiped grit from his flesh and looked apprehensively back over his shoulder. Was that movement, there in the night? Or only wind stirring the trees? Hastily, he scrabbled to his knees and began searching the area where he had fallen. On contact with the ground, he'd dropped both of the prized packages. He found the one containing the molly almost immediately. Like most modern forms of portable information storage, it was well made and had survived the fall with no visible damage. The second envelope . . .

The second precious, irreplaceable envelope had ripped on impact. While a small portion of its contents lay scattered nearby, the bulk had thankfully remained inside the transparent glassine container. Rising to a kneeling position, he started to pick up what had fallen out, when he heard what was a loud cough somewhere behind him.

Utterly consumed with sheer terror, he struggled the rest of the way to his feet and ran on, heading for the pickup point located just inside the preserve's fence line. He would have used the communicator zippered into his inside shirt pocket to request an immediate pickup instead of the one already scheduled, but he did not want to spare either the time or the wind to make the call.

If the general outline of the massive heat signature that had appeared so suddenly and unexpectedly on his spinner had not been enough to identify its source, the reverberant snarl that traveled through brush and across trees to the place where Keshu had set up his temporary command post was confirmation enough.

"Vishnu!" Johar muttered as he stared at his own readout. He looked over at the chief inspector. "Seems to me I remember seeing something on the news about a rogue cat taking people in this part of the preserve."

"I knew we'd have to coordinate this operation with Transport, but not with Wildlife and Game." Keshu's words came sharp and fast. His difficult decision had been made for him. By an animal. "Tell the two flying squads to head this way. Instruct everyone on the ground to move in." He took a deep breath. "Pick up the Frenchwoman."

Johar eyed his superior uncertainly. "But Chief Inspector, you've been saying all along that without unassailable proof, a court case can't be—"

Keshu cut him off. "It doesn't matter now, Lieutenant. We've done as much as we could, and it's all flown to pieces. I won't risk letting this woman slip away and hide."

"What about the others—these other people?"

Keshu adjusted his turban as he regarded the officer. "One crisis at a time, please, Lieutenant Johar. First the Frenchwoman. Then we'll see if we have a need, or responsibility, to deal with these others." Motioning for the officer to follow, he started forward along a pre-determined route that led through the jungle. "Inform everyone as to what is happening out there and instruct them to be extra alert, though all the noise and activity should be enough to frighten off—"

Johar reached out and gestured with his spinner. "Chief Inspector —look."

Frowning, Keshu rechecked his own instrument's readout. Some-where overhead, above the ground and below the clouds, the drone was still doing its job. Only now the images it was transmitting made no sense: no sense at all.

When the new arrival had shot the big man and then confronted the others by the water hole, a puzzled Jena had decided that events had become too complicated. Her redemptions were models of simplicity and purity. Not knowing how to proceed under such increasingly baf-fling circumstances, she had decided to give up on her evening's orig-inal intent and had begun to withdraw.

And then the tiger had appeared, striking out of nowhere, slicing through the night like the incarnation of a god. The assassin had found himself slain. It had been a paralytic moment, one of those instants of unforeseen stupefaction capable of numbing even

those who thought themselves permanently inured to all manner
and kind of violence.

Unlike those clustered by the water hole, Jena hadn't screamed.
She had just stared, hardly breathing, looking on as the tiger proceeded to first slay efficiently and then begin to dine on its prey. She
crouched in awe, looking on in admiration. She was not frightened.

She was envious.

Never before had she been witness to such studied ferocity. Was
the tiger nothing more than a big cat? Or was it truly, as the sacred
scriptures declared, the mount of the goddess Durga herself? Jena's
mind was awhirl, overwhelmed with the rigors of the long night's
stalking, the warm enveloping smells of the jungle, the heat, and now
this unexpected miraculous presentation right before her very eyes of
death by tiger. From where she knelt she could smell the blood. It was
something they shared. Deep, deep within herself, she knew she was
more closely akin in spirit and desire to the tiger than she could ever
be to its victim.

Was not the great goddess Durga, more properly known as
Mahadevi, shown riding upon a tiger? Thus mounted, had not she
defeated the demonic Mahisha against whose powers the combined
might of all the other gods had shown themselves to be useless? And
afterward, was not Durga acclaimed by all and anointed the leader of
the gods in all matters of battle?

Why should she not be the same? Would not Mother Kali look
with approval on her servant who, taking such initiative, would
thereby render herself even more capable of serving? With her daily
dose of drugs coursing through her system, dizzy with delusions of
divine approval, she rose slowly from her place of concealment and
began walking—not away from the scene of primeval carnage, but
toward it.

Mesmerized, a flabbergasted Keshu and Johar stared at their readouts. It was the lieutenant who broke the temporary trance.

"Lord Krishna," he muttered, "she's not running away: she's heading right *for* it."

Holstering his spinner, Keshu broke into a run. "Tell everyone to *hurry*." He pulled his sidearm. "We have to get close enough so we can fire and scare it off, but I don't want to hit her!" He broke into the brush. Johar was right behind his superior, barking frantically into his spinner.

As she emerged into the small clearing by the water hole, Jena was chanting a favorite mantra to herself. Full of allusions to innocence lost, Mother Kali, India, loves gone astray, and murders committed, it would have provided ample fodder for even the least-demanding clinical psychologist.

It was doubtful that it had much of an impact on her present audience.

Instantly alert, able to see infinitely better at night than any human, the tiger looked up from its meal, raising its bloodied snout from the hollow it had chewed out of the center of the dead tracker's midsection. It stayed like that, staring unblinkingly at the creature that had interrupted its feeding, slowly and unconcernedly licking the blood from its exquisite muzzle.

Removing her clothes, singing softly to herself, Jena reached into her shoulder bag and pulled out the sword. The same sword that had, in the name of Mother Kali, sped so many on their journey away from this sordid, unhappy world. Jena had no necklace of skulls to dangle from her neck, no belt of dead men's hands to encircle her waist, but she had studied with the dedication of a true acolyte. She knew the reputed moves as well as any disciple.

Holding the sword tightly in one hand, regretting she had no head of a demon to display in the other, completely naked to the Sundarbans night, she began to dance.

Her movements were as graceful as those of the ballerina she had once thought, long, long ago, to become. As gracile and fluid as those of a sambar deer, as polished and controlled as those of a mass murderer. Twirling the razor-sharp weapon over her head and breathtakingly close to her sides, eyes half shut as if in a delirium of pleasure, she spun and twirled to the corrupt, unhealthy, soul-crippling music only she could hear. She alone, and Mother Kali, who was forever her lord and savior from the complete and utter insanity that years ago had threatened to overwhelm her completely.

Closer and closer she drew to the tiger, which lay on its belly, alert and watchful. Nearer to death but also nearer to Nirvana, to the transformation that would make her invincible, unconquerable, indomitable. Soon nothing would be able to touch her, nothing would be able to harm her. Not ever, ever, again.

Voices sounding, coming rapidly nearer. Urgent voices, cajoling but not convincing. She knew those voices. The were the voices of men, that had never done anything but deceive her. She was very close now. She could smell the rancid stink of the dead man's eviscerated torso. She fancied she could smell the bloody perfume of the tiger's breath.

"Cher père," she whispered softly as she bent forward. "Do you have my mother's finger?"

"Nahi, no!" Keshu raised his pistol as he burst through the brush. So did Lieutenant Johar, and the half dozen officers who had closed in behind him.

Uttering a thunderous roar, the tiger leaped from where it lay crouched beside the disemboweled corpse of the tracker Schneemann and slammed into the slim, pirouetting form of the human that had dared to decisively intrude on its personal space, stepping over the invisible, imperceptible line the feeding cat had defined for itself. For just an instant smacked out of her self-imposed dream state and back to harsh, unforgiving reality, Jena had a second or so to stare with unglazed eyes up at the monster. Then she thudded into the ground with the big cat on top of her, her head twisted and bent unnaturally backward as she struck the unyielding earth.

Gunshots rang out. Intended to startle and not to kill, the multiple shots caught the tiger's attention immediately. Unsettled by the appearance of so many bipedal shapes and confused by the loud noise, it bounded away from the figure beneath its paws and raced off into the night, abandoning its latest prey and leaving behind only smells and shadows.

Night-goggle-equipped junior officers fired off a few more shots and continued to pursue the fleeing cat. But not too energetically, and only to the edge of the clearing. The huge animal could be anywhere, and special starlight-magnifying goggles notwithstanding, night was its ally, not theirs. Keshu and Lieutenant Johar slowed to a stop near the supine figure of the suspect. Other than a quick, repulsed glance in the direction of the partly eaten carcass, neither showed any interest in the dead man.

Attractive, Keshu thought as he stared down at her. More so than the computer-conjured composite suggested. The sword that lay in the dirt not far from her outstretched right arm was traditional in shape and style. It looked almost as if it had been modeled after a museum piece. That was hardly surprising, he reflected. The multiple murder victims whose killer he had been tracking had not had their heads and limbs cut to pieces with an épée.

At first, he had trouble interpreting the expression on her face. Then it struck him. Ecstasy. That made no sense. In which case, it fit with everything else that had transpired recently. Opposite him, on the other side of the body, Johar was kneeling to examine the motionless form more closely.

"No bite marks." He paused, studying harder. "No claw gouges: not even a scratch." Obviously confused, he looked up at his superior. "But she is dead. I do not need someone from Forensics to tell me that."

Kneeling on the other side of the corpse, Keshu slipped his left hand beneath hair and head and started to lift it. Though he applied very little pressure, it moved freely. Too freely.

"Neck's broken. Must have hit awkwardly and then the cat fell on her. Too much weight for small bones." In death, she looked quite peaceful. At ease. Now he would never know what had motivated her to commit all those killings, all those senseless murders. Because even without conclusive proof, based on everything he had seen this night he was confident that the department had found its serial killer. The stealthy stalking, the presence of the sword: everything pointed to not just a suspect, but to one who was as guilty as he and Subrata and all the others who had participated in the hunt for this woman believed.

And while he might have preferred it to have turned out otherwise, at least he would be spared the need to produce irrefutable evidence at a trial.

He straightened. Overhead, the first of two backup choppers was descending toward the water hole clearing on noise-cancelled blades. "Pack her up. Make sure Forensics handles the weapon carefully. There might be indicators present: blood, DNA, hair. Like sins, evidence is not easily washed away. Minute amounts can get caught between blade and hilt, or on the decorated handle."

"Yes, Chief Inspector." Turning, Johar gestured in the direction of the two unknown dead men. "What about them?"

Keshu was only mildly curious, but wholly professional. "Full body workup. Might be some kind of connection that can be established later. In a case like this, when you can't be sure quite what's going on, you don't want to overlook anything."

The lieutenant nodded. Pulling his spinner, he began establishing contact with the arriving teams. Walking slowly away from the increasingly busy site, Keshu halted at the place where the clearing gave way to dense undergrowth. The tiger had vanished within, swallowed up as if it had never been. A specter, a wraith, a phantom of the jungle. But one that had left behind all-too-graphic evidence of its presence.

They would have to notify Wildlife and Game of the incident, he knew. He did not think he would have to remind Johar to do so. The lieutenant was very efficient. Standing there in darkness increasingly filled with the noise of men and their machines, an old rhyme came to him.

Tyger, tyger, burning bright,
In the forest of the night.

Turning, he looked back to where specialists were now swarming around the broken body of the foreign woman. Was she truly, for certain, inarguably, the serial murderess? Or were the improbable events of this night no more than a fantastical sequence of misattuned coincidences, and the real mass murderer was still out there somewhere, stalking the depths of the city?

Well, there was one way he would know for certain. If the killings stopped. In that event, he did not know whether to thank the tiger or condemn it. If the woman lying dead on the ground behind him was in truth the one responsible, then victims unknown and unnamed should give thanks to the big cat. If not . . .

He decided he was confident. The circumstantial evidence might not be conclusive, but it was credible. There would be no court trial, no summoning of witnesses, no lengthy parade of long-winded authorities. The thing was done.

Sometimes, he reflected somberly, in spite of what its tens of millions of fractious, exuberant, milling inhabitants might want, or even just one very weary police inspector, India went ahead and took matters into its own primordial, indomitable hands.

chapter xvii

Finding a restaurant that was open all night was not a problem. In a city the size of Sagramanda, there were hundreds of establishments of every variety that never closed their doors; not for Holi, not for Ramadan, not for Christmas. Finding one that offered privacy booths required a little more searching.

Hesitant to head for any of the dining spots in the neighborhood where he lived in secret with Depahli lest they were being watched, Taneer led his fiancée and his middleman to another busy part of the surging metropolis where they were likely to find what they needed. The Uzbek fast-food eatery met their needs admirably. Furthermore, a restaurant was a good location in which to hold their final meeting, because in addition to being exhausted, fearful, and in a hurry, they were also all ravenously hungry.

Over a meal of vegetables, potatoes, and Uzbek horseburgers, they discussed their final business behind the shimmering privacy screen the booth provided. Looking out through the light-distorting waveforms was like trying to see through melted glass. Not trusting even a restaurant he had never visited before, Taneer used his own portable instrumentation to check out the booth's security before settling down to business.

"Will not that European gentleman and his associates come looking for you?" Sanjay asked him as he sipped his Kanacola.

Taneer worked on the briefcase he had placed on the table between them. Beneath the case, the tabletop displayed a constantly shifting panorama of scenes from Uzbek legends. The display could be tuned for adult, juvenile, or child consumption, but no one was paying any attention to the built-in diversion. All eyes were on the case.

"Why should they?" Taneer ran through the specified sequence required to open, rather than explode, the case. "Our Mr. Karlovy got what he came for." He smiled as a soft beep indicated that he had entered the unlocking sequence correctly. "And we got what we came for."

In an age often defined by its universal use of credit, it was a strange sensation to set eyes on so much actual money. Though little more than stamped-out rectangles of electronically embedded paper and plastic, it still had real presence. Cash still stood for something, which was why it remained in use.

"Got your bag?" Taneer asked the man seated across the table. Next to him, eyes very wide, Depahli was clinging to his left arm with one hand while the delicate but strong fingers of the other were moving along his leg. Though it was difficult, at the moment he would not let anything distract him.

Wordlessly Sanjay placed on the table the takeaway bag he had requested when they had entered the restaurant.

"How would you like your fee?" the scientist inquired politely, his hands resting on the case's implausible contents.

A captivated Sanjay hardly knew how to respond. Even after all the time and effort he had put into this piece of business, even after enduring and surviving all the very real risks, not to mention nearly being shot, and nearly being eaten, he had never really believed, deep down, that he would be faced with something as solid and real as the contents of the case that rested on the table before him. He felt like a character in one of the movies he had so loved as a child, the viewing of which had been such a special treat for himself and the dirt-poor family out of whose unrelenting poverty he had slowly managed to raise himself.

"I . . . I suppose I will have it just as you wanted yours. A little of each."

Nodding amenably, Taneer began passing large wads of currency across the table, riffling briefly through each bound packet before surrendering it to his middleman. Dazed, Sanjay did not even bother to count the money. Three percent of the total agreed-upon price that Chhote Pandit had negotiated. In return for one standard-size mollysphere and a small packet of material whose contents, Sanjay realized with a start, he had not even had a chance to see clearly for himself. But he could see the money plainly enough.

When he had finished counting and distributing, Taneer carefully closed and relocked the case. "There you are, Mr. Ghosh. Three million in U.S. dollars, euros, and rupees. Three percent of the total payment due me. I thank you for a job well done and for assistance far beyond what was originally agreed upon."

Sanjay regarded the takeaway bag, with its colorful external designs promoting Uzbek fast food. His gaze shifted back to the case lying in front of the scientist. Without a word, he slipped his right hand inside his bogus hitman-style vest. Alarmed, it abruptly occurred to Taneer that in asking this shopkeeper to emulate a bodyguard, to render the illusion complete the shopkeeper might actually have brought a weapon with him. And neither he nor Depahli had one.

Seeing the sudden shift in their expressions, the perceptive Sanjay divined the reason behind their reactions. He did not have a weapon on him—but they didn't know that. Already this night he had bluffed his way through a much more nerve-racking confrontation. What if he chose to take the whole case, and all the money? They were in a very public place. If they thought he had a gun, would they still try to stop him? Could he not walk out with the entire ten million?

Licking his lips, his right hand still resting inside his vest, he let his gaze shift from scientist to siren. "I have a confession to make." They both tensed. "I am, sometimes to my own detriment and regret, an honest man." Withdrawing his hand, he revealed that it held nothing grasped in his fingers. He had only been scratching an itch.

"I know what you are thinking," he went on. "I can see it. I will not deny that the thought has occurred to me. But I am scrupulous even when I am dealing with such things as certain recreational pharmaceuticals that are frowned upon by society at large." He sat a little straighter on his hard-backed bench seat. "A man may be poor, but he can still be honorable. I am no longer poor. If I were to try and cheat you, I could not look again into the eyes of my beloved wife Chakra and those of my children." Somberness gave way to a wide, engaging grin.

"Then there is the matter of how I would be reincarnated. Thieves and crooks do not, I believe, come back as handsome men or virtuous women, or tall trees or fine-looking animals. It is a measure of mankind's failure that there are so many whose karma causes them to be reincarnated as rats and roaches." His right hand drew the stuffed takeaway bag closer to his side of the table. "Better to be able to live with three million and oneself than with ten million and a stranger."

Obviously and unabashedly relieved, Taneer exhaled sharply. For her part Depahli rose, put both hands on the table, and leaned across to reward the simple shopkeeper's honesty with a kiss. Though he suspected it would be a kiss the likes of which he could no more imagine than he could envision walking away from the restaurant with three million dollars in a takeaway bag, Sanjay drew back and turned his face slightly away from her.

"Please, miss. When I said I was an honorable man, I meant truly in all things. I am well and surely married."

Pausing halfway across the table she smiled, nodded, and sat back down. Taneer eyed his middleman admiringly. "You are more than honorable, Sanjay Ghosh. You are steadfast."

"Perhaps, but I am also not made of clay." With the table once more separating them, he felt safe in smiling at Depahli. "Please do not tempt me again, Miss De. I fear I would not be able to resist a second time."

She laughed amusedly. "Don't worry, Sanjay. You're safe with me."

Smile fading, he nodded, serious once more. "You must have considered many options for this moment, but I have only my shop and my home village. Do you think the police will now be looking for me?"

Taneer shook his head. "I think not. Why should they? You've done nothing wrong. I am the one who skipped out on a company contract. If anyone *should* contact you, feel free to tell them the truth." He grinned. "As much or as little of it as you see fit. Your involvement required you to expedite some small business for me, that's all."

"Yes." Sanjay eyed the takeaway bag. "Some small business. I know nothing beyond that."

A smiling Taneer spread his hands. "See? You have nothing to worry about. No one even knows that I paid you. Or if they suspect, how much I paid you. Which does not matter, because the money came from outside the country. You are quite in the clear, my honorable friend." He rose.

"It's been a long as well as eventful night. I am sure you would like to deposit your money in an all-night security box or a bank or two." He put an arm around Depahli and gazed affectionately into her eyes. "We also have much to do, and all of it should be done quickly."

Sanjay stood, making sure the heat-seal rim of his paper bag was locked tight. While on public transport, it would not do to have any of his takeaway spill out. One last time, his eyes met those of the scientist who had been instrumental in transforming the shopkeeper's life. "I suppose that we will never meet again."

Taneer steepled both palms together in front of his lower face and dipped his head. "With luck," he agreed succinctly.

They parted. Heading for transport that would take him to the section of the city where he lived and had his little shop, Sanjay reflected on everything that had befallen him. It all seemed a dream now. There was so much he would never forget. Not least of all the providential tiger, who might as well have been sent by the gods. As someone who had been raised to be logical as well as spiritual, he knew that was unlikely. The tiger had been motivated by hunger, not an intrinsic desire to save him and his employer. If it had chosen to steal up behind them instead of behind the tracker, it would have taken him or Taneer or the scientist's girlfriend. Nature was an opportunist, not a meddler.

He slowed, frowning slightly. An autocab had come up alongside him to inquire courteously if the gentleman with the takeout food might be needing a ride. Heading for the nearest west-going public transport it occurred to Sanjay that it would not only be safer to take the cab, it would be faster and easier.

Besides, he could afford it now.

Depahli had never thought she might one day be part of the great Indian Diaspora. As an abused child and later as an exploited adolescent, the likelihood of traveling overseas had seemed as remote to her as voyaging to the moon.

Now as she and Taneer stepped out of the transport and hurried along the street that led to their apartment building, all possibilities seemed open to her.

"Where shall we go first, my love?"

"Anywhere you want, Depa," he told her softly. "Anyplace you've ever seen in the movies, or on the vit, or heard about. Anywhere you've ever dreamed of." He looked back down the modest but neatly land-scaped street. This late (or rather, this early) in the day few vehicles were about, and even fewer pedestrians. Off to the east, the sky was just beginning to lighten.

"We'll need to establish a base of operations first, acquire a home. Maybe in the U.S. I hear the Indian community in Los Angeles is very accepting, and the weather is not too cold. Vancouver I think we would both find beautiful, but chilly. The same for the U.K. There is always Trinidad, or Fiji." He slipped his left arm around her. "We'll find a place, a place where we will both be happy." He squeezed her tightly against him, and she did not resist. "A place to raise our children.

"But first, we need to make a short detour and a quick visit. In Switzerland, to a certain banking institution, in the city of Zurich."

Entering their building, they made their way in the empty lift up to their apartment. Though it had been her residence for many months now, Depahli found that she was not going to be sorry to leave it. It had been a refuge, but not a home.

A home. She had not experienced one since childhood, and that offered little worth remembering. She was going to start her own, and with the man she loved. Eyeing Taneer as he began pulling suitcases down from the shelf in the living room closet, she knew that she would follow him anywhere, even if he was dead broke.

"I'll start getting things together in here, my love," she told him. "Grab a case and take what you think we'll need out of the bedroom."

Turning, he nodded to her. What a woman, he found himself thinking as he watched her pack only what was necessary from their temporary existence. Not only beautiful and street-smart, but efficient. They were going to build a life together that would rival the fabled cohabitation of Vishnu and Lakshmi.

In the bedroom, Taneer set the empty travel case down in front of the four-drawered dresser and murmured a command for the lights to turn on. As they did so, he was startled not by the intensifying illumination, but by a voice. A voice he recognized and had not expected to hear ever again.

"Namaste. Hello, Taneer—my son."

Anil Buthlahee sat on the bed. The same bed in which his son and his son's Untouchable harlot had doubtless consummated their filthy, unnatural, offensive relationship many times. The vision nauseated him, and he put it out of his head in order to concentrate his attention on his startled offspring. And also to focus his aim.

Taneer stared at the weapon in his father's hand. It was not large, but guns these days did not have to be, often possessing as they did killing power all out of proportion to their size. So tightly was his father's hand gripping the weapon that the skin of his fingers had turned pale.

Looking tired but alert, as if he had come to the end of a long and difficult journey, the senior Buthlahee glanced in the direction of the door into the living room and inquired quietly, as if he had all the time in the world, "Where is the whore?"

"Please, don't do this." Calm in the face of Karlovy's bodyguard Punjab, fleet of foot in reaction to the attack of the tiger, in the presence of his father Taneer found himself shaking uncontrollably. He might have been shaking even if his father had come unarmed.

The fear he felt was not for himself, since he had been prepared to die ever since he had fled the company and absconded with its property, but for Depahli. Depahli, whom he loved more than the money he had been promised. Depahli, who had risen from nothing to devote herself to him, and to them. Depahli, who was trapped in the living room with no way to escape. To try for the front door, she would have to cross in front of the entrance to the bedroom.

"She's not here," he said quickly. Perhaps a bit too quickly. "She's shopping."

Anil Buthlahee grunted disappointedly. "Do you think I am

nothing more than a dumb, ignorant merchant? I heard you talking." He gestured with the muzzle of the compact little pistol. "I will do what must be done, to salvage the honor of our family."

Within Taneer, fear was giving way slowly to anger. "Why, Father?" He gestured aimlessly. "Why do this? Why do you *think* this way? This isn't the seventeenth century. This is *Sagramanda*; now, today. Enlightened people don't go around committing suttee anymore, or honor killings! Caste is no longer what determines the worth of a human being. Things have *changed*."

"Not all things," Anil replied unyieldingly. "I am my father's son. As such, I must honor him and preserve the reputation of the family, which you have so uncaringly desecrated." He blinked, as if he had something in his eye. "I only wish *you* were your father's son."

"I *am*, Father! I am."

"No! No," Anil added more quietly. "My son would not sleep with an Untouchable. That is abomination enough. But to contemplate *marrying* such a person, living with one . . ." He shook his head sharply. "Having *children* with one . . ."

Desperate, Taneer tried another tack. "If you would only set aside your outdated cultural baggage, Father, long enough to just meet Depahli, I'm sure you would come to—"

Moving the muzzle of the pistol slightly to one side, Anil fired. The muted puff of the silencer was followed by a crashing sound as the vase he had aimed at was blown to bits. It had the intended effect of shutting up his son. Words can be more powerful than bullets—but only when spoken or printed outside the range of the intended target.

The gun's aperture shifted back to point at the stunned scientist. "I will meet her, Taneer. And then I will kill her. Then I will kill you. Afterward, I will walk out of this room and this building and this sin-ridden city. I will go back to my business and the rest of my family, that respects me and our common history, and I will try for the rest of my life to heal the hole in my heart."

Taneer swallowed. "It doesn't have to be this way, Father."

Eyes that had seen those of the other when they had first opened onto the world locked on them. "Yes, it does, Taneer."

In the living room, Depahli had been standing pressed up against the other side of the bedroom wall, listening. Everything had been going so wonderfully well. From standing outside the gates of Nirvana, she had suddenly found herself thrust into the pit of hell.

She could not get across the room to the front door without Taneer's homicidal fanatic of a father seeing her. The communicator she could use to call the police was in the purse lying on the entryway side table. Not that calling the police would be a good idea or a final solution anyway. Even if by some miracle they could arrive in time to keep the senior Buthlahee from killing them both, she knew from experience that police had a habit of asking awkward questions. If they decided to do a quick search of the apartment and found the briefcase containing the equivalent of seven million American dollars, they might ask some that could not properly be answered.

She could not stand there forever, frozen against the wall, paralyzed by indecision. At any moment, the elder Buthlahee might decide it was time to stop talking to his son and walk into the living room. She could not even reach the bathroom to hide in there. Besides, she did not want to hide. As a child, she had tried hiding repeatedly to avoid her uncle. Each time, he had found her. Each time, her unhappy life had been made a little more miserable.

She remembered the tiger that had jumped out of the jungle to kill the enigmatic tracker. The tiger had concealed itself, only to attack with complete surprise when no one was looking at it. Frantically she searched the living room. There was nothing within reach she could use as a weapon; not even a letter opener. All she had were her hands and fists.

She remembered something else. Like the tiger, she was the master of her immediate environment. Maybe she could use that. Sucking in air, she screamed rather than spoke the familiar commands, spewing a steady stream of them into the air. Recognizing her voice, the instrumentation that had been installed in the bedroom responded accordingly.

A pair of naked apsaras appeared at the head of the bed and leaned forward, while two mightily thewed royal attendants whose origin could be traced to a passage from the Mahabharata rose from its mattress and straightened as they moved to engage the apsaras. Typically, she and Taneer would be kneeling on the bed between, awaiting the slightly warm but otherwise noncorporeal arrival. Instead, the apparitions closed on the preoccupied Anil Buthlahee. Startled and surprised, he whirled and fired wildly at the surrounding figures. Gun gas slammed miniature explosive shells into the wall, the headboard. In a moment, even the traditional merchant would recognize the quartet of unexpected visitants for what they were: high-tech, state-of-the-art virtuals.

Reacting as quickly and with as much presence of mind as he ever had in his life, Taneer scooped up the finely carved reconstituted stone statue of Ganesh from its alcove, rushed forward, and brought it down on his father's head just as the old man realized the deception and started to turn back to him. The blow was not hard enough to knock the merchant unconscious, but it was sufficient to stun him. Dazed, he fell to his knees.

"Depahli!" Still holding the statue, Taneer sprinted toward the doorway.

She met him there, slamming into him and wrapping her arms around her beloved tightly enough to squeeze the wind out of him. He forced himself to break the embrace. Both of them regarded the figure of the old man on the floor, who was moaning and struggling to rise. The muzzle of the gun he held wavered dangerously, like a drunken asp.

"Taneer . . . ," Anil grunted. "No good, Taneer, no good. I'm . . . coming. . . ."

"Run!" Pushing Depahli into the next room, the scientist followed. A wild shot flared through the space he had just been occupying to blow a dark hole in the living room ceiling. Behind them, Anil Buthlahee could be heard cursing and stumbling into furniture as he fought to recover his equilibrium and reload.

As he set Ganesh aside to grab the case and its precious contents, Depahli snatched up her bag, which contained their passports and other critical documentation. Breathing hard, Taneer followed her out the door and into the hallway. Disdaining the elevator and ignoring the probing stares of the recently awakened, they raced down the fire stairs. The building lobby was deserted when they reached it, as was the street outside. Off to the east, the sun was now showing itself over the nearest structures.

As they started running up the road, a third figure emerged from the entrance to the apartment building. Shouting and screaming threats and imprecations, it waved in the air a small, deadly object.

To their great good fortune, the infuriated, raging Anil Buthlahee chose to first look down the street instead of up it, to the north. It gave them just enough time to frantically hail the passing rickshaw, climb in, and deliver instructions to the confused but willing driver. Behind them, Anil Buthlahee finally turned, just in time to see his son climb into the vehicle. As it accelerated up the road, the old man broke into a run, gesturing threateningly with the gun in his hand. He might have fired once; neither Taneer nor Depahli could be sure. But the determined merchant was still dizzy from the blow to his head and could not take proper aim.

Standing behind counters and sitting at a desk had not prepared him for trying to run down a public vehicle. He slowed, staggering, and stopped. Bending forward at the waist, hands resting on his knees, he gasped for air as the silent rickshaw sped on out of sight.

"There's nowhere you can go, you and your slut!" he wheezed loudly. "Wherever you go, wherever you run to, I will find you! On my honor, I will find you!"

Scientist and dacoit did not hear him. The unpretentious,

unadorned interior of the electric rickshaw enveloped them, shutting out the outside world, blocking out the last, ineffective threats of Taneer's hidebound father. Once again there were only the two of them. Soon it would be that way forever.

Then the scientist started laughing. The rickshaw's owner glanced back briefly, eyeing him through the window of the passenger compartment before returning to his driving.

Alternately smiling and confused, one hand on her beloved's shoulder, Depahli looked at him with some concern. "Taneer—Taneer, my darling, my sweet man—are you all right?"

Choking back tears, he took her other hand in his and looked into her beautiful face, perfect down to the single red jewel that glistened on her forehead. "I was just thinking, Depahli. Though I have great respect for all the traditions of my family as well as those of my ancestors, I'm not really what you would call a religious person. But after all the prayers of my childhood, and all that were never answered, I have to admit that Lord Ganesh finally came through with some help."

"Very substantial help, I should say." Her smile grew suddenly uncertain. "Do you think that your father will ever be able to find us and make trouble for us again?"

He shook his head. He was confident now, sure of himself and his future. Of their future. "My father is a smart and clever man, but only within the world he knows. That is the world of eastern India, from Sagramanda south to Puri and onward as far as Visakhapatnam. He knows nothing of the world beyond except what he has seen in movies and on the vit, and that will not be enough to enable him to find us— even if he can find the will and the money." He smiled at her. "Besides, he knows nothing about skiing."

She cocked her head sideways at him, one golden earring dangling. "Skiing? You know nothing about skiing either, Taneer."

"I know. But I will, and soon. You will, too."

Turning, pressing her back into the single bench seat of the rickshaw, she snuggled close, his hand still holding hers. "I have never seen snow, my love, except on the tops of the Himalayas, from a distance. In the movies, everyone is always talking about how cold it is."

"They're right." He let his cheek rest gently against the top of her head. "It is cold. But we won't be."

Forensics had largely finished their work, and the morgue detail was cleaning up. Even for those who dealt daily with the violent consequences of the seemingly endless conflicts that characterized Sagramanda's merciless underbelly, the remains of the bodies of Jena Chalmette and the tall assassin were sufficiently grisly to make a strong man blanch. It was what they were paid to do, however, and the crew went about its gruesome work enveloped in a respectful professional silence.

Keshu and his people were able to readily identify the foreign woman not only by matching her image to that of the carefully crafted computer composite, but through the false identification papers she carried in her large shoulder bag. The assassin proved more problematical. He had no individual ident on his person, and they could not attempt a visual match because, due to the tiger's brief but ferocious intercession, the dead man's face had largely gone missing. The chief inspector was not concerned. Subrata and his resourceful colleagues would work their magic with research and reconstruction to produce an identification.

He knew that not only had they found the mystifying, secretive serial killer they had sought, but that the government of India and the municipality of Greater Sagramanda were to be spared the expense of incarcerating and trying her. It was not the resolution he had sought, but it was one he was content to live with. Of course, there remained the mystery of what the three, and subsequently five, people she had been stalking had been doing in the middle of the night in a restricted area of the Sundarbans Preserve, but that was not a problem for him to puzzle out. Others should, and would, attempt to follow up on that.

Then what was he still doing here? he suddenly asked himself. The sun was up, the temperature was doing likewise, he had been awake all night, and he ought not only to be on his way home—he should *be* home by now, snug and asleep in bed beside his wife. If she was awake, she would be concerned at his absence, but not frantic. Time and experience had taught her years ago that her husband's profession was not one that was respectful of regular hours.

Morning was always the most beautiful time of day. The ambrosial time was even more enchanting in the forest preserve. As a city cop, except for formal vacations and the occasional case that took him into Sagramanda's municipal parks, the only greenery he encountered was in the form of vegetarian meals in the departmental cafeteria.

The team from the morgue was wrapping up its macabre labors, their exertions chilling even on an increasingly hot morning. Lieutenant Johar and several of his colleagues were compacting the crime scene, recording the last bits of environment and evidence for official records. They were taking extra care because a foreign national had been at the crux of the investigation, and details would have to be provided to Interpol, the EEU, and the French government. That left him free to take a walk: something else he rarely had time for.

Two trails lined with brush that had been snapped and broken by those who had fled the tiger led off into the undergrowth. Given all the intensive human activity, including the presence of choppers, the chief inspector felt confident that the big cat was now nowhere in the immediate vicinity. Informing Johar of his intentions, Keshu struck off into the bush.

It was marvelous in the forest. Still cool enough to stroll, with the nocturnal biting insects having clocked out and their diurnal counterparts not yet having clocked in, he was able to wend his way through the tall trees in comparative comfort. Monkeys gamboled in the branches, occasionally pausing to inspect the perambulating inspector. Rollers and other birds sang songs of awakening. Ants, the true masters of the planet, scurried everywhere, busy at the same work they had performed for the forest since time immemorial. He was enveloped by green and brown, with not a machine in sight. He wandered through surroundings that were scenic, stunning, picturesque.

After ten minutes of it, he found himself starting to grow irritable.

City boy, he chided himself lamentingly. Who are you kidding here? Better stick to what you're familiar with, with what you know. Concrete and rubberized walkways are your real paths, nanocarbon pillars and glass sheathing your jungle. He started to turn to retrace his steps.

As he did so, sunlight reflecting off something on the ground caught his eye. Squatting, he reached down to pick up the piece of folded glassine. Its torn edges showed that it had been part of a larger packet. Now it was empty, except for what looked like a clutch of small seeds. Frowning, he turned the fragment of see-through envelope over in his fingers. Definitely seeds. Rising, he looked up the trail, then down. Dropped by someone, probably, in their headlong flight from the tiger.

Even ordinary seeds deserved a chance at life. Almost absently, he shoved the piece of transparent wrapping into his shirt pocket, making sure to fold it double to keep its humble contents from spilling out. Plants were just like visiting relatives, he reflected. He might not be comfortable completely surrounded by them, but in moderation and kept at a reasonable distance they could make for pleasant company.

When they finally sprouted in the self-watering window box he kept in his office, he was mildly disappointed. Hoping for something exotic, he found himself caring instead for a dense fresh growth of jugla. A common roadside weed, jugla at least had somewhat attractive, small yellow flowers. The upside was that they wouldn't require much attention to thrive. That quality would help them survive in the office of a man who very often was not there.

He had spent the morning dealing with the inevitable endless flow of paperwork, a river of reports as long and wide as the Ganges. Now it was time to go out into the field and try to follow up on half a dozen ongoing cases, not to mention the usual riots, political protests, and preholiday confrontations. His driver today was a Corporal Abuya; young, attractive, and puppy-dog eager. He smiled thinly to himself. A few days tramping through the underbelly of Sagramanda would put a damper on that just-out-of-the-academy enthusiasm. Seasoning, it was called. He wondered at what point he had stopped being seasoned and had started being aged.

As soon as he seated himself in the cruiser, pleasantries were exchanged and the corporal efficiently guided the fuel-cell-powered patrol car out of the underground motor pool garage and up into the barely controlled chaos of the city streets. Its clean-burning hydrogen-fueled engine emitted no pollutants into Sagramanda's brown but increasingly tolerable atmosphere while pushing the car along at more-than-adequate speeds.

High above the street, a miniature forest of unassuming roadside weed prospered in its window box. Looking just like any other batch of unpretentious jugla, the plants growing outside the window of Chief Inspector Keshu Jamail Singh's office were in fact slightly different from their commonplace country cousins. The end product of decades of research that had in its most recent stage been supervised by a brilliant and now-vanished biochemist, this particular variety of jugla had been genetically engineered so that, without any extra effort or special nutrients or additional attention, it emitted not one but two gaseous by-products. The usual oxygen, and most unusually and remarkably, free hydrogen.

In secret fields somewhere in central Asia, tens of thousands of acres of cotton and wheat had been plowed under to allow for the planting of a new cash crop. Much to the puzzlement and amusement of the local farmers whose lands had been bought out for the new project, the disciplined agriculturalists who had been brought in to take their place had sown neither of those traditional crops, nor millet, nor sorghum. No, the newcomers had spent a minimal amount of money and had put in place the most simple, basic farming equipment to raise—weeds!

Over tobacco and strong, heavily sugared tea, this outlandish development was much discussed on the streets and in the bazaars of neighboring towns. What did the investors expect to get out of such a planting? How could they possibly hope to recoup their investment from dirty, worthless weeds?

The investors were not worried. In fact, they were much pleased when their first crop came in. Requiring virtually no water and practically no fertilizer, the visitors gazed proudly at the sight of the billions of little yellow flowers that soon covered their extensive fields, the slender green stems erupting from even the poorest soil. With the success of the project speedily proven, plans were already in the works to greatly expand the plantation and to export it elsewhere. Multiple crops of such hearty, naturally disease- and insect-resistant plants could be raised all year beneath the specially treated impermeable plastics that protected them from the weather.

Protected them, while also channeling to collection reservoirs the millions upon millions of cubic meters of virtually free hydrogen fuel being generated by the weeds whose natural photosynthetic process had been genetically modified to emit the precious gas.

At the cost of a hundred million dollars, the consortium of investors reckoned the purchase of the jugla's genetic code to be something of a bargain.

Khatm karma

about the author

Born in New York City in 1946, Foster was raised in Los Angeles. After receiving a bachelor's degree in political science and a master of fine arts in cinema from UCLA (1968, 1969), he spent two years as a copywriter for a small Studio City, California, advertising and public relations firm.

His writing career began when August Derleth bought a long Lovecraftian letter of Foster's in 1968 and, much to Foster's surprise, published it as a short story in Derleth's biannual magazine *The Arkham Collector*. Sales of short fiction to other magazines followed. His first attempt at a novel, *The Tar-Aiym Krang*, was bought by Betty Ballantine and published by Ballantine Books in 1972. It incorporates a number of suggestions from famed SF editor John W. Campbell.

Since then, Foster's sometimes humorous, occasionally poignant, but always entertaining short fiction has appeared in all the major SF magazines as well as in original anthologies and several "Best of the Year" compendiums. His published oeuvre includes more than one hundred books.

Foster's work to date includes excursions into hard science fiction, fantasy, horror, detective, Western, historical, and contemporary fiction. He has also written numerous nonfiction articles on film, science, and scuba diving, as well as having produced the novel versions of many films, including such well-known productions as *Star Wars*, the first three *Alien* films, and *Alien Nation*. Other works include scripts for talking records, radio, computer games, and the story for the first *Star Trek* movie. In addition to publication in English, his work has appeared and won awards throughout the world. His novel *Cyber Way* won the Southwest Book Award for Fiction in 1990, the first work of science fiction ever to do so.

Though restricted (for now) to the exploration of one world, Foster's love of the faraway and exotic has led him to travel extensively. After graduating from college he lived for a summer with the family of a Tahitian policeman and camped out in French Polynesia. He and his wife, JoAnn Oxley, of Moran, Texas, have traveled to Europe and throughout Asia and the Pacific in addition to exploring the back roads of Tanzania and Kenya. Foster has camped out in the "Green Hell" region of the southeastern Peruvian jungle, photographing army ants and pan-frying piranha (lots of small bones; tastes a lot like trout); has ridden forty-foot whale sharks in the remote waters off Western Australia; and was one of three people on the first commercial air flight into Western Australia's Bungle Bungle National Park. He has rappelled into New Mexico's fabled Lechuguilla Cave, white-water rafted the length of the Zambezi's Batoka Gorge, driven solo the length and breadth of Namibia, crossed the Andes by car, sifted the sands of unexplored archeological sites in Peru, gone swimming with giant otters in Brazil, and surveyed remote Papua New Guinea and West Papua both above and below the water. His filmed footage of great white sharks feeding off Southern Australia has appeared on both American television and the BBC.

Besides traveling he enjoys listening to both classical music and heavy metal. Other pastimes include basketball, hiking, body surfing, scuba diving, collecting animation on video, and weightlifting. He studied karate with Aaron and Chuck Norris before Norris decided to give up teaching for acting. He has taught screenwriting, literature, and film history at UCLA and Los Angeles City College as well as having lectured at universities and conferences around the country and in Europe. A member of the Science Fiction Writers of America, the Authors Guild of America, and the Writers Guild of America, West, he also spent two years serving on the Planning and Zoning Commission of his home town of Prescott, Arizona. Foster's correspondence and manuscripts are in the Special Collection of the Hayden Library of Arizona State University, Tempe, Arizona.

The Fosters reside in Prescott in a house built of brick salvaged from a turn-of-the-century miners' brothel, along with assorted dogs, cats, fish, several hundred houseplants, visiting javelina, porcupines, eagles, red-tailed hawks, skunks, coyotes, bobcats, and the ensorceled chair of the nefarious Dr. John Dee. He is presently at work on several new novels and media projects.

Visit him online at www.alandeanfoster.com.